HEARTH & CAULDRON

A HEARTH & CAULDRON MYSTERY, BOOK 1

SHAWN MCGUIRE

CHAPTER
ONE

Seven-year-old Peony nearly broke my heart the way she played with her fingers and sniffled so hard her shoulders jerked with each sharp inhale. My heart was safe with thirteen-year-old Clover, but she was trying her darndest to break my spirit. Leaning forward with elbows resting on her widespread knees and a glare on her face, Clover was as defiant a child as I'd ever seen.

I could have said no . . . No, no, I couldn't have. My whole life, I'd never been able to say no to people. I did need to move this along, though. I had a shop to open and customers to tend to. Something to bake. There was always something to bake.

"We're so sorry to bother you with this, Reeva," their father, Alder, insisted.

"We didn't know what else to do," added Aster, their mother. "They say it takes a village to raise a child and well . . ."

"It's fine that you came to me," I assured with an empathetic smile. "As high priestess, I see my role as being both guide and rule enforcer. Before I say anything to your girls, however, I have to ask something from the two of you."

They both froze, their eyes wide. If only they could be that in sync as parents.

"I need to know," I continued, "that you'll enforce whatever punishment I give. While it does sometimes take a village to raise kids, and you happen to live in one where the residents are always willing to help when there's a need, ultimately your daughters are your responsibility."

"Of course." Alder gave a firm nod, eyes shifting from me to his daughters, issuing a silent warning.

"Whatever you say, Reeva," Aster vowed, a beat too late. "We'll follow it to the letter."

I glanced at the girls perched on my patio bench. For an instant, they'd both become my daughter. Yasmine at seven after getting caught red-handed cutting into the cake I'd told her was for our neighbor's birthday party that night. Yasmine at thirteen after sneaking in through the front door at midnight when she'd been told in no uncertain terms that she couldn't go to that party. I didn't like the authoritarian side of parenting any more than Alder and Aster Flowers did. But oh, what I wouldn't give to have my girl sitting before me now, alive and well, anxious for the words about to come out of my mouth.

"First, let's be sure I've got my facts straight." I took a few steps closer to the girls. "Please correct me if I get anything wrong."

"You're wrong," Clover sassed instantly.

"Clover," Aster snapped, "I swear to the Goddess, if you don't check that attitude, I'll triple whatever punishment Reeva gives."

The girl remained quiet but made a face at her mother. They should have named her Saguaro or after some other kind of cactus flower. The girl was prickly as a porcupine.

"My understanding," I continued, raising my voice slightly, "is that you broke into a villager's garden and helped yourself to several plants. And not just any villagers. You broke into the

Barlows' garden. The two most powerful green witches in Whispering Pines." And the entire Midwest for that matter.

"W-we w-were h-harvesting," Peony stuttered and wiped her nose on her sleeve.

I couldn't wait, Momma. Your cakes are soooo yummy.

"I've spoken with Briar and Morgan," I told Peony, using the voice that always made Yasmine cringe and me feel like a tyrant. "Harvesting would mean using a set of shears to carefully remove only as much from the plant as you needed. They say you pulled whole plants from the ground—sweet pea, lavender, mandrake, and rue. Doing so upset the other plants around them as well. Is that accurate?"

"W-what are shears?" Peony asked, her legs swinging, her feet not reaching the ground.

"They're scissors for the garden," Aster explained as though she was a gardening pro. Ironically, all four of the Flowers had thumbs that were far more brown than green.

Peony shook her head. "W-we didn't use shears. C-Clover didn't s-say we had t-to."

Clover shrugged. "I tried to break off what we needed. Didn't work, so I yanked."

You can't understand, Mom. You're too old. I had *to go to that party.*

"I'm not sure that's quite accurate," I corrected both the girls before me and the one ever-present in my mind. "I think you yanked because you were afraid that either Briar or Morgan were going to come out and catch you."

"Because that stupid rooster wouldn't stop crowing," Clover blamed.

Pitch, Morgan's all-black pet, served as an avian version of a watchdog or scarecrow for the Barlow garden. If he spotted anything out of line, he sounded the alarm.

I shook my head. "By the time they heard Pitch, the damage had already been done. They showed me what you did. It was significant." I set a chair in front of them and sat so I could look them in the eye. "Vandalism is punishable by law. Briar and Morgan could have reported you to Sheriff Reed and asked him to charge you. He probably would have sentenced you to community service. The Barlows left it up to your parents to decide your punishment." Since Clover was the instigator, my gaze stuck to her as I said, "They seem to be at the end of their rope with the two of you, however, and asked for my help. I know your parents are raising you to follow the Wiccan Rede—"

"What's a rede?" Peony interrupted, her sniffles finally under control.

"It's a rule or guideline that Wiccans follow. It states that we are free to do whatever we choose to"—Clover sat taller at this pronouncement—"as long as our actions don't harm anyone. The problem is that *harm* can mean different things to different people. Each of us has to decide for ourselves what that definition is."

Clover, once again fueled by attitude, declared, "I decided that I needed those plants and the Barlows had plenty. We didn't take them just to mess up their garden. We needed them for spells."

Alder stepped forward and demanded, "What spells?"

"A girl at school is telling lies about me," Peony wailed.

"That's not very nice," I empathized. "What were you going to do about it?"

"We did *tons* of research first," Peony explained and nudged her sister. "Tell her, Clover."

The teen sighed. "Peony needed sweet pea to make the girl tell the truth."

Peony nodded. "The book says if you hold sweet pea in your hand, you have to tell the truth. So I was going to make her hold it and ask her why she lies about me."

For that exact purpose, sweet pea could have come in handy a few times in my life. "And what about the other plants?"

"Clover wants to steal her friend's boyfriend," Peony announced.

"Peony," Clover groaned and looked at me. "That's not exactly it. He and I like each other, everyone knows that, but this other girl put a hex on me, and now he won't even look at me. If you put rue in your bath, it'll break the hex. Rub it on your floor, it sends spells back. If you use a sprig of it to sprinkle salt water, it clears negativity."

I made a mental note to check my garden for rue. My cottage was full of negativity. "What about the mandrake?"

"Mandrake is good for both things," she informed as though giving a presentation. "If you wear some, like pinned to your shirt, it attracts love. If you carry it in your pocket, it banishes negativity. Before you can use it, you have to activate it, so you're supposed to set it someplace it won't get disturbed. After three days, you put it in water and let it soak overnight. Then it's ready. You can sprinkle the water in doorways or windowsills or, better still, sprinkle it on the person who's bugging you. The book says demons can't stay where there's mandrake."

Would it work on personal demons? I had a few of those to banish. Maybe I'd stop by the Barlow's and get some mandrake. "And the lavender?"

Clover shrugged. "Guys like it. It works great in love potions."

"Love potions?" Alder cried, and Aster patted his shoulder to calm him down.

I looked down at the girls long enough to make them squirm. "I have to say, I'm impressed with how much you know."

Peony beamed, and one corner of Clover's mouth turned up a little.

"Can you imagine, though," I continued, "how chaotic things would be if everyone decided for themselves what did and didn't constitute harm? There have to be guidelines for people to follow, and enforcing those guidelines, in this situation at least, falls to me. The two of you have broken the Rede by damaging the Barlows' plants. That directly causes harm to them because they use those plants in their religious practice. And they sell them at Shoppe Mystique, so this affects their customers as well."

All four of the Flowers stared at me, ready to hear my decision, but it seemed the girls needed a reminder of the basics first. It couldn't hurt for Aster and Alder to hear it either.

"The Rede is backed up by something called the Threefold Law. Do either of you know what that means?"

Peony's hand shot into the air. "It means that whatever you do will come back to you three times. If you do something bad, like run your bike into someone else's bike, your bike will get a flat tire, you'll lose your bell, and you'll forget the code to unlock your bike from the stand. That happened to one of my friends."

"A perfect example." I reached out and laid a hand on her shoulder. "While not one of our guidelines, we also do all that we can to live in harmony with nature. We respect what it has to offer, and in return, it provides us with many treasures. Food, shelter, water, and medicine for example.

"So, how many bad things are gonna happen to us?" Clover asked, a tiny tremor of fear laced into the defiant question.

"How many plants did you disrupt?"

Peony counted on her fingers. "Four."

"Four times three times two Barlows." I met Clover's stare. "That's a lot of bad. Since the two of you committed this infraction together, I want you to work together on your punishment. Under Briar's and Morgan's supervision, you need to clean up the mess you made in their garden. Since you enjoy doing research, I'd like you to learn how to properly care for each of the plants you harmed and then write a paper detailing those steps. As magical properties appear to be of special interest to you, include those too."

Aster had taken a small notepad from her purse and scribbled every word I said. She tapped it with her pen and announced, "I'm taking notes, girls. Don't think you'll be able to say you forgot—"

I cleared my throat, and she stopped talking.

"To end the paper," I continued, "I want you each to include a paragraph that explains why what you did was wrong. Make two copies. Give one to me and one to the Barlows. Before doing anything else, you need to apologize to them face to face."

They nodded but didn't say a word.

I turned my attention to the older girl, who seemed to have lost a bit of her bravado. For a moment, she was Yasmine again. Then she turned into my sister. Her attitude was so much like Flavia's at thirteen it scared me.

"Clover, I'm concerned about the path you're leading your little sister down. Your role with her is like mine with the coven. You should be guiding her in directions that will be helpful and positive. Right now, she looks up to you. Trust me, the day will soon come when she won't anymore."

Memories of growing up with Flavia skittered through my brain. Her wicked side first came out when she was old enough to realize she had to share our parents' time and attention with me. If I'd done more to lead her down the right path when she was Peony's age, things might have turned out better. For all of us. The guilt over that still ate at me.

"Clover, I'd like you to write an additional paper on the role siblings play in each other's lives. I expect both papers to be well thought out with perfect spelling and punctuation. Think of it as a final exam that will allow you to pass on to the next grade at school. If you fail the exam, you'll need to repeat it until you get it right."

Peony looked excited to be working on this project with her big sister. Still so innocent and malleable. Clover looked miserable, which meant she would likely learn the most from this exercise.

"Aster? Alder? Any questions or concerns?"

Taking on a sort of tough-guy role, Alder crossed his arms and, in an all-business tone, asked, "What's the due date on this assignment?"

"They need to clean up the garden, per the Barlows' directions, immediately. They can take the time they need with the papers. I'm more concerned that they learn from this rather than getting it done by a specific date. Sometime before the end of summer is sufficient."

"Did you hear that, girls?" Aster asked. "Head straight over to the Barlows and you can bet I'll be checking with Briar later." To me, she added, "This is so embarrassing."

We watched the girls head to the dirt road that crossed in front of my cottage. It would take them straight to the Barlows.

The university is only two hours away. You'll see me all the time, Mom.

I blinked away yet another memory flash and turned to Alder and Aster. "I'm glad you're both behind me on this. Lessons learned this way aren't easy, but they often have the greatest impact."

"Cleaning up the garden is a must," Aster began. "I'm a little surprised about the papers. That will certainly take a chunk out of their summer." She paused as though thinking I might change my mind. "But, as you said, this lesson will really be driven home."

Alder shot his wife a disapproving look. "Better than if Sheriff Reed charged them with a crime and made them do community service all summer. I agree with Reeva's decision."

"Well, I do too," Aster insisted. "Just saying it's a shame. Summer should be time for them to relax and play."

Overall, Yasmine had been a good kid, but that didn't mean parenting wasn't a challenge. I empathized with the Flowers and was glad that they asked for help rather than giving up and letting their daughters run amok. Lately, though, they had been turning to others first when the girls needed disciplining. That needed to be their last resort rather than the go-to item on their list.

"Am I safe to assume you're both committed to Wicca?"

"Of course," Alder stated.

"Absolutely devoted," Aster added.

"Great, because I also have a little assignment for the pair of you."

Like a sunset fading beneath the horizon, the color drained from their faces.

"I'd like you to work together on a plan for how you will enforce the Rede and Threefold Law with your girls. Give me plenty of details. Tell me how you'll teach them to be intentional every day. List activities you'll do together, such as full moon or new moon rituals either with the coven or on your own at home. How you'll celebrate the sabbats. Those types of things."

I nearly laughed at their shocked expressions, but this wasn't funny, and I was dead serious. The residents of this village had lived far too many years with Flavia thinking she could do as she pleased. I was determined to not let someone else pick up where she left off. This wasn't the first time Clover had been in trouble. She was looking for attention and wanted it from her parents, not other people.

Aster's jaw dropped. "I don't understand, Reeva. *We* didn't do anything wrong."

"You didn't, and I don't want you to think I'm punishing you. Instead, look at it as another tool for your parenting toolbox. It's an exercise that's almost guaranteed to help your family. You came to me for help, and I'm happy to do so this one time, but it's up to you as their parents to ensure that this kind of thing doesn't happen again. If it does, I doubt the next punishment will be up to me. Sheriff Reed will almost surely step in at that point."

Worse, karma was waiting to see if they kept their promise to abide by my decision. The last thing I wanted was to get between someone and their karma. Never again.

CHAPTER
TWO

Despite the early-morning intervention with the Flowers family, I still made it to my shop by shortly after eight o'clock. Plenty of time to perform my morning tasks. This meant starting with anointing the outside of a white pillar candle with a drop of my Blessing oil—four parts grapeseed oil and one part each of sandalwood, rose, and frankincense essential oils. I used only white candles in the shop because, among other things, white symbolized peace and protection, which was exactly how I wanted my customers to feel. Peaceful and protected.

As I lit the candle, I whispered, "Light my way."

Hearth Witch Tip
Use unscented candles in the kitchen
to prevent unpleasant aroma combinations.

To bless my shop, I held the candle in both hands and stood in Hearth & Cauldron's kitchen, the center of the building where I did demonstrations and held classes. I closed my eyes, took a deep cleansing breath, and then envisioned a bright light flowing like a mist from the pillar. Turning in a slow widdershins or counterclockwise circle, I said, "Protect my shop and all who enter it. Fill it, them, and me with creativity, curiosity, and positivity."

I paused my rotation to allow the mist to flow into the dining room to the left of the kitchen. I paused again when I faced the retail room on the right. Once the circle was complete, I set the candle on a silver plate on a high shelf and placed a clear glass hurricane around it. There, the flame could continue working its magic from open to close.

The other part of my opening process was to record the previous day's sales in my ledger. I found this was a task best done with a rested mind, and I was always tired at the end of the workday. When the clock ticked over to 9:00, I finished my last sips of tea and closed the doors of the long, narrow coat closet I'd converted into an office. Many mornings, shoppers were already on the front porch waiting to be let in.

"Blessed be," I greeted. Or, "Merry Meet."

My assistant, Bee Wallace, arrived at ten o'clock and would stay until three five days a week—she had Sundays off and didn't come in until noon on Mondays. Whenever Bee wasn't there, I handled things on my own. I needed to hire another assistant. Ten or eleven-hour days, seven days a week, from Memorial Day to Samhain took a toll on even the youngest, spriest villagers. But Hearth & Cauldron had been my dream since I was a teenager. It was my passion so that helped on those extra-tiring days.

After the initial round of early birds, I announced, "I'm going to step outside for a few minutes."

"Take your time," Bee sang out from the retail room. "We

need to take advantage of every minute we can get outside on days like this."

Whispering Pines was tucked into a dense forest in the Northwoods of Wisconsin. The darker, colder months were long and quiet. The lighter, warmer months were glorious but crazy busy once the tourist season started.

I met my best friend, Ruby McLaughlin, right where I expected to on the wooden Fairy Path that wound through the pines. As I gave her the shortened version of the Flowers' intervention this morning, she fiddled with the crescent moon pendant nestled at the base of her throat and stared at me, head tilted to the side.

"Why are you looking at me like that?" Was I missing an earring? Did I button my blouse wrong? Was there a smudge of jam on my chin? Speaking of which, I was down to my last two jars of raspberry. I needed to make more soon.

"Something's different about you, and I'm trying to figure out what it is."

That was a widely cast net. I'd always been different in nearly every way. Although, this was true for most of the residents of Whispering Pines. The village was known as the place where *All are welcome and those in need may stay.* Also *A place for those who don't belong.* In other words, if a person didn't fit in anywhere else, this was the perfect place for them.

I grew up in the village—was one of the Original families, in fact—but because I lived elsewhere for so many years, plenty now considered me an outsider. No, not even an outsider. For some, I simply didn't belong anymore.

After another few seconds, Ruby snapped her fingers. "It's the apron."

"Do you like it?" I smoothed my hands over the pale-lavender cotton apron currently covering my jeans and black blouse. "Are you ready to be impressed?"

She shook her head, still studying. "No, that's not it. I mean, it is, but it's more than just the apron. Did you say impressed? Why should I be impressed?"

Pushing my shoulders back, I proudly told her, "I made it myself. Remember that bolt of cotton muslin I bought from you a few months ago?"

"Forty yards of midweight white. So many uses for that. I ordered a bolt of heavyweight for myself at the same time and made a slipcover for that beat-up armchair I love so much. I'm thinking about coordinating café curtains to keep LaVonne LeBeau from peeking in my windows. Why can't she just ring the bell like a normal person?" She mimed peering into a window and knocking on the pane. "Wait. Your apron isn't white. It's purple."

"I made a dye with red cabbage."

Ruby's mouth dropped open. "You what? But you're not the crafty one."

"I've also got a beautiful light-gold one I dyed with onion skins."

"What a great idea for a class." Ruby ran The Twisty Skein, the village hobby shop, a few yards up the path from Hearth & Cauldron. "Fabric dying can be messy when only one person is doing it. If there's a group, it'll be best to do it outside. Perfect now that the weather has warmed up." She circled me, inspecting my creation. "Nice even color. Oh, a cross back style."

"I prefer aprons that just slip over my head. No straps to snag on drawer pulls or dangle in the batter bowl." A white cat with startlingly azure eyes was currently weaving a figure eight around my feet. I bent to pick up Blue before he tripped me.

"Or catch fire because you stand on a stool to get something in the cupboard above the stove and got too close to the burner flame. Don't ask." She returned to her inspection. "Great deep pockets. Straight even seams. Perfect. I give you a B-plus."

Blue purred as I dug my fingers into the thick fur by his ears. "If it's perfect, why don't I get an A+?"

"Because crafts are my domain. Stay in your lane, witch." While a smile stayed on her mouth, the sparkle faded from her eyes. Witches could be so territorial. Even when it came to their best friends. "Don't worry, I'll give you credit for the idea when I teach the class, which I think should last two days."

"That's about how long it took me," I agreed. "Two days."

She ticked off the steps on her fingers. "Scour and mordant the fabric, create the dye, color and rinse the fabric the first day. Cut out the pieces and sew the apron on the second. Or they can take the fabric home with them and use it for whatever they want. Or they can buy pre-dyed fabric from me and attend the second-day apron assembly class without dealing with the dye mess."

"Or you could do a long one-day class," I suggested. "Prepare the fabric in the morning and assemble in the afternoon."

Ruby blinked as though realizing I was still there. She tended to get lost in her thoughts when a new idea struck. "Now, as much as I love that you made your own aprons, back to the matter at hand. Something's different about you. You wear a chef's coat at the shop. You only wear aprons at home. And why is Blue letting you hold him? He never lets anyone hold him."

I gave the cat a final ear scritch, set him on the ground, and he immediately trotted into the woods. Blue was a community cat. He appeared a few years ago, belonged to no one, and lived in whichever villager's home suited him best at the moment.

"Guess he likes me," I replied with a shrug. "He pops over to play with Dot every few days. When we had that intense cold snap in February, he stayed for two weeks."

Ruby crossed her arms. "You're avoiding my observation."

"I'm explaining your observation about Blue. As for the first, I decided that a chef's coat is too pretentious. When a customer enters Hearth & Cauldron, I want them to feel like they've stepped into my home. Most people don't wear chef's coats when they cook in their homes, they wear aprons. I've decided it's time for a life reset, and pretty new aprons sounded like a fun way to start."

"A reset?" Ruby declared, hands over her heart. "I love that, Reeva. More than anyone I know, you're entitled. And this is the perfect time."

It was because it wasn't just a matter of *wanting* something new for myself, I *needed* it. The difference between a perfect cake and one fit only for the garbage bin could be a matter of a minute or two too long in the oven. Some days I felt like my life's timer was ticking perilously close to the crumbling, overbaked cake stage. I needed an infusion of excitement. The question was, would a reset work for me, or would something happen, once again, to destroy my plans?

Ruby asked, "Is this why you asked the coven to meet at your cottage tonight?"

"Pretty much. The moon is full, and my cottage is filled with shadows. And not the kind cast by light. I want to solidify my intention for a fresh start by having the coven bless my home and property."

"Nice," she approved and then nodded toward the east. "Uh-oh. Trouble's coming."

For a heartbeat, I thought she meant Flavia. I still worried I'd bump into her while strolling through the village. Turns out, bruises received over a lifetime took longer than two weeks to heal. Instead, I found Tripp Bennett coming our way. He looked relaxed as always in cargo shorts, a Pine Time T-shirt, and flip-flops. His blond waves were loose instead of tied back in the ponytail he wore when cooking.

"Not trouble." I waved at him. "He's here to pick up aprons."

Ruby blinked at me. "How many did you make?"

"I'm not sure, but I spent every night this past week dyeing and sewing. It was very therapeutic."

"Planning to sell them in your retail side? Let me know and I'll add your logo using my embroidery machine."

I glanced down at my creation. "That's not a bad idea. I'll monitor customer interest for a day or two, but get ready to order more bolts of cotton. And I'll need to get more produce for dye."

She gave me an over-the-shoulder finger wave as she headed back to Twisty, pausing to say a few words to Tripp as she passed him.

"Hey, Reeva." He kissed my cheek in greeting, a habit he'd started a few months ago. Charming and chivalrous. Qualities I highly approved of. "Is this one of the aprons?"

I did a slow spin. "This one is mine, but the others are this style. They're hand dyed and hand sewed, so no two will be the same."

"Reeva originals. Can't wait to see them."

"Let's go, then."

THREE

"Scones tomorrow?" Tripp asked, checking the schedule on the framed bulletin board hanging near the front door.

"Yep. Students can make lemon-lavender or ginger-lime." I paused at the bit of nostalgia that suddenly swelled in me. Teaching people to make scones always did that. "Did I ever tell you that Mr. Graham, Sugar and Honey's father, was making his first batch of scones the day they hired me to help at Treat Me Sweetly? Of course, it wasn't called that yet. We just knew it as the Grahams' place." I smiled at the memory. "He thought he was so cosmopolitan, bringing this exotic pastry to Whispering Pines."

"Scones? Exotic?" Tripp chuckled.

"Mr. Graham was a wonderfully uncomplicated man." And his *exotic* scones became his shop's signature item. They still were.

"I'm secure on scones. I make them often for our guests at the B&B. What else have you got coming up that I might be interested in?"

"There will be a men's only class tomorrow afternoon," I taunted.

"Men's only?" He checked the schedule again. "It's not listed. And tomorrow's Tuesday."

Normally, I only held classes on Wednesdays, Fridays, and Saturdays. I also did short, usually impromptu demonstrations on the other days except Sunday. Those were the short and sweet days for the village shop owners since many tourists headed back home on Sunday. Most of us only stayed open until two.

"This is a last-minute class," I explained. "Do you recall Ruby's men's only craft class a few weeks ago?"

"I do. She taught me how to etch glass. I've been etching Pine Time's logo onto everything I can find. Wine glasses, water glasses, pitchers . . ."

"It was a huge success."

"It was. There were probably a dozen of us there. Rourke O'Connor started it. He wanted to make April something for her birthday. Ruby taught him how to crochet an afghan and decided the rest of us needed a 'safe place' to unleash our creativity." He chuckled. "Safe place."

"I know you're not shy in the kitchen, but others are. This is short notice, but the concept worked so well for Ruby, I thought I'd give it a try. If it goes well, I'll do it regularly. Tomorrow we're making hand pies." I pointed at the clipboard hanging next to the corkboard. "There's a sign-up sheet beneath the scone sheet."

He immediately added his name to the list.

Tripp warmed my heart. Like my nephew, Martin Reed, also the village's sheriff, Tripp had come to be like a son to me. He was constantly learning and tweaking his skills, determined to be the best cook possible for Pine Time, the bed-and-breakfast he ran with his girlfriend, Jayne O'Shea. I'd never admit it to anyone, but

I held my Wednesday classes in the late mornings or early afternoons specifically so Tripp could attend. He made breakfast for his guests every morning and held wine and cheese gatherings on their back patio next to the lake in the late afternoons. He had free time between 11:00 and 2:00, and I was happy to oblige.

"You did hand pies before, didn't you?" he asked.

"I did before I officially opened. I believe you, Jayne, Morgan, and River took that class." I smiled, remembering how precise River Carr had been with his dicing. Probably not all that surprising for a man who owned a billion-dollar business. He knew how important details were to success.

"I'm secure with hand pies, too, but I'm also surrounded by women every day at Pine Time. Don't get me wrong, I love them all but could do with some guy time."

"We'll do both savory and sweet this time."

"Dinner and dessert that you can shove in your pocket. Perfect guy food."

"I'm glad you approve. Ready for your aprons? Or rather, Jayne's aprons?"

"Ready."

I set the pair on the table. Being an instructor at heart, I needed to explain the process. "The fabric was white to start, so I created dyes for them using food. Since green is Pine Time's prime color, I used spinach. I used black beans to make your secondary shade."

Tripp held the second apron up at arms' length. "Black beans make blue dye?"

"Isn't it beautiful?"

"It is. And the colors are spot on. Pine trees and Lucy Lake. Jayne's going to love these."

"If you have time, stop in at Twisty before you go home. Ruby will add your logo."

"Great idea. She's got it on file because she puts it on kitchen towels that we give as thank you gifts for guests who stay a week or more. Are you prepared to make more aprons? We'll probably get orders."

"I'm prepared to teach you and Jayne how to make them. They're a little fiddly but not hard. How is Jayne, by the way?"

Her life was in reset mode too. Two weeks ago, she was still the village sheriff. Then she locked up my sister for her crimes, promoted Martin to sheriff from deputy, and called it quits so she could run the B&B full-time with Tripp. That last decision, quitting, felt a little hasty to many of the villagers.

"She's figuring things out," Tripp replied. "She wants to learn how to cook so will be taking some of your classes eventually. For now, she's my sous chef. Which is why she needs an apron. This morning, she's weeding the herb garden. Later this afternoon, she'll go kayaking and then help me with the wine and cheese gathering tonight. Other than hanging out at the Barlow cottage, that's basically how she's spent every day of the last two weeks. Sometimes she'll mix it up by reading or sitting on the rooftop deck with her sketchpad."

"Is she driving you crazy yet? Karl would always get underfoot during the off-season. Of course, I like my routines and don't like anything or anyone messing with them."

His smile indicated he knew all about me and my routines.

"I can't say she's bothering me. This is an adjustment for both of us, but so far so good. I'm not willing to give up the cooking but it's not a bad idea for her to know how to make a few things." He fingered the aprons, a faraway look crossing his face for a moment. "Maybe creating a line of Pine Time products would keep her busy. She could set up a display case in the sitting room."

"That's a great idea. Making aprons would be a good project for her."

He nodded and then blurted, "She's questioning her choice."

"Which choice? She's made a number of them lately."

"The sentencing. She had no doubt about it at the time. She

was so afraid that if Flavia went to prison, she'd get let out early or escape. Even though she and River agreed with Flavia serving her sentence here, Jayne's scared that the villagers don't like it."

"No matter which decision she made, she'd second-guess herself. Tell her that the folks in our little village are more upset that I'm still here than that Flavia is." At his skeptical look, I added, "I'm serious. Some of them believe, like Jayne does, that Flavia has a mental disorder and if she can be helped, that's more important than serving time in prison. Some feel prison is the only place for her. Others only care that she's being punished and isn't roaming free. Believe it or not, the chatter about her is already dying down."

His head tilted in surprise. "It's only been two weeks. How can they be over it already? Flavia caused a lot of damage."

"Yes, but you have to remember that until Jayne uncovered everything, only the Original villagers knew all of what Flavia had done. The other villagers didn't like the mean old witch in the weird black cottage, but they didn't know the full story. Now, those folks just want the dust to settle so they can have their quiet little village back. Well, quiet after the tourist season."

"How do you know all this?" He tapped his fingers to his forehead. "Have you got a little fortune teller in you?"

I laughed. "No, I'm friends with a nosey barista. Violet keeps me well informed."

Tripp grinned, then took on a defensive air. "Wait a minute. Why would anyone be upset that you're still here?"

"For no other reason than I'm related to a person who did horrible things. It's like when a serial killer is finally caught, and the family gets accused of knowing what the killer had been doing."

"No one should be held responsible for the sins of their families." He pulled me in for a hug. "Before you know it, the people thinking those things about you will have moved on to something else."

I fought the hug for a second, I had customers in the shop after all, but then I melted into it.

"I hope you're right." I gave him a grateful smile when I pulled away.

Tripp unfolded the green apron and inspected how it was made. "I'll let Jayne know you offered to teach her how to make these things. And I'll encourage her to take a cooking class. That would be good for her. Right now, she's almost hoping for a crime that Martin will need her to consult on. It's hard to walk away from a lifestyle you've become used to."

He was singing to the choir on that one. I was so happy with my life in the little town of Port Washington, Wisconsin, with Yasmine. Dear Goddess, I missed her every day.

"Jayne is welcome any time," I assured. "And if cooking doesn't turn out to be her thing, Ruby has tons of options."

Tripp promised to be here for the hand pies class, gathered his aprons, and headed next door to have Ruby add the logos.

"The retail room is spic and span," Bee announced and then frowned. "What does that mean? I know it's a saying that has something to do with cleanliness, but what do the words 'spic' and 'span' mean?"

"It may have come from the old Dutch word *spikspeldernieuw.*"

I waited for Bee to give me a go-ahead nod. She often questioned things, but many times it was simply an out-loud thought, to hear her own voice, or to fill airspace she dubbed too quiet. The first few times I responded right away, she gave me a stare that could curdle milk. I learned to present an opening and then wait to see if she'd step through. This time, she nodded.

"While I don't recall the verbatim explanation," I proceeded, "the word breaks down to *spike splinter new* and refers to something being like a new spike forged in a blacksmith's fire. Spikes were made of iron, which tarnishes quickly so only looked new for a short time. Splinters from a piece of wood are lighter and cleaner than the outside. The phrase could also harken back to the fact that a knife and fork were sometimes called a *spike* and *spon*. One uses utensils instead of one's fingers and remains clean."

Bee squinted as she took all of this in and after a few seconds of processing, asked, "Really?"

I shrugged. "One of my instructors at culinary school was a big history and trivia buff. There were days when he spent half the class period giving us the history of whatever it was we were supposed to be making. History is interpreted differently by different people so we can't be positive, but my instructor inspired me to learn what I can about how recipes came to be. I read more books on the history of food than any other kind."

Bee pinched her lips together. A look that meant she wasn't convinced. "That explains why we have such a unique collection of cookbooks and antique housekeeping books in the retail room. I should borrow a few. See what I can learn."

"By all means, feel free to read all you want. Let me know if you're going to bring anything home."

The poised woman with the short blond bob looked offended.

"I'm not saying you would steal anything, Bee. I know you'd bring back whatever you borrowed. You know how some of our items can be, though. If you want to take something home, I should bless it first."

She relaxed. "Speaking of which, I noticed some new things on your desk. I didn't put them out because I didn't know if you had cleansed them yet."

"I didn't." I glanced around the shop. "How many customers do we have right now?"

"Just a handful. A mother came in with her daughter and young granddaughter while you were helping Tripp."

A smile turned my mouth. "Maiden, Mother, and Crone. Perfect. Perhaps they'll want to observe the ritual."

"You get set up," Bee told me, "and I'll gather folks around."

CHAPTER
FOUR

E very item in my shop was blessed twice. Once before being put on the shelf and again before being placed into a brown paper bag for the new owner to take home. Many of our customers liked to watch this cleansing and blessing process. So while Bee scurried off to the retail room to see who wanted to observe the ritual, I got ready.

I started by collecting a trio of antique wooden spoons, an old handmade pottery, and my basket of cleansing supplies from my office closet. Before I was able to take a single thing out of the basket, the grandmother, daughter, granddaughter, and two other young women were at my side at the farm table.

"Merry meet, ladies," I greeted. "Bee told you that I'm about to cleanse some new items?"

They nodded.

"What does that mean?" asked the little girl, who I guessed to be about twelve.

"What's your name, sweetie?"

"Erica."

"That's a very good question, Erica. Every time we touch something, we leave a tiny bit of ourselves behind. Whether it's a fingerprint or tiny fleck of skin, that object has now picked up a little of our energy. I like to clear away any negative energy that might have accumulated on the pieces. But, since many of the items I sell are antiques and people like antiques precisely because they have a history to them, I take care to not strip that away."

"How do you do that?" Erica asked.

"Well, that's exactly what I'm about to do, so you'll see in a minute. Are there any other questions before I begin?"

"I have one." The grandmother pointed at the wooden spoons. "Are those for sale? I have a collection."

"A big collection," added Erica.

"They are," I confirmed, "and I can tell by the look in your eyes that they're meant to be yours. I'll bless them specifically for you."

She clapped her hands lightly.

"If there's nothing else, we'll start. Once I've begun, please hold your questions until the end."

From my basket, I took a small spray bottle. "This is my cleansing spray. This little bottle is easier to work with, but I make a quart at a time by filling a jar about one-third full of witch hazel."

I smiled as the young women—one with black hair, the other white blond—scribbled notes into what looked like small grimoires.

"To the witch hazel, I add a palo santo stick and a couple drops each of myrrh, rosemary, lavender, and cedarwood essential oils. Finally, a pinch of salt, a few black tourmaline and rose quartz chips, and then top off the bottle with moon water."

Erica's hand shot into the air. "What's moon water?"

"Water that has been left out to charge beneath a full moon." I gave her a little wink and reminded her, "No more questions until I'm done, okay? I need to concentrate, or the blessing won't work."

She frowned at my gentle scold but nodded, her auburn curls bouncing as she did.

Using the small bottle, I spritzed a section of the table. "With this liquid, I cleanse this surface of any lingering negative energy." Next, I laid down a cotton cloth printed with a variety of old-fashioned kitchen items. "An altar is a place to hold useful or symbolic items for worshipping, praying, or casting spells. It can be as ornate or plain as you choose. I put down a cloth to both protect the surface and reflect the occasion. This cloth makes me smile every time I use it, which helps me infuse positivity into the objects."

They watched as I took more items out of my basket.

"A pentacle represents the five elements—earth, air, fire, water, and spirit. We place items that represent the elements on the altar in those positions. I choose salt for earth." I placed a small bowl of salt to my upper left. "A feather is light like air." To my upper right, I set a feather I found while walking through the forest. "This tealight candle represents fire and sits at my lower right. A goblet of water is obviously the water element, and that goes to my lower left. And finally, this small cauldron represents spirit for me and sits at the top of the pentacle. A proper altar will include other tools such as a chalice, wand, athame, crystals, a small broom, or objects of significance for the individual witch. For a cleansing, however, this is all I'll need."

The two notetakers scribbled furiously and then silently compared to make sure they got it all.

I held a long match to the flame of the white candle still burning inside the hurricane on the shelf and then lit the tealight with it. Then I added a good pinch of salt to the water and smiled at Erica standing across from me. She clasped the edge of the table, eyes sparkling with anticipation. Yasmine used to do the same thing when I baked. Erica was clearly dying to touch the little cauldron but kept her hands on the edge. Good girl.

Taking the pottery bowl, beautiful in its simplicity and the perfect size for whipping up a batch of muffins or cupcakes, I closed my eyes. "I'm envisioning a bright light enveloping me, absorbing into my body, flowing out of my hands, and into this object." I opened my eyes again, dipped the tips of two fingers into the salted water, and touched them to the bowl. After holding it over the flame and waving the feather around it, I held the bowl over the cauldron. "In the name of the five elements and under the light of the sun, moon, and stars, I bless this bowl. I declare that it will reside peacefully in my shop until the person it's meant for finds it. So mote it be."

As always happened, my focus had narrowed to this small area of the shop. I registered that a few new customers had paused to watch the cleansing and then continued to the retail room while others stayed. Those gathered around gazed differently at the bowl after the blessing, like it was now something magical. To me, anything that brought joy or peace must have a bit of magic in it.

"Now the spoons." I looked at the crone. "What is your name?"

"Grandma," Erica answered.

The woman chuckled and placed a hand on top of her granddaughter's head. "She's very excited. My name is Meredith."

"I'm excited too," I told the little girl. "It's wonderful when the perfect item comes into our lives. For your spoons, Meredith, I'll take the ritual one step further."

I repeated the steps in the exact same way—anointing the spoons with salt water, passing them over the fire, stirring the air with the feather and holding them over the cauldron—but changed the words of my blessing slightly. "In the name of the five elements and under the light of the sun, moon, and stars, I bless these spoons for Meredith. I ask that they bring her joy and declare that their power now belongs to her. So mote it be."

"So mote it be," the little girl repeated and reached for the spoons.

I held over Erica's head and handed them directly to her grandmother instead. "You know I blessed these spoons for your grandma, right?"

"Yes, ma'am."

"That means they're even more special now. Make sure you get her permission before using them."

She pouted but lowered her hands to her sides.

Erica's enthusiasm and strong will reminded me of Yasmine at that age.

I know I was supposed to ask first, Momma. I'm sorry I broke your mug.

My mother's favorite tea mug. Did I tell Yazzy it was okay? Did I tell her the mug was just a thing, not my actual mother?

I blinked and Meredith came into view, clutching the trio of spoons to her heart. "Whether you use those to make wonderful things in your kitchen, as a tool to dig small holes in your garden, or opt to hang them on a wall where they will bring you joy every time you look at them, their magic is now a part of you. Because you have claimed them, you are also a part of them."

Meredith glowed a little brighter than she had before she crossed my threshold. "We were here last summer, but I don't remember this shop."

"The building was here," I told her, "but Hearth & Cauldron has only been open since Yule. This shop has been my dream for forty years."

"Why did you wait so long?" the dark-haired notetaker asked.

"Because sometimes a dream requires more than just desire to come to fruition. Sometimes, you have to live for a while and let life knead that dream like a ball of bread dough until it's just right." In a flash, my mind skipped through the almost six decades I had lived. All the sorrows and joys that had shifted and reformed my dreams and plans. As though understanding exactly, Meredith, being a few years older than me, smiled knowingly. I held my hand out to her. "If you're done shopping, I'll—"

"Oh, no," Meredith's daughter interrupted. "There are some things I've got my eye on."

"Let me know when you're ready and I'll bless those pieces too."

As the maiden, mother, and crone wandered back into the retail room, the notetakers stepped forward.

"Do you do that for every item?" the blond asked.

"I perform this full pentacle ritual, as I call it, for every item I place on the shelves. As I mentioned, we leave some of our energy on everything we interact with. After an item sits on my shelf with so many people picking it up and commenting about it, it needs to be charged for its new person. Bee or I bless every item a customer purchases, no matter how small. Usually, it's with a spritz of blessing water." I pointed to the candle on the shelf. "A candle burns in this shop all day, every day. Passing items over the flame while chanting the blessing also works."

"I believe that too," the dark-haired one murmured. "About the energy transfer."

"What are your names?" I asked.

"I'm Trixie," the blond one said, "and she's Ember."

"You're both studying Wicca?"

"Oh yes," Trixie agreed. "We have been for a couple of years. We were so excited to find out about this village."

Ember added, "We're always looking to enhance our practice by trying things that work for others."

"So you're solitary witches," I concluded. "Taking what works for you and creating your own practice."

Trixie's smile slackened. "Is there something wrong with that?"

"Not at all. When I was a little younger than you, I started down a kitchen witch path. It didn't take long for my practice to move beyond the walls of our kitchen. If it has to do with hearth and home, that's where my path and passions lie, so I started calling myself a hearth witch."

Ember tapped the open page of her grimoire. "You said that a cauldron represents spirit to you. What else can represent the elements?"

"A mirror or crystal ball symbolizes spirit to many witches. A seashell could mean water. Incense, air."

They scribbled again.

"I have a question about your cleansing water." Trixie read the list of ingredients I had quoted. "Do I have everything?"

"You do." I pointed northwest. "Do you know where Shoppe Mystique is in the commons area?"

They both took on the giddy expressions we often saw on green witches young and old. Like rock stars of the Wiccan world, Briar and Morgan Barlow had developed a huge following simply by word of mouth.

"We've been there." Trixie practically swooned. "Willow told us Briar helps in the morning and Morgan will be coming back in the afternoons starting Friday."

"She will?" It had only been a month since her twins, Talon and Juniper, were born. Last I knew, Morgan had planned on at least six weeks of leave.

Ember winced. "Maybe we shouldn't have said anything. Willow said their helper, some girl name Keiko, needs more supervision than she can give. Willow has to focus on helping the customers first."

Keiko Shen was another young woman trying to find her way along the Wiccan trail. And through life in general, I suspected. She helped here at Hearth & Cauldron on occasion.

"I'd gladly change places with her," Ember offered. "To work with the Barlows? Or even Willow. She seems cool too."

I was ashamed to admit, even to myself, that I was a little envious of the way people flocked to the trio. There was no denying that they were wonderful women. And for the tourists, the Barlows and Willow looked like what people envisioned when they thought of witches, less the pointy hats. Morgan with her flowing black hair, long dark dresses, and so much silver jewelry she jangled. Briar leaned toward all black, always had, and could still give her daughter a run for her money, just at a slower pace since her stroke two years ago. Long, tall Willow with her waist-length red hair and earthy ways. Perhaps my life reset should come with an image tweak or two as well. Like the new aprons. And I'd been letting my blond bob grow out over the past year.

As though reminding me to mind my karma, the flame on the white candle encased by the clear glass hurricane guttered.

I thought an apology to the Universe and checked my envy. My shop had only been here for a few months, after all, and Shoppe Mystique had been open for decades. Hearth & Cauldron was slowly gaining followers too.

Bee came over and stood next to me then. I could tell by the look on her face something was wrong.

"Sorry to interrupt," she said softly.

"Feel free to browse," I told the women and then turned to Bee. "What's wrong?"

"Did you make any sales today?"

What a strange question. "You'll need to give me more direction. I sold a few spots for Wednesday's scone class, and people are going crazy for your bumble bee cross-stitch kits. The *cute as can bee, bee happy*, and *bee-utiful* are almost sold out. Assemble more when you have time. We'll sell them. Ruby wants some for The Twisty Skein too."

Bee pushed her shoulders back proudly. "Benji and Abner

are putting together more for us. Keeps the old codgers out of trouble." Her husband and neighbor were always getting into mischief. "I've designed a few new ones that Ruby can sell. *Bee good, meant to bee,* and *bee mine.*" Her expression shifted from proud to perplexed. "Anyway, I think an item is missing."

Missing? "You're sure one of the customers isn't carrying it around?"

She shook her head. "I checked."

"What item is it?"

"Do you remember the pair of fluted muffin tins?"

Of course I remembered them. They were quite unique. The cups were molded with narrow channels that started at the bottom center and curved up to the top rim. Muffins or cupcakes baked in the pans would come out looking like miniature Bundt cakes but without the hole in the middle. I believed they were from the mid-1900s so definitely vintage, but my primary rule for any item I acquired was that it either made me smile or gave off a good vibe. I wasn't concerned with monetary value. An item didn't need to be expensive to be perfect for one's home. These little pans hit high on the good vibe and smile scale the moment I saw them.

"You did cleanse them," Bee confirmed, "right?"

"I did before putting them on the shelf like I do everything." I glanced toward my retail shop and spotted Erica peeking at me from around her mother. "Did you check the little girl?"

Bee sputtered, "You think a child stole from us?"

"I reprimanded her during the blessing. She wasn't happy with me about that."

"Well, she's not carrying a bag or backpack. She's wearing shorts and a T-shirt so she couldn't be hiding them in her clothing."

"You're probably right, then. They were stolen." I'd need to cleanse the room before leaving tonight. Other than the obvious, a theft was concerning on multiple levels and left a great deal of negative energy behind.

"Maybe whoever took them loved them so much they simply had to have them despite not having the money to pay for them."

Dear Bee. Always trying to put a positive spin on things. "Whatever the reason, there's never a valid excuse for stealing. And you know I believe that a stolen item is a cursed item."

"Nothing will bake properly in those pans now."

Even though she didn't follow Wicca, Bee respected the religion and my personal beliefs completely.

"When did you last see the tins?" I asked her.

"Yesterday," she recalled, staring at the ceiling, her habit for remembering details. "I'm positive. I straightened and dusted the shelves before I left yesterday and remember seeing them. They're just so cute."

I smiled. "They are. That makes them easy for customers to notice." I closed my eyes and pictured myself doing the morning candle blessing. I was focused on the shop as a whole and wasn't paying attention to the inventory. "Yesterday was Sunday. You left at noon, and there was little business those last two hours. I spoke with everyone who entered and hung out in the retail room to answer questions. Those pans must have been on the shelf this morning. No one broke in overnight. I'd know if they had. That means it happened since we opened."

"This is very upsetting." Bee worried her hands together then flapped them at her sides as though shaking off her upset.

Even more worrisome was that baked goods were often shared with others. *If* the thief got them to cook properly, sharing muffins with this kind of dark shadow hanging over them could lead to trouble.

CHAPTER
FIVE

I blinked and roused from the trance I'd slipped into to find fireflies flitting around me. Decades earlier, Karl had planted a hawthorn, an oak, and an ash tree in a triangle in our backyard because I had mentioned that the trio was supposed to attract fairies. Sweetest thing he'd ever done for me. All these years later, the area inside that triad provided the perfect meditation space. Along with my home and my shop, it was one of my favorite places.

"What's a person to do," I asked the firefly-fairies, "when they're exactly where they want to be but still want to be somewhere else?"

I'd felt this undefinable, unsettled yearning my entire life. No matter where I was, I felt unsettled and like I didn't fit in, even in Whispering Pines. There was a German word for that. The Germans had great words. *Sehnsucht* basically meant *a yearning or longing for something unknown or indefinite.*

Unexpectedly, the jailing of my sister made this feeling worse instead of better. I'd been sure that once the biggest thorn in my side was removed, I'd be able to settle in and be comfortable. Flavia was evil, and there was no doubt she needed to pay for her crimes. My problem was that even though her wickedness had been weighing me down my whole life, she was still my sister. Now that we had no contact with each other, I realized she had served as a sort of anchor for me, something I could attach myself to in a world where I often felt adrift. Yasmine had done this for me as well.

Of course I still had Martin and wonderful friends. In the past year, Ruby and I had become so close we considered ourselves sisters. Better than sisters in my situation. Our friendship was something I never would have predicted at fifty-eight years of age.

My attention strayed now, as it often did, to a spot between the hawthorn and ash. The air there seemed to blur or shimmer at times. It was probably a spiderweb or simply the way the light shone through the branches. Sometimes, the pain of losing my daughter became so great all I could think of was being with her again. I would stare at the shimmer and imagine it was a thin spot in the veil, a gateway to Summerland and those I loved who had passed before me. What would I do if my Yazzy appeared there, her hand outstretched? *Come with me, Mom.*

"We're ready for you."

I jumped and looked over my shoulder to find Gardenia Nakamura peering in at me.

"Sorry, Reeva. I didn't mean to startle you."

"No, my fault. I was lost in thought."

"I could tell. I tried to get your attention a few times."

Twirling my finger around the triad, I explained, "This spot is almost soundproof. There have been days where I've lost hours in here without a clue so much time had passed."

"That sounds lovely," Gardenia said, a wistful edge to her voice. "Anyway, the coven is ready to begin."

"I'll be right there."

It hadn't felt right for me as high priestess to lead a coven blessing on my own home. There was no reason I couldn't. It's not like the ritual would change because it was my cottage instead of another villager's. Morgan, our previous high priestess, said she would do it, though, so that was the plan. Except now I worried that letting her take the lead might not be the right decision either. It was almost like telling the coven I needed backup and couldn't handle things on my own. I was already certain half of them believed I wasn't qualified for the role. Either way, it was too late now.

I found the coven gathered on the dirt road in front of my small stone cottage. At some point, Karl had covered the original stone with barn-red pine planks. When I decided last fall to return it to its original charm, I could have sworn the house exhaled with the first plank removed. Maybe that's what stirred up all the negativity inside.

"Blessed be, all," I greeted. "I believe you know why I asked to have our full moon gathering here this month instead of at the Meditation Circle."

"You want us to clear the negative energy from your home," Rourke O'Connor called out from the back of the half-moon-shaped crowd. They always stood in a half-moon formation.

"And to bless it with love and light," added Iris Nakamura. The tiny Asian woman was one of the village's elder witches. Gardenia, her granddaughter who could be her twin born decades later, put a proud arm around her shoulder.

"Yes, I need help clearing my home of the harmful energy of the past year." And the many, *many* years before. I let my gaze take in all of them. "You all know what I mean."

Nodding heads and a murmur of "Oh, we know" met the comment.

Even though he was well aware of everything she'd been doing, my husband, the former sheriff, had done nothing to stop or even slow Flavia's rampage. In my book, that meant Karl had been as wicked as she was, and much of it had dropped off him like loose hairs over the years and crawled into the corners of my cottage.

"I've smudged every room multiple times," I continued, "and conducted my own rituals. I can still feel a heaviness, though. Working together, I think we can get those bits still hiding under the furniture or, Goddess forbid, in my pantry."

"Which could cause even bigger problems." Morgan stood next to me, her hand on my shoulder. "A cursed pantry for Reeva could be disastrous."

The group chuckled at that.

"It's been a few months since we've done a cottage blessing," Morgan reminded the coven. "If I remember correctly, Suzette Thibodeaux's was the last one."

They nodded their agreement.

"After she died," Lorena noted with little warmth. Suzette had been a hard person to like. "Then again before Gabe Grace moved in."

"Tonight, Reeva will go inside first," Morgan explained, "and light a candle in the kitchen, the heart of her home, and state her intention for this blessing. Then we will go room to room, starting with her bedroom upstairs. I'll mark each window with sage water to prevent evil from reentering and then use a sage, cedar, and sweetgrass smudge stick in each room. As I finish in a room, a group of three of you will go in and sweep. Remember to start in the corners and sweep in a slow widdershins circle. As a trio, you should direct that energy out of the room, down the stairs, and out the door between the kitchen and sunroom. Any questions?"

Keiko Shen raised her hand. "Can I help?"

Morgan shook her head. "Not this time. We always ask new members to observe a home blessing first."

"Stay by my side," I told Keiko. "I'll be following Morgan to each room and will explain what's going on."

Morgan moved to the center of the group. "To begin, everyone hold your brooms in both hands."

I pulled Keiko a few steps away so my whispers wouldn't distract anyone. "Contrary to popular belief, a witch's broom is not for riding on." She rolled her eyes at my little joke. "Whether a full-length one as the group members have or a handheld whiskbroom, it's a tool meant to stir the air and sweep away negative energy, not dirt."

"Spirits of protection," Morgan called out, "I ask that you instill the members of this coven with your power. I ask you to walk with us through Reeva's home, help us rid it of any harmful energy, and ensure that only peace and light remain. As I have asked, so mote it be."

We followed Morgan to the open side door and were met by a loud screeching, squawking sound.

"Is that your owl, Reeva?" someone asked.

"Sorry. Yes, that's Sanny." All these people in the house would surely upset her. At only six inches tall, she might be tiny, but she had a huge voice. I stepped inside, let her hop onto my finger, and set her on my shoulder. "She'll stay quiet there."

Morgan dipped her finger into a small cauldron of sage water, marked an X at the top of the doorway, and stated, "No evil shall enter through this marked opening. So mote it be." She then lit her sage/cedar/sweetgrass bundle and waved it around and across the opening.

Even that little bit of a blessing made the cottage feel lighter to me. "I'll go light the candle. Keiko, you may come with me, but no questions yet."

Morgan smudged the two of us with the bundle—starting at our toes, going up over our heads, and down to our heels—as she would herself and each of the twenty-four coven members before they entered to do the sweeping. In my kitchen, a white pillar candle anointed with blessing oil and a box of matches waited on the counter. To be sure I was very clear and didn't miss anything in my intent declaration, I'd written it down. After I lit the candle, I read from the paper.

"With this blessing, I intend for my home to once again be a place of peace, comfort, and safety for myself, my animals, and all those I welcome inside. With this blessing, I ask that any lingering pain or suffering be banished, leaving me with a clear space where I can have meaningful relationships and create good new memories for the rest of my days. So mote it be."

With Keiko shadowing me, I returned to Morgan and the others still waiting outside. "You're up." As they entered, I turned to Keiko. "What questions do you have?"

She immediately asked, "What's in the cauldron? Moon water?"

"No, that's sage water. To three-quarters moon water and one-quarter witch hazel, we add a sprig of white sage, a few drops each of clary sage and hyssop essential oils, and some black tourmaline and rose quartz chips. It works much like a smudge stick. Let's follow them upstairs. They'll be in a sort of meditative state and likely won't acknowledge us at all, so be sure to stay out of their way."

For each room, starting upstairs with my bedroom, Morgan entered first. She went to every window and at the top marked an X with sage water and repeated the words, "No evil shall enter through this marked opening. So mote it be."

"Shouldn't she do the doorways too?" Keiko whispered.

I shook my head. "Only exterior windows and doors, because evil enters from the outside. She marks the openings first so nothing can enter while they're sweeping. To keep the house clean, I will repeat this entire process on my own every few weeks."

After marking the openings with the water, Morgan smudged each corner floor to ceiling and across the walls. Then she signaled for three witches to enter and begin sweeping. Once every room, including the bathrooms, closets, and hallways had been marked, smudged, and the witches had all swept their way outside, Morgan declared, "Reeva's cottage is clean. The property, however, also holds on to angst from the past, so there is one last thing we need to do."

I nudged Keiko with my elbow. "We can join this time."

Her eyes were wide. "What am I supposed to do?" She was so anxious to do the right thing or, more specifically, to not do the wrong thing.

"Just listen. Morgan will tell us."

Morgan chose five members and sent each to an elemental point at the edge of my property. Verne went to the water point. Violet to spirit. Basil earth, Luna air, and Honey fire. "Once they're in position, the rest of us will space ourselves evenly between them. Stand with your hands at your sides, palms facing Reeva's home. Envision a bright light of peace surrounding you. Watch it soak into you, flow out of your palms, and toward the cottage. Softly chant the words *peace, comfort,* and *safety* over and over like a mantra. This will surround Reeva's home and property with a circle of protection and positivity."

Keiko and I chose spots between Violet and Verne. Once everyone was ready, the chanting began. "Peace, comfort, safety" became an indecipherable buzz as each member repeated the words using their own pace and intonation. As I chanted, I gazed around the circle, fixing this moment in my mind. Next to me, Keiko fidgeted.

"So mote it be," Morgan declared loudly three minutes later. "Our work is done."

"Is something wrong?" I asked Keiko when we all separated. "You seemed distracted."

"I screwed up your blessing, didn't I? I'm sorry. I was chanting and watching everyone, and it seemed like . . ." She looked at some of the other coven members, a genuine look of concern on her face.

"Keiko, what's wrong?"

"It's . . . nothing. Sorry. I hope I didn't ruin the blessing."

CHAPTER
SIX

With Morgan's role as fill-in high priestess done for the evening, she took my arm and walked me toward the front of my cottage. "Mama asked me to give you her regrets for not coming tonight. River is busy with something at work, so she opted to babysit the twins. She hopes you're not upset."

Briar and I had a complicated relationship. As teens, we often butted heads. Quietly. It wasn't like we erupted into cat fights. She and her mother were the first to join the O'Shea family here. While her mother, Dulcie, made a big impact on villagers over the years, Briar couldn't always accept that she was just a kid like the rest of us. She liked being the leader, so even if a plan was someone else's, she always wanted to be the one to direct the group. She had mellowed significantly over the years and became less the person in charge and more a gentle mentor to many. We got along fine now, despite a few shadow wounds.

"If I had the option to babysit grandchildren," I replied, "that's where I'd be as well."

Morgan offered a sad smile, knowing that would never be

possible for me. "I hate to leave so soon, but I need to get back." Her gaze dropped toward her swollen breasts. "Feeding time."

"I understand." Giving her a gentle hug, I added, "Kiss those babies for me, and thank you for stepping up tonight."

Despite my earlier worries, I was glad we did it this way. It seemed someone needed to keep an eye on Keiko.

"You know I'm here anytime you need me," Morgan promised. "And not just for coven reasons."

"Same holds true for you. We live a literal minute apart. If you need someone to watch the twins . . . or River, say the word."

She laughed, throwing her head back. "Goodnight, Reeva, and blessed be."

Heads turned to watch her leave, and the mood mellowed a tick. I stepped up to address the coven, but before I could, Sanny let out a screech and series of squawks from inside the house. I put her in her cage after the blessing was done. She probably wanted to be let out. It was almost dark, and owls were nocturnal, after all.

"If I can have your attention?" The coven turned to me. "I can't thank you all enough for what you've done for me tonight. You know that tonight's full moon is the Flower Moon or the Corn Planting Moon. That meaning behind the second one is obvious, I think."

Laughter sounded from a couple areas in the group.

"The Flower Moon," I continued, "is a time not only for flowers to bloom but humans as well. It's a great time to consider a new career or job, or to spend some time on self-reflection and evaluation." I glanced at Ruby. "In other words, the perfect time for a life refresh or reset."

Heads bobbed up and down and murmurs of agreement rumbled.

"I have a firepit in the corner of my property. While it's nowhere near as big as the Meditation Circle fire ring, I'm happy to hold a ritual for anyone who may want to do so. In the meantime, knowing how tiring cottage cleansings can be, Laurel graciously brought scones for us." I looked toward my cottage. Luna and Verne were just coming out with trays. "Looks like they're ready to pass them—"

A gasp rose from somewhere in the group, and a woman's voice called out, "Can we get a chair please?"

I rushed to where I'd heard the voice and found Gardenia supporting Iris.

"What happened?" I asked, waving for Basil to hurry with the chair he'd grabbed from my patio.

"I think doing the blessing tired her out." Gardenia looked worried. "Her heart . . . you know."

We all knew. Iris was a dear woman, happy to putter all day in her garden like any good green witch. Her specialty was, no surprise, irises. Of the 300 or more species, she knew everything there was to know about 200 of the beautiful flowers. Iris's heart started failing a few years ago, and since she was quickly approaching her nineties, even if a heart to replace her breaking one became available, she wouldn't accept it.

"Let some young ducky have it," she told me with total sincerity when I'd asked about a transplant. "We can't expect our parts to hang in there forever, and I've had a long, wonderful life."

Once she was seated, I knelt in front of her. "Tell me you didn't wear yourself out on my account."

She smiled tiredly. A look that made me worry. "If this is my last full moon, I consider myself blessed to spend it with my coven doing something good." She pointed a crooked finger at me. "You deserve to be happy, Reeva. You stood like a shield between the village and Flavia for too many years, taking the brunt of her abuse. It's time for you to reap the rewards of always putting others first."

Tears filled my eyes, and I couldn't speak to reply.

Fortunately, Verne showed up with a tray of Laurel's scones, so I had a moment to collect myself.

"How about some refreshments, ladies?" he asked. "Laurel made both chocolate and cinnamon chip scones. Do you have a preference?"

"Either is fine." I held out a hand, too concerned about Iris to care about scones. He handed me a chocolate one as Gardenia took a cinnamon chip from the tray.

"This might perk you up, Mimi," Gardenia suggested. "How about some tea to go with it?"

Iris nodded. "Tea sounds nice."

I pointed toward the cottage. "There are carafes of hot water, cups, and a variety of teas on the kitchen counter. Help yourself." As Gardenia hurried off, I set down my scone and took the old woman's hand in mine. "Should I call over to Unity for you?"

"Good Goddess, stop fussing. I got a little tired. The world isn't coming to an end. A bit of tea and a bite to eat and I'll be good as new. Or good as I can get, at least."

My cat appeared next to us then and leapt onto Iris's lap.

She laughed. "Animals always know, don't they?"

I smiled at Dot. She loved laps.

"Holding a cat is good for the heart. Lowers your pulse." Iris ran her fingers through Dot's fur, then tilted the cat's face up to hers. "Bright-orange eyes. What a beauty. But I never thought of you as being cliché, Reeva. A witch with a black cat?"

Iris's color was getting better, and her breathing steadier and stronger. Good job, Dot. I relaxed and explained, "Dot is an American Bombay. They resemble miniature panthers, don't they? Those eyes sealed the deal for my daughter. She was Yasmine's cat."

"Oh," Iris exhaled. "And now she's yours."

I scratched Dot's forehead. "She's great company."

"Did I understand you adopted an owl too?"

"Close. Sanny adopted me. She showed up on the patio one day and again the next and the next . . ." I held my hands six inches apart. "She's fully grown and about this big, also has large orange eyes, and her head is on a swivel. Or so it seems. She sits with her back to me and rotates her head to look straight at me." I shivered playfully. "That's a little disturbing."

"As is her call. I heard her earlier. Not happy with so many people in her house."

"No, she's not. And she has many calls. One sounds like a combination of a hoot and the ping of a ship's sonar. Another is kind of like the squeaker in a dog's chew toy. The most disturbing one reminds me of a screeching cat."

Iris arched her eyebrows. "And you allow this creature to stay in your cottage?"

"We have an agreement. I let her stay inside as long as she remains quiet." I narrowed my eyes at Dot. "Other than warning calls when strangers are about, the only time she makes any noise inside is when Dot teases her."

"Here you go, Mimi." Gardenia handed a mug to Iris. "A nice calming chamomile."

"That sounds lovely," Iris agreed. "But I'd rather have one of those chocolate scones than a cinnamon."

I picked up the napkin and small scone from where I'd set it on the grass. Just the right size for a nighttime snack. "I'll trade you. I'm not particular about flavor."

"Thank you, my dear." Iris took a bite of the scone. "Oh, very tasty."

I looked between the pair. Maiden and Crone. Iris's daughter was in her forties when Gardenia was born. She passed away when Gardenia was only four years old, so Gardenia grew up here in the village with her doting grandmother. Iris tried to lead her granddaughter down the green witch path and teach her about plants, but the girl wasn't interested. Gardenia still seemed to be struggling to find her way, which I suppose was normal for many in their twenties.

"If either of you needs anything," I began but was interrupted when Laurel arrived and practically hip checked me out of the way to take my spot next to Iris.

"I heard there was a little trouble over here. Are you all right? Is there anything I can do?"

Laurel hired Gardenia at The Inn a few years ago and, like she did with all her employees, cared very much about Gardenia's personal life. She purposely assigned Gardenia to whichever task needed doing, hoping something would spark an interest in her. Gardenia did whatever was asked of her but seemed happiest when taking care of her ailing grandmother.

"Nothing wrong with me that a cat, a scone, and a cup of tea can't fix." Iris set her napkin on Dot's back, broke off another bite of the scone, and held it up to Laurel. "These are quite good. I understand you made them."

"I did and thank you." Laurel smiled, but it quickly turned into a deep frown. "Maybe you should go home and get some rest. Let me give you a ride."

When Laurel reached for Dot, Iris slapped her hand. "A ride will be welcome, but only after I finish my snack." She looked past Laurel. "And spend a bit more time with my beloved witches."

A line had formed behind Laurel. Seemed others had heard of Iris's episode and came to check on her.

Laurel stepped aside and told Gardenia, "Let me know when you're ready to leave. I'll drive you." To me, she said, "I heard she collapsed. As in fell to the ground."

"She might have," I agreed, "if her granddaughter hadn't been at her side."

"That poor girl. She's afraid Iris won't be with us much longer. So worried, in fact, she's cut her hours at The Inn to ten or twelve a week and still calls in sick some days."

Laurel was such a protector. *Smother Hen*, some of her employees lovingly called her. A quality passed down from her mother, who had built The Inn as a home next to the lake for the two of them. Its original version was much smaller, but as Whispering Pines' popularity grew, Fern added to the building during each off-season. First came the addition of more bedrooms, a bigger kitchen, and living room off of what was Fern and Laurel's personal apartment/living quarters. Then another floor with five more bedrooms with private bathrooms. Next, Fern converted the first floor's bedrooms into a lobby and large dining room that was now The Inn's restaurant. When that was complete, she added a third floor with another five bedrooms and bathrooms. In the end, there were ten rooms in which she could accommodate a maximum of thirty guests and a restaurant that was almost always full.

"You need to hire more people," I mused. "We all do this year. With the arrival of the twins, even Morgan needs someone part-time at Shoppe Mystique to help Willow. She agreed to give Keiko a try."

"Our wannabe coven member? I guess that's not going so well."

"I heard the same thing from some customers today. Did I tell you that she's been helping out at Hearth & Cauldron?"

"You didn't. What's she doing? Can she cook?"

"No, but that's my territory anyway. She cleans and stocks and asks a million questions." I laughed. "So far, she's doing a fine job, so I'm thinking about putting her on a regular schedule. Ruby needs someone, too, but that's been true for the last two seasons. She's never organized enough to bring someone on before the season starts."

"And then she's too busy to train someone once the tourists arrive," Laurel concluded. "Quite a conundrum. I hate to say it, but we're running out of villagers looking for work. What we need to do is bring in seasonal help, but we don't have any place for them to live. Rental cottages, rooms at The Inn and Pine Time, and campsites go to tourists first." She crossed her arms and pondered the problem. "Maybe we could work out a deal for monthly rates with the hotels on the other side of the village limits. I'll talk with the manager over there and see if that's a possibility."

We watched as the line to check on Iris grew shorter.

"Were you serious about driving them home?" I asked. "I think they came here with the O'Connors, but Ruby also has her car here. Or I can take them."

"I'll take them," Laurel insisted. "You've got to be ready to drop after . . . everything over the past few weeks. And while I'm sure the O'Connors would take them, April gets a little chatty after a coven gathering. Iris needs quiet."

"Sounds like we have a plan. I should circulate. Thank you for taking part in the blessing and bringing those scones. That was very thoughtful. And for caring so much about Iris and Gardenia. If everyone cared just a little bit more, the world would be a much better place."

She gave me a warm smile. "It's got to start somewhere, right?"

As I walked away, I wondered why Laurel and I had never gotten closer. Like Briar and me, Laurel and I also had a complicated history but for a different reason. We grew up together but both preferred to keep to ourselves rather than hang out with the other kids. If only we would have realized then how similar we were, we might have been good friends. We still shared similarities. We were both businesswomen concerned with hospitality and making our customers feel at home. Most days, during tourist season especially, we barely had time to breathe, but we both needed to eat. Maybe we could squeeze in a lunch sometime.

"I don't think I've ever been inside your cottage, Reeva."

I blinked, clearing childhood memories from my mind, and found Violet standing before me.

"Karl never had anyone over," she continued, "and this is the first time you have. Right?"

"It's the first time I've had the coven over," I amended.

"I'm over all the time," Ruby said as she joined us.

"*All* the time," I moaned and winked at Violet.

"Well, it's charming," Violet praised, "and that kitchen is exactly what I imagined for you. I'm so happy we cleared out all that bad energy." She shivered. "I felt it as soon as I walked in."

"You felt it?" Ruby asked. "Really?"

Violet was a cross between a green witch and a fortune teller, or so it seemed. No one anywhere could roast, brew, and blend coffee the way she could, and while we all teased her about being a gossip, it was more that she just seemed to know things before the rest of us did. Of course, like with Laurel and The Inn, hundreds of people went through her coffee house every day during tourist season, so she overheard their conversations.

"Oh, sure." Violet nodded. "That cottage was holding on to a lot of secrets." She brushed her hands together. "All gone now. By the way, Reeva, your beans are ready. You can pick them up anytime."

Along with the super-secret blend she served and sold exclusively at Ye Olde Bean Grinder, she also roasted a blend for the local shops. Smart of her to save the best stuff for herself. The local blend meant a cup of coffee at Hearth & Cauldron would taste the same as one at The Inn's restaurant, Treat Me Sweetly, Biblichor, or Grapes, Grains, and Grub. It was a subtle thing that united the village. Alert tourists would comment on the similarities, but few figured out our secret.

"I'll stop by in the morning," I promised.

"Great. See you then. Basil and I are going to head out. The Grinder opens early, you know. People need their morning joe."

"That rhymes," Ruby noted. "I could cross-stitch it on a picture for your wall."

"Or we could put it on T-shirts." Violet wiggled all ten fingers in a wave. "See ya, ladies."

"I wanted to let you know," Ruby pointed toward the fire pit in the corner of my yard, "a few members have gathered for a full moon ritual—"

I saw the fire. "On their own? I thought we'd do that as a coven. Or as much of the coven that wanted to." Looked like they didn't want my guidance.

"Stop it," she scolded. "I can tell what you're thinking by the look on your face. Trust me, they love that you're our high priestess. Everyone's just doing their own thing tonight. I'm going to start tidying up."

Ruby was right. I wasn't so sure they *loved* me, but Morgan chose me. With Briar's blessing. Why was I so self-conscious about this?

Maybe the problem was that I came after Morgan, and anyone would have a hard time following her. The woman was almost half my age and had twice my confidence. She commanded attention simply by entering a room and could keep the group hanging on her every word until she declared a gathering over.

Dot appeared at my feet then, headbutting my leg and winding around my ankles. She stared up at me, glanced across the yard at the two clusters of coven members that were still here, then up at me again. Then back to them.

"Fine, I get it. I need to spend more time with them."

I crossed the yard to one of the clusters. Verne, Luna, Gil, Peyton, and Lorena were discussing Verne's latest hobby. The man had many.

"I'd love to come see this setup," Gil was saying. "An aquarium at the marina seems fitting."

"Too matchy-matchy," Luna teased.

"If you get one," Verne cautioned, "go with something small, like a ten-gallon freshwater setup that you can lift without having to remove too much water. You shut down the marina over the winter and will want to bring it home. Saltwater setups can't be moved. They're far too complicated."

"What brought up this discussion?" I asked, trying to casually insert myself into the conversation. "Have you done something new to yours, Verne?"

I'd heard that he had an impressive hundred-gallon saltwater tank that had taken him years to establish.

"He had to set up a second tank," Lorena teased with an eye roll and shake of her head.

Verne blushed fiercely. "I admit, I didn't do adequate research. I read that puffer fish and clownfish need space and figured a hundred-gallon tank had plenty of room so added two puffers to start." He held his thumb and forefinger about two inches apart. "They're just little guys. Turns out they're very aggressive. They started nipping at my other fishes' fins."

"Nipping?" his daughter, Luna, scoffed. "They're actually eating the other fish."

"She's exaggerating," Verne insisted. "One weak fish got eaten. Shame. They're cute little beasties, but they don't play well with others."

"You all know that I travel in the off-season," began Peyton, owner of Sundry, the local groceries and more store.

We nodded. Peyton traveled with a friend every year, and they took turns choosing the location. Peyton learned about the local food, while his friend studied the customs of the area. I had to admit, I was a bit envious of his adventures.

"I went to Southeast Asia this past winter," he continued, "and learned about the seafood there. I was thinking of selling some exotic varieties in our fish case."

"I don't think so," insisted Lorena, his assistant manager.

"Some of those fish are not only crazy expensive, they're hard to prepare."

Peyton added, "Yeah, I should probably ditch that idea. If I'm going to ask someone to spend that much money on dinner, I want to make sure it won't require a degree to make it."

"Perhaps," I stated, "you need to hold a cooking class."

"Are you volunteering?" Peyton asked, hopeful.

"I don't know a lot about seafood," I confessed. "I'm happy to look into it, but it would take me as long to learn as it would you. Maybe on your next adventure, you could arrange to learn the skills from the local experts."

He considered this and nodded his head. "I like that. I'll check into it for this winter. Good idea, Reeva."

We chatted a bit more on various topics, the remaining coven members slowly joining us. After another half hour had passed, India announced, "I'm going to say goodnight. I bid on and won a collection of vintage books in an online auction. They arrived late this afternoon. I want to get to Biblichor early in the morning so I can look through them and get them on the shelves."

The others agreed it was time to go.

I held my hands over my heart. "Thank you all again for the blessing."

"We were happy to do it for you, Reeva," Rourke assured with a pat on my shoulder.

"One last question before you leave," I begged. "I got to the village just before Midsummer last year. Is it true that the villagers celebrate Litha in their own homes?"

"I don't remember exactly when Midsummer turned into a family and friends celebration," April stated. "Probably when the tourists started taking over the commons."

Gil shook his head. "They make a lot of noise, eat, drink, and dance around the bonfire."

"You're off the hook for this one," Peyton said. "No one expects you to arrange a gathering."

"So mote it be," I replied with a laugh. "Merry leave, everyone."

Naturally, I'd respect the villagers' wishes, but I didn't like the idea of celebrating another Litha by myself. Yasmine and I had always looked forward to preparing a Midsummer feast of grilled salmon and vegetables and a fresh fruit salad. She loved being able to stay up all night. We'd watch the sun set on the longest day of the year and go to bed when it rose again in the morning. She called it our backwards day when she was seven and finally old enough to understand what we were doing.

Martin was the only family I had left, but he'd stopped following Wiccan traditions years ago. Besides, he'd be busy with either Rosalyn or patrolling the commons that night. Maybe I could convince Ruby to stay up all night with me. I really didn't want to be alone.

CHAPTER

SEVEN

By eleven o'clock, Ruby and Keiko were the only ones left at my cottage. Ruby helped me with dishes while Keiko bagged the garbage.

"Looks like I got here just in time," Keiko commented.

"For what?" Ruby asked.

"To help liven up the place," she replied as though it should be obvious. "Does the coven always turn in this early?"

I took my tea collection to the pantry. "Not at all. We started early tonight. Most gatherings don't begin until midnight."

"Remember, we all live by our own schedules from November through May," Ruby added. "Now that we'll be working seven days a week until Samhain and have to care what the clock says again, we need to readjust. Give us a couple of weeks and we'll be party animals right along with you."

Keiko cringed. "Party animals? No one says that anymore."

Ruby frowned. "I do."

Keiko gave her a blank stare. "Like I said, just in time. This village needs more young blood."

I first met Keiko two weeks ago, just before my sister was sentenced. Jayne had told me that Yasmine and Keiko had been friends here and that the young woman might be able to give me insight into my daughter's last days. I acknowledged their friendship but hadn't been able to talk with Keiko about it yet.

The other thing both Jayne and Morgan had warned me about was that a year ago Keiko was new to Wicca and determined to learn negative magic. She tried to get a job working with Morgan at Shoppe Mystique, hoping the green witch would teach her. Morgan sent her away, instructed her to immerse herself in the religion, and invited her to come back once she realized how dangerous messing around with negative spells could be. Keiko reappeared in the village during opening weekend and declared she now saw the error of her ways. Desperate for help at the shop, Morgan agreed to give her a chance, and we made a pact to help the girl get on the right path but to tread carefully while doing so.

On that topic, I asked Keiko, "How are things going at Shoppe Mystique? I understand Morgan will be coming back for the afternoon shifts starting Friday."

She nodded and bounced on the balls of her feet, her waist-length black pigtails swaying as she did. "I'm so excited. It's been my dream for almost two years to work with the Barlows. Morgan in particular. She's just so . . ." She let out a fangirl sigh that seemed to come from somewhere around her belly button.

"You'll learn a great deal from her." I thought of Ember's comment about Keiko needing more guidance. "Willow is a talented green witch as well. Has she had time to teach you much?"

"Not a lot. The store is packed, especially in the afternoons, so they have me on the schedule eleven to three." She shrugged. "Makes sense for helping out, but she doesn't have time to teach me much. I'm doing my best, but I think I made some mistakes. When I got there today, Willow showed me how to run the register. Looks like that's where I'll be until someone can teach me more. I'm allowed to tell people where to find things in the shop, but I can't give advice. Guess I suggested the wrong herbs for a stomach ailment."

She said that last bit like it was no big deal.

Ruby pressed the dishwasher's start button. "You do understand the kind of problems that could cause. Right?"

"Yeah, I get it." She tossed the garbage bag out the side door. "I'll put that in the can when I leave."

Not wanting to dismiss the *wrong herbs* statement, I told her, "My sister nearly killed me with the wrong combination of herbs." I left out the fact she had purposely created the mix and intended for me to die.

"Wow," Keiko replied, with a little more compassion.

"Morgan grew up learning from her mother," Ruby recalled while snatching a piece of dark chocolate from the tin in my pantry. "Briar learned from her mother. It took three seasons before Morgan let Willow run the place alone and then it was only for a couple of hours at a time. She wasn't allowed near the deadly stash for five years."

"I get it," Keiko sang out a little louder.

"I'm sure you've learned many things about green witchery over the past two years," I added, "but it'll take a good two more to learn the healing aspects."

"I said I get it," she snapped. "Geez. If I wanted to be lectured, I wouldn't have left home."

She stopped talking so quickly it was obvious she'd blurted something she hadn't intended to.

"Keiko?" I pressed cautiously. "Did you run away from home?"

I expected her to bolt out of the cottage. Instead, she braided one of her pigtails partway and then shook it to unwind it again. "I left home when I was sixteen. To answer your next question, I'm nineteen now."

She *left home*. What did that mean? Was it the same thing as running away, or had something else been going on? "Where did you live? Don't tell me the streets."

"Sometimes. If it was warm enough. We slept on park benches or other places."

"We?" Ruby asked.

"Me and some other kids. We watched out for each other."

That would explain her occasional street-tough attitude. I saw the scared little girl behind it, though.

"Okay, hang on." I sat on the edge of my kitchen table. Keiko leaned against the built-in china cupboard. "You sometimes lived on the street if it was warm enough. What about when it wasn't warm enough?"

Something wasn't adding up here. I could spot a nineteen-year-old who thought she could hide things from me from forty paces.

"Breast implants? Really, Yazzy?"

"You snooped through my stuff?"

"I didn't snoop. I saw the brochure sitting on your dresser when I brought your shoes to your room. Is this what you've been so secretive about lately? You barely look me in the eye."

"You can't stop me. I'm nineteen. A legal adult."

"No, I can't, but I'd like you to research this thoroughly first."

Keiko's response pulled me from the memory. "I went back home when it got too cold." She grew quiet, her expression clearly showing she was remembering something she didn't especially want to. Her flippant, "That was fun," confirmed it.

There was a lot she wasn't saying. "Your parents knew where you were?"

She let out a heavy sigh. "Look, what happened, happened. My parents and I came to an understanding. Yes, they know where I am, and I know where they are. Not that it matters because, like I said, I'm nineteen and all legally my own problem."

"An understanding?" Ruby echoed. "What does that mean? And where are they?"

"I don't want to get into what that means," Keiko insisted. "Where they are is back in Japan. Specifically, some dinky little village northwest of Osaka. Don't know if I'll ever see them again, and I'm not sure I care. Or that they do." She held her hand up at me. "Don't look at me like that. It's not like we hate each other. It's that they don't understand me and don't want to and I'm not willing to live by their rules. I need to be who I am. You know? That's why I fit perfectly here. As long as there are some people my age. I mean, I'm fine hanging out with you oldsters to learn Wicca stuff and for the coven gatherings 'cause that's pretty cool."

Ruby cocked an eyebrow at her. "Oldsters? Not sure I can handle the gush of love coming off you."

Keiko made a face at her.

That's why I fit perfectly here. She wanted to move to Whispering Pines. The village had all sorts of stipulations around that. The big one was that a newcomer had to have a job in the village in order to become a resident. They could rent a place, like one of the rental cottages or a room at the B&B, for as long as they wanted, but that got pricey quickly.

The more I'd learned about this young woman, the more my heart had warmed to her. "You'll find plenty of non-oldster people here. I promise. You know Gardenia and Luna from the coven. Gardenia is a couple of years older than you, and Luna is a bit younger. Close enough to be friends, though. Rosalyn O'Shea is in her mid-twenties. Lily Grace and Oren just graduated from high school in May. Lily Grace is also trying to find her way."

"Introduce me?" Keiko clasped her hands together, pleading.

"You already know Gardenia and Luna," I reminded.

"Yeah, I mean this Lily girl. Who is she?"

Right now, Lily Grace would run the other direction if I

even looked at her for too long let alone tried to introduce her to anyone. Her mother, my childhood best friend, Rae, died at my sister's hands two weeks ago. Lily Grace needed to blame someone and chose me. She claimed if I would have *done something* about my sister decades ago, the evil swirling beneath the surface of this village never would have formed. I couldn't argue against or agree with that. What I knew was that for more than fifty years, no one had been able to stop my sister from doing anything.

"Lily Grace," I corrected. "She always goes by both names."

Ruby nodded. "If you call her Lily, you'll be looking at her backside before you can finish saying hi."

"How about some tea?" I asked. "We can settle into the sunroom and chat a little longer."

"Not too long." Ruby glanced at Keiko. "Building stamina and all that."

"So glad you two are getting along," I teased.

"Oldster," Keiko hissed, but I saw the grin playing at her mouth. "You two stress me out. Can I play with your cat?"

"Her name is Dot." I filled my kettle with water. "Let her sniff the back of your hand before you pet her. Sanny, my owl, will peck your fingers if you reach for her, so let her come to you too."

"Her beak may be tiny, but it's sharp." Ruby shook her hand as though freshly pecked. "Are you still living at the campground?"

"Yep." Keiko shrugged. "It's working okay. For now."

"I live at that end of the village," Ruby clarified. "If you trust someone my age to drive, I'll drop you off at your tent later."

Keiko shook her head and wandered into the sunroom. "You're not as funny as you think you are, Ruby."

"She called me by name. That's a big improvement over oldster." Ruby waited until we heard Keiko talking to the animals. "Okay, what's wrong?"

"With what?" I asked.

"With you. You're awfully quiet tonight."

"That episode with Iris really upset me." I recalled the elderly woman's shaking hands and her velvety soft skin. "She seems so frail."

"She does. But you were quiet before the coven got here. I thought you were excited for the blessing."

"I was more anxious to have it done than excited about it." I inhaled deeply. "The cottage feels lighter now. The darkness Karl left behind is finally gone. I tried many times but couldn't get rid of it on my own."

"Just going to make me say it, hey? You're free of Flavia. Why are you so glum, chum?"

"I'm not glum. I'm going through an adjustment. You were an only child so don't understand. Whether you get along with a sibling or tear each other to shreds, they're still your sibling. They're still your blood. It hurts me that my sister's life was so awful and that I couldn't do anything to help her."

"Not your fault." When I didn't reply, she pressed, "What are you thinking?"

"That I miss her."

"You what?" Ruby shrieked, appalled by this. "I can't believe—"

"Not the person she is. For years, I've missed the person she could have been and the relationship we could have had. When I was a kid, I used to daydream about what it would be like to have a sister who was also my friend. She never tried, though. Barely even talked to me. I hoped that at some point she'd want to meet and get to know her birth daughter. I thought, if anyone, Yasmine could lighten that heart of hers."

"Not sure that's possible when something's inky black through and through." Ruby took three mugs from my cupboard and set them on a tray with a small pitcher of milk and a bowl of sugar.

"Through and through," I agreed. "Flavia never once asked about her. Yasmine had known she was adopted since she was very young. On her twentieth birthday, when Flavia still hadn't shown any interest in her, I decided she deserved to know the truth about her birth parents."

So I told my daughter about how Flavia's husband was attacked by a bear as he walked through our woods late one afternoon. About how one night a short time later, my husband *comforted* her. Flavia tried to disguise the pregnancy with oversized dresses, but everyone knew what had happened between her and Karl. A few supported me—Laurel, Briar, Sugar, and Honey. Ruby had gotten married and left Whispering Pines at that point. Flavia and I left the village to ride out the final weeks of her pregnancy in a small, comfortable house in small, comfortable town north of Milwaukee.

I had worked in different restaurants for top-notch chefs for five years after college. When I realized I'd never achieve my dreams by working for someone else, I returned to the village to figure out my next step. That's when I married Karl. I had just settled in and was finally feeling comfortable with a life here when my sister upended everything.

I didn't tell Yasmine that Flavia left the day after she gave birth to her and returned to Whispering Pines.

I did tell her, "After about a minute, I was so in love with you, Yazzy, that I was honored to be the one to raise you."

I didn't tell her how my sister's final words before leaving were, "If you want her father to retain any sort of reputation in that village, you'll deal with this problem now."

Karl could have left Whispering Pines with me. We could have raised his baby together. Instead, he chose to stay in this secret-filled village with my evil incarnate sister. What did I care about his reputation? I kept that to myself too.

Instead, I let my sister believe she was ruling my world once again while secretly accepting the ticket out of Whispering Pines for what I thought would be the last time. I gladly took the money, from her husband's life insurance policy and our parents' will, that she deposited into my bank account every month. And I loved every single day with my daughter.

"Reeva?" Ruby asked, bringing me back to the present. "Why did you let Yasmine come here last year?"

"It's not like I could have stopped her." I dropped pinches of Morgan's Relax tea into the teapot on the tray and added hot water. "It was and will always be the biggest regret of my life. I never, ever dreamed it would come to what it did." I stared out the window toward my triad. I couldn't see the trees now, it was too dark, but I itched to run out there and lose myself in the magic of the firefly twinkles again. Maybe Yazzy would be there in the shimmer this time. "What I should have done was come with her." I inhaled and shook away the memories and regrets. Can't go back. Only forward.

Ruby frowned at me from the corner near the cupboard where I kept my cookbooks and mixing bowls.

"I'm okay, Ruby. Just having one of those days. Let's go sit with Keiko." I checked to make sure we had everything for our tea and noticed, "Look, Laurel left her scones. Would you like one?" I lifted the tea towel, uncovering a half-dozen scones, and gasped. "Oh my Goddess."

"What's wrong?" Ruby rushed to my side.

I plucked one from the basket. Earlier, I had recognized that they were round, the way the British traditionally made them, instead of the triangular shapes Americans preferred. I'd been so distracted by Iris's health scare I hadn't noticed that instead of being rolled and cut with a round cutter, they'd been baked in a pan. With shaking hands, I turned the scone over.

"They're fluted."

"How pretty," Ruby gushed. "How did Laurel make them look like that? She always says she's a frustrated kitchen witch who never could quite get the hang of cooking. These scones are really good, though. Did you try one? What's the matter?"

"The pan she used to bake them had cups with this design." Before she could ask, I explained, "I had two pans with this pattern on the shelf at the shop. They disappeared sometime this morning."

"Disappeared as in someone stole them?"

"That's what I'm saying."

"You think Laurel stole your pans?" Ruby crossed her arms and scowled at me. "I can't believe she would do that."

"I can't either, but the coincidence can't be ignored. She brings fluted scones to the coven gathering the same day my pans went missing?"

Ruby struggled with this. "Did your pans have this exact pattern?"

"Good question." I forced myself to relax a bit and tried to picture them. "I can't remember. Bee might know, though. Let's not have these with our tea. I've got some sugar cookies we can nibble instead."

"Why not the scones?" Ruby flipped the towel over the basket again and set them aside. "I told you, they're really good."

"When an item is stolen, dark energy attaches to it. Food made in a stolen pan could cause all sorts of problems."

"Oh my." Ruby paled. "And most of the coven just ate these scones."

CHAPTER

EIGHT

Despite my concern over the potentially tainted scones, I slept better than I had in more than a year. The cottage didn't give off any bad vibes and instead made me feel as though I was protected and safe. Just the way one should feel in their home. I had opened my bedroom window wide and fell asleep to the sound of the pine trees whispering to each other. A noise woke me in the middle of the night, and then Sanny let out a screech, but she quieted quickly, and I went right back to dreamland.

I woke rested and energized, ready to pop out of bed before my alarm went off. This turned out to be a good thing because after all those feet trampling through my home, the energy was clean but the floors were a mess. After letting Sanny in, I vacuumed the carpet and then mopped the kitchen. The main floor bathroom also needed freshening. I admit, I was a bit obsessive when it came to the level of messiness I could tolerate in my home, but the benefit to living alone in a small cottage was that a refresh took less than an hour.

The bird and cat followed me as I finished my tidying by straightening things that had been displaced during the sweeping. "No wonder I prefer the coven meet elsewhere. It was worth a bit of dirt and disorganization this time, though. I slept like I'd been drugged."

My gaze unintentionally traveled to the basket of scones still sitting on my counter.

"Laurel did not drug us."

Dot weaved around my ankles, mewing to be picked up, so I did and let her drape herself over my shoulder.

"She's a good person. A very good person. There has to be another explanation for this scone thing."

Sanny flew down from where she'd perched high on a shelf and landed on the counter next to the basket.

"If she put anything in them, it was good vibes."

Laurel's way was to quietly bring happiness to people's lives with comfort. And an infusion of comfort was exactly what the villagers needed after all the deaths here last year.

This, of course, made me think of my sister and how rather than restoring the peace, her incarceration had divided the village. It felt a bit pie in the sky, but I appreciated Jayne's stance that while criminals needed to be punished, they should also have a chance to right their wrongs. Perhaps with little else to do during her incarceration and the spiritual guidance of Sister Agnes, our resident excommunicated nun, Flavia could change her ways. I prayed to the Goddess that would happen but didn't hold out a lot of hope.

"As for Laurel," I told my twosome, pushing away the thoughts of my sister, "there's only one way to find out. I have to talk to her."

Dot let out a *mrow* of agreement. Sanny flapped her tiny wings.

"I'll go over to The Inn and have a chat with her before I open Hearth & Cauldron. Like I said, there has to be a simple explanation. But first, breakfast."

After a poached egg, an English muffin with homemade jam,

half a grapefruit, and tea, I took five minutes to wash my dishes and put them away. My kitchen might be stuffed full of gadgets, but it was always clean. No crumbs on the counter or floor, no dirty dishes in the sink or clean ones drying in the drainer. This was the heart of my home, the space that energized me like no place else. We had an understanding: I kept it clean, and it fed my body and soul.

With my cottage back to rights and belly full, I was ready to leave. "All right, girls, play nice today."

Sanny let out a squawk. Dot hissed. For as much as they wanted me to believe they didn't get along, I'd never once found feathers or tufts of fur on the floor.

On my way to the garage to get my bicycle, I discovered what must have been the noise that woke me last night. Across the yard, the chairs around my fire ring were all tipped over and the wood I'd neatly stacked in the rack was tossed about. All I could think was that an animal must have come through. There were occasional black bear sightings here, but they generally stayed away from residences unless desperate for food. I glanced at my garbage can. Untouched. So not a bear. If one had been in my yard, it would have raided the can for scraps. To be safe, I dragged it inside the garage. No time to put things to rights now. I'd re-stack the wood tonight. Instead, I pulled my bicycle out of the garage and hopped on to ride the mile to the shop.

One thing people had to understand about living in or visiting this village was that there would be a lot of walking or bike riding. Cars weren't allowed, and the closest parking lot still meant a half-mile walk to the commons. The residents were used to the forced exercise, and even in the winter, it wasn't a problem because the maintenance crew was diligent about keeping the snow cleared from all walkways. On rare occasions, if I had many items to bring to the shop or things that were too big for my bike's basket, I could leave my vehicle in the small lot behind the sheriff's station for a short time. From there, I pulled a cart the quarter mile to Hearth & Cauldron.

"You're here already." Ruby was sitting on The Twisty Skein's front steps when I rode by. "It's not even eight o'clock."

"You're here too. I figured you'd sleep longer since you were up past midnight."

She sighed. "Couldn't sleep. Probably all the energy from the coven gathering." She squinted at me. "You look really good. What did you do?"

"For the first time in over a year, I slept soundly. The coven should run around and bless everyone's cottage. Can you imagine the positive energy flowing around this place if everyone got a solid night's sleep? I seriously haven't felt this comfortable in my home since Karl and I first moved in."

"That's great, Reeva. Is that the only reason you're here early? An energy surge?"

"Not the only reason. I want to talk to Laurel about those pans." I bit back a grin. I knew why Ruby was here already and it had nothing to do with disrupted sleep. "You want to go with me, don't you?"

She sprang to her feet. "Since you asked."

"To be clear, I don't believe she stole them, but this coincidence is too great to ignore. Like I told the girls, if she infused those scones with anything, it was peace and good vibes. You know how edgy the villagers have been with each other lately."

"Did *the girls* have a reply for that theory?"

Ruby didn't have a pet. She didn't understand.

I parked my bike in the rack to the right of Hearth & Cauldron's main entrance and continued down the Fairy Path with Ruby hot on my heels. "Talking to animals is often more rewarding than people. They don't talk back."

I gave her a pointed look. She stuck her tongue out at me.

"When we get to The Inn, please let me handle things." When

she didn't respond, I pushed, "You'll get all confrontational. That's not what I want. Promise me."

"I heard you."

"But you didn't promise."

She drew a teeny tiny *X* on her chest with the tip of a finger. "Cross my heart."

As we stepped off the wood plank walkway of the Fairy Path and took a left onto the red brick that encircled the commons area, I thought, as I often did, that if the kitchen was the heart of the home, the Pentacle Garden was the heart of Whispering Pines. While not at the center of the village, the garden was the center of the commons. And dead center in the garden was the white marble Negativity Well. That well was the true heart of the village. For decades, people had whispered their worries into their hands and threw them to the bottom to be washed away.

"Do you remember," I asked, feeling nostalgic, "Dulcie telling the tale of how the negativity well came to be?"

"Oh, sure. Fifty-some years ago, she and Lucy were searching for a Yule tree with Briar and Dillon and found a natural spring. They both claimed that the spot where the water burbled to the surface was like stepping into a bubble of serenity."

That spring not only filled the well, it supplied water to the entire village.

"The commons area is still like that," I mused. "Calm and serene. A place where people want to hang out."

After a moment of silence, Ruby asked, "Have you ever wondered how throwing all those bad thoughts and feelings down there affects things?"

I blinked. "I never thought about it."

"All those worries and complaints swirling around. We all drink, bathe, water our plants, and cook with that water."

"Maybe for the next coven gathering we'll bless the well."

We'd taken a dozen or so steps toward The Inn when three small children darted in front of us on the brick path, screaming and laughing.

"Sorry!" their father called out.

"No harm done," I assured. Letting kids burn off steam by running laps around the garden was fine right now. In a couple of hours, however, the area would be packed with tourists.

Ruby sighed. "The laughter of children. Isn't that a wonderful sound?"

She would have been a great mom. She'd been married once, and I often wondered why she never had kids. Ruby not only refused to talk about it, she'd blatantly change the subject or remembered she had something else to do if I asked.

"Good morning, ladies," greeted The Inn's assistant manager, Emery, from behind the registration desk. Even though he was only twenty years old, Laurel had found the perfect business partner in this boy.

"Morning, Emery." Ruby gave a little finger wave. "Is Laurel busy?"

I elbowed her in the ribs and hissed, "You promised."

"All I did was ask about Laurel."

I arched a brow.

"Fine." She clasped her hands behind her back. Innocent as could be.

Emery pointed to his right, past the creaky staircase that led to the guest rooms. "She's in her apartment talking to Mr. Powell. A sink in one of the rooms on the third floor is leaking. We need someone to get over here and fix it ASAP."

From his tone, Emery considered this plumbing problem to be a smite from the Universe. As he did any time a guest wasn't pleased. Grievances must be rectified immediately.

"Just knock," he added before I could ask. "She must be off the phone by now."

"I've never been inside Laurel's apartment," Ruby whispered as we made our way there.

"I was a handful of times when we were kids, but since the whole inn was available, Fern made us gather in the dining room or out on the patio by the lake." As free as the Gale women could be with sharing their home, they tended to keep their private quarters private. "I was in there once before I left twenty years ago, but I don't remember why. Probably stopped to drop something off."

I knocked and took a step away from the door. When there was no answer after thirty seconds, I was about to knock again when the door yanked open.

"Oh, Reeva. Ruby." Laurel pulled a fringed linen shawl tighter around her shoulders. "I expected to find Wesley out there. He says there's a problem with the walk-in freezer in the restaurant's kitchen." She hesitated before opening the door wider and saying, "Come on in and have a seat. Give me a second to let him know Mr. Powell is sending someone to fix that too."

A burst pipe and a broken freezer? As she went back to the bedroom I knew she used as an office, I couldn't help but wonder if the Threefold Law was at work in her world for taking those pans from my shop.

"This is charming," Ruby said of the apartment decorated in shades of pale golden yellow, soft Wedgewood blue, rosy pink, and creamy ivory. As we took opposite ends of the striped love seat, Ruby gazed up at the stained wood beams that formed a grid pattern on the ceiling. "You know what this reminds me of?"

"A cottage in the English countryside?"

It had been a long time, but it looked to me like very little had changed. Even the furniture was in the same place. I remembered Laurel and her mother having very similar tastes.

Laurel even dressed like Fern in flowing pants, loose-fitting blouses, and her hair tied up in a messy bun.

"The whole inn has that appearance," Ruby agreed. "This apartment looks like she got her furniture from someone's grandmother's estate sale. Or multiple grandmothers."

"You're close." Laurel took a seat on a cozy-looking armchair covered in pink and blue chintz. "A lot of it came from my grandmother and great-grandmother. Proof that if you buy what you love and make sure it's quality, it will last many lifetimes. My mother recovered the chairs and loveseat about ten years ago, shortly before she passed. Anyway, what can I do for you two?" She noticed the basket in my lap then. "Returning my basket? There was no hurry for that."

She held out her hand, and I took a scone from beneath the tea towel.

"Goodness, Reeva, you could have kept those." She suddenly looked insulted. "You didn't like them?"

"I wanted to ask you about the pattern." I turned the fluted bottom toward her.

She smiled. "Isn't it a nice touch? My pan makes the design."

"Yes, that's what I thought." Now that I was here in front of her, my comfort level with my mission had weakened. I had to ask, though, or I wouldn't be able to let it go. "I had some pans like that at the shop."

Laurel's blue eyes were bright, and a smile turned her mouth. We were sharing something about cooking, her secret passion. And I was about to rain on it. When I waited too long to say more, the stern expression she used when dealing with unreasonable guests or business contacts slid into place.

"I've got a room on the third floor with a sink pipe that has sprung a leak. Fortunately, my mother thought to put in separate waterlines to each floor when she added on to this place, but I had to shut off the water to the third floor. I'm sure you can imagine how happy the folks up there are. Also, my walk-in freezer has stopped freezing. A potential kitchen disaster you can surely appreciate. *And* Gardenia called in sick again. Whatever you're here to say, Reeva, just say it."

I inhaled and calmly stated, "Those pans went missing from my shop yesterday."

She pursed her lips—disturbingly similar to the way my sister did—and shot to her feet. She stormed off to the tiny kitchen where we heard the clatter of glass and metal items being shifted about.

"Glad you're handling this," Ruby murmured and sat back on the loveseat.

I scowled at her. "Shush."

Laurel returned with a pan in hand. Hers had a dozen cups. The ones in my shop were smaller with six cups each.

"Is this your missing pan?" she asked. "I doubt it, because my grandmother gave this to my mother along with many other things as a housewarming gift when we moved to the village. A decision I sometimes curse."

"You don't mean that," Ruby soothed as though talking to an upset child.

Laurel dropped the pan down on the blue velvet tufted ottoman sitting between the chairs and the loveseat and then lowered onto the chintz chair. "No, I don't."

I moved over to the edge of the ottoman closest to her. "I'm sorry. Truly I am. But the pans went missing and then you showed up with the scones—"

"So you decided I stole your pans?"

"I'm sure you can see how I might draw the conclusion."

She glared at me for a long moment then let her tight shoulders relax. "I can, but we've known each other for forty years. You know me better than that. If you're going to start playing private eye, you'd better learn to gather more facts before accusing people."

Ruby scooted forward on the love seat. "In Reeva's defense,

she didn't accuse you. She told you the pans were missing, and you made the assumption . . ."

Laurel let out a sigh that clearly said we were wearing out our welcome.

"Your apartment looks just the way I remember it," I told her, attempting to break the tension. There were bookcases tucked into corners and beneath windows. Collections of candles in every size sat on side tables, the fireplace mantel, and on top of the many bookcases. "I love it when people actually use candles instead of just decorating with them."

Laurel smiled at that. "Guess it's a witch thing."

"It is. I'm sorry if I offended you. Are we okay?"

She rolled her eyes. "We're fine. As I said, I'm having a challenging morning." The phone she'd set on the ottoman buzzed. "That's the intercom. Hang on." She held it to her ear. "Yes? Okay, send him up to the room and tell him I'll be right there." She clicked off and set the extension in her lap. "Emery says Schmitty is here."

"Schmitty can fix anything," Ruby offered.

"Is this what you're doing today?" Laurel asked. "Running around and hunting down the pan thief?"

I winced apologetically.

"Well, at least you can eliminate me now. And the scones were good, right?"

"I had a chocolate one," Ruby volunteered. "I thought it was great."

"I heard great things about them but never tried one," I admitted and immediately added, "not because you made them. I took one but was so distracted by poor Iris that I never got to eat it. Then, when we found the basket on my counter and I saw the fluting, I worried they were tainted."

Laurel's eyes went wide. "*And* you thought I poisoned you? Honestly, Reeva—"

"By karma," I insisted. "Tainted by karma. You know, because the pans were stolen?"

She shook her head but didn't respond otherwise.

Changing topics, I said, "The blessing seems to have worked. My cottage hasn't been this peaceful in more than twenty years."

"I'm glad." She picked up the basket I'd returned, folded back the tea towel, and held it out to me.

I took one of the chocolates and broke off a bite. "Oh, Laurel. These really *are* good."

She beamed. "High praise from you."

"I've always believed that home cooks can be as talented as trained chefs, and you just proved it." I stood then. "We'll let you get back to handling your crises. I need to stop and get my beans from Violet and then open the shop."

Laurel walked us out, and we waved goodbye to Emery as we left the building.

Ruby frowned. "Strike one on tracking down the pan thief."

"Sometimes, the obvious answer is the right one," I mused, "and other times it's merely a distraction from the truth. I'll talk more with Bee. A bit of Focus tea might help too."

"But just a bit," Ruby cautioned. "A few weeks ago, I was trying to clean and tidy Twisty but was distracted with thoughts of the opening of tourist season and couldn't focus. I had two cups of the stuff and ended up so focused on dusting and straightening I never opened the shop that day. Jayne stopped by to get more sketching pencils and watercolors. She's quite good, by the way. Has some hidden talent she never took the time to explore. Anyway, she said she could see me in the back and tried three times to get my attention. I never heard her."

I chuckled and led us northwest along a pea-gravel path through the Pentacle Garden to Ye Olde Bean Grinder.

"My first experience with Focus tea," I recalled, "was a mug Dulcie Barlow offered me when I was eighteen. I had so much going on in my life at that time, my mind was spinning. She told me to think of one thing to focus on while I drank it. The tea worked so well for me I nearly passed up an offer from the Grahams to work in their bakery after school."

"What? Why?"

"I chose helping my sister find her path as my thing to focus on. I thought kitchen witchery might be an option for her and suggested they hire her instead."

"I didn't know Flavia could cook."

"She can't boil water without burning the pan. Fortunately for me, the Grahams insisted on someone with skills."

Ruby took hold of the coffee shop's door handle, shaped like an arc of coffee beans. The moment we walked in, I could tell something was wrong. Violet didn't welcome us with her normal hundred-watt smile.

"Good morning, Violet," I greeted cautiously.

She turned away from the shelf on the wall behind the counter that held ceramic mugs, personalized for the villagers who came in regularly.

"Oh, Reeva." Violet's eyes were red.

"Are you crying?" I asked. "Good Goddess, what's wrong?"

She sniffed. "Iris died last night."

I couldn't believe it. "Iris died?"

Not that I doubted her. Violet spread a lot of information but rarely was anything untrue.

"Martin stopped in for a cup earlier." Violet explained. "While he was standing right where you are, Jagger called him over his walkie-talkie. He said there was a problem at Iris's house and Gardenia wanted him to come."

"We were just at The Inn," Ruby stated. "Laurel said Gardenia called in sick this morning. She didn't say anything about Iris, though."

Violet dabbed at her eyes with her apron. "Iris has been getting worse and worse over the last few weeks. Gardenia stopped talking about it. It was too upsetting for her."

"But she told you?" Ruby challenged.

Ruby was lucky looks couldn't kill.

"Gardenia and I have been close friends for years." Violet turned away from Ruby and focused on me. "Not long after Martin left, I saw Jagger patrolling the commons. I ran out there and asked him what was going on. Before he could answer me,

Martin called on the talkie and told Jagger to switch to their 'secure' channel."

"And you listened in?" Ruby asked. "Knowing it might be confidential?"

Violet looked at Ruby like she'd lost her mind. "It's a walkie-talkie. It's got a speaker, not an earpiece. And it's not like Jagger didn't know I was standing there. Anyway, Martin asked him to contact Dr. Bundy and send him to Iris's cottage."

"The medical examiner." My heart sank. There was only one reason they'd summon him. Violet had to be right about poor Iris. "How long ago was this?"

"Let me think." She stared at the clock on the wall as she recalled, "Martin was one of my first customers. He got here around six fifteen. I talked to Jagger between six forty-five and seven."

"And now it's quarter after eight." I recalled Jayne saying that it took Dr. Bundy an hour to drive to Whispering Pines from his office. If he came right away, he would have gotten to Iris's place about an hour ago.

"Are you thinking about going over there?" Violet asked.

"I am. When Iris had that episode last night, I wanted to contact someone at Unity, but Iris said no . . . I should have anyway."

Violet shook her head. "She wouldn't have gone, and if one of them would have come to your cottage, she would've sent them away. Iris accepted months ago that her heart would give out before long. She made sure to enjoy every day she had left and didn't let anything stop her."

"That's why she came to the gathering last night," Ruby concluded, her attitude softer now.

Violet nodded. "That's why. 'You've got to live until you die, duckies,' she told Gardenia and me all the time. I'll get your beans for you, Reeva. And since you're going, you can bring Gardenia a coffee too."

A few minutes later, my cloth bag was filled with ten pounds of beans, and I had an insulated mug with a special creation for Gardenia.

"Tell her I'll stop by after I close tonight," Violet called out when we reached the door. "In fact, I'll let Basil close and leave a little early."

It was upsetting to see normally upbeat, unflappable Violet so subdued.

"I'll tell her." As soon as Ruby and I were outside, I demanded, "What is wrong with you?"

Her spine straightened. "What did I do?"

"Asking Violet about why Gardenia shared things with her and listening in on the walkie-talkie conversation. You know she doesn't spread lies. Why were you being so confrontational with her?"

"Haven't you ever watched Jayne or Martin interrogate a suspect?" She made a jabbing in the knife and twisting it motion. "Gotta be pushy to get the answer you want."

"When did you ever see either of them interrogate a suspect? You watch too much television. Violet isn't a suspect and didn't do anything to deserve that."

Ruby wasn't listening to me. Instead, she set the scene. "This can be our schtick. I'll be the pushy one, and you can be the sensitive one."

"What are you talking about?" Sometimes Ruby exhausted me.

"Laurel said it. If we're going to be private investigators, we have to learn how to gather facts. We need to fine-tune our process."

"First, that's Martin and Jagger's job. If they need help, they'll consult with Jayne. Second, we aren't, nor do we have time to be, private investigators. Third, Laurel was being facetious."

As we walked along the Fairy Path, I realized I'd be cutting it close if I was still going to open on time. I needed to pick up the pace. Or maybe Bee could come in early. I dropped my bag of coffee beans on the table inside Hearth & Cauldron and called her.

"I'll explain when I get back, but there's an emergency with a coven member that I need to attend to."

"Iris," Bee uttered sadly. "The poor dear. Go on over. I'll be to the shop in half an hour."

How had she heard already? Why did I even ask? Word spread eyeblink fast in this village. "Thank you, Bee. I shouldn't be long."

"Take your time. I'll be fine. You do have a class this afternoon, though."

"Right. Good. You're a Goddess-send, Bee."

She giggled, like she did every time I said that. Which was partly why I said it, but also because it was true. Then, with the travel mug Violet had filled for Gardenia in hand, I stepped outside to find Ruby waiting on her bicycle.

"Where are you going?" I asked.

"You said we were going to Iris's cottage," she replied and clipped the strap of her helmet. Her *very* sparkly helmet.

One slow day at The Twisty Skein this past winter, Ruby grabbed a container of crystals, a bottle of glue, and a mug of tea. She started a fire in the circular fireplace that filled the center of her shop, which made a perfect spot to sit and do crafts, and proceeded to create the blingiest bicycle helmet anyone had ever seen. Halfway through her project, villagers came in for supplies. The next day she was open, because shops only opened a few days a week in the winter, she had a dozen people show up with their helmets. She sold out of every crystal and sequin in the shop, most of her glue, and had a dozen pre-paid orders for more of everything.

"I said *I* was going to Iris's cottage. You don't have to come." I secured the mug in the wicker basket on the front of my bike and clipped my blah by comparison helmet beneath my chin.

"We're partners in this private investigation thing," she insisted. "I have to come."

I pushed off, knowing she'd follow. "I already told you, there is no private investigation thing. I'm going as high priestess to offer sympathy to a coven member."

"Okay. Then I'll be a coven member offering sympathy."

Glancing suspiciously at her, I asked, "Has Ruby McLaughlin finally reached her limit with crafting? Are you bored?"

"Bite your tongue. I'll never tire of crafting, but one can always benefit from different experiences."

I couldn't argue with that. Considering the discussion we'd just had with Violet, Ruby could do with a lesson on empathy.

During quieter hours or when there weren't so many tourists, we could ride through the commons. It was the shortest route to Iris's cottage. By this time of morning, however, there were enough people around that cutting through the commons or even riding along the Fairy Path was nearly impossible. Instead, we made our way along a secret path running through the woods that paralleled the Fairy Path and took us all the way to Unity, the village wellness center. There, we darted across the highway and continued west along the dirt road that crossed in front of my place, the Barlow cottage, the Meditation Circle, and eventually to Iris's cottage. Or maybe I should say Gardenia's cottage now.

"It's so peaceful through here," Ruby commented. "I'm always up before the tourists and leave after the shops have closed so don't usually have a problem taking the other route. Maybe I'll go this way now and then, pick you up, and we can finish the ride together."

"Any time," I agreed with a smile. While Ruby could be a little over the top at times, she was the dearest, most loyal friend I'd ever had.

Iris and Gardenia lived in the same area as Sugar and Honey. The sister bakers lived in side-by-side cottages that had identical layouts but decorating schemes that couldn't be more different. Honey, who decorated cakes that were so full of detail I found something new every time I looked at one, preferred a more minimal look for her home. Sugar, who could be as bold and brash as they came, surrounded herself with crystal and lace.

As we passed by, I noted the garden they'd set up between their homes. While neither of them had any green witch talent, they had created a cozy little sitting area to enjoy at the end of their busy days. Very nice.

After another minute of pedaling, we came to Iris's place. My heart stuttered at the sight of an ambulance and what had to be Dr. Bundy's SUV. When Jayne stepped down, she gave the Tahoe with "Sheriff, Whispering Pines, Wisconsin" emblazoned on the side to Martin. That vehicle and the station van, which Jagger now drove, were also here.

"Not a very joyful gathering," Ruby commented.

"Not at all," I agreed.

Gardenia, standing with Martin and the medical examiner, saw us and waved us over. Martin looked like he was about to object to our presence, but Gardenia held out a hand for me to hold.

"I want Reeva to be here," she told Martin. "There's nothing being said that she can't hear. Ruby too."

Dr. Bundy nodded to us in greeting. "As I was saying, in a situation like this, when the deceased has a known health condition, we don't do an autopsy unless the family requests it. That said, I did a cursory examination and found no foul play. I have no reason to believe this was anything other than her heart finally giving out."

"She did have that episode last night," I reminded Gardenia, probably unnecessarily, but wanted to make sure Dr. Bundy knew.

Gardenia nodded. "She'd been having more and more of

those lately. One every week or so. That's why I cut my hours at The Inn. I needed to be here for Mimi."

I squeezed her hand and gently asked, "Do you want Dr. Bundy to do an autop—"

"No," she blurted. "I hate the idea of her being . . . you know. I do have one request."

"I'll do what I can," the balding, slightly pudgy man promised. "What is it?"

"Can you arrange for a blood test?" Gardenia asked. "I think she stopped taking her heart medication. I'd give it to her every night and never found any pills lying around, but she was getting sicker and sicker so fast."

"I obviously don't know the specifics," the doctor told her, "but that could simply have been the progression of her disease."

She nodded. "I know. I asked her flat out one day if she was taking the pills or flushing them, and she insisted she was taking them. It will eat at me if I don't know for sure. And she wanted to be cremated. So it's now or never, I guess."

He handed her a small notepad. "Jot down your email address for me. I'll have my secretary send you a form stating what you'd like done. You'll need to sign it, digitally is fine, and send it back. Then I'll collect a blood sample and get it to the lab. I know how overwhelming something like this can be, so rest assured your funeral director will—"

"I spoke to her briefly before you got here," Gardenia stated. "Fortunately, I guess, we knew this was coming, so those details are all set."

The doctor smiled. There was so much empathy and experience in the expression. "It will still be overwhelming."

"Thanks for coming so quickly, Dr. Bundy." Martin held his hand out to the man he'd seen far too many times over the past thirteen months.

"I swear," he replied while shaking Martin's hand, "my vehicle heads this way on its own sometimes. I hoped now that Jayne has handed over the reins, things would settle down."

Martin stiffened slightly. "This wasn't a murder, so in that respect, I'd say they have."

"Guess you're right about that." Dr. Bundy signaled for the ambulance driver to go ahead and turned to Gardenia, taking the pad back from her. "I'll call my secretary once we're in cell range, so look for an email from Joan within the hour. I'll get that blood sample drawn right away and call in a favor. Hopefully the lab can come up with an answer for you quickly."

"Thank you, Dr. Bundy." Gardenia watched as the ambulance took her grandmother away and then slipped inside the cottage.

"You seem upset, Martin," I observed.

"Not sure how to define it." He blew out a heavy breath.

"Under pressure?"

"There is a lot of that. Jayne set a pretty high bar."

"You know she wouldn't have handed over the keys if she had any doubt about you." I rubbed my hand over his back, then snatched it away. A coddling aunt wasn't what the sheriff needed people to see right now. "And River wouldn't let someone without proper experience take care of his village."

"That's true. Both things, but River more so than Jayne. She stretched herself way too thin trying to do two full-time jobs and ended up feeling really guilty about Tripp having to run Pine Time alone. She had to choose one. I hope she made the right choice."

"From what I can see, she absolutely did." I smiled at my nephew and resisted the urge to pull him in for a hug. "I saw Tripp yesterday. He says she's trying to find her footing like you are. Give yourself time and know that you've got the whole village supporting you and backing you up."

"Not so sure about that," he said in a way that made me think he had a reason to doubt it.

Were some of the villagers giving him a hard time like they were me? Did they think that he also should have known what Flavia was up to?

"I don't imagine you came here to see me," Martin stated, pulling me out of my troubling thoughts.

"No, but since I've got your attention, Sheriff Reed, I can take a minute to talk with you." I must have had a proud aunt look on my face. Like I could help it. He blushed and shoved his hands in his pockets. "I'm holding a men's only class at two o'clock this afternoon. We've got room for a couple more." I looked at Jagger. "You should come too. We're making hand pies." I held my hands in a half-circle shape. "Perfect for lunches on the go."

"Jagger doesn't eat bread." Martin locked eyes on his deputy. "Or sugar. Or bacon. Guy's a freak."

Jagger was an enormous man. He stood a good four or five inches taller than Martin, who was five-eleven, and had to be a hundred pounds of pure muscle heavier. Jagger was lean and strong as an ox.

"I eat bacon," Jagger objected. "He's right about the bread, though." He tapped his stomach. "Makes me gassy."

"Do you ever have guests in your home?" I arched my eyebrows at him. "I know Martin cooks for Rosalyn on occasion."

"Um," Jagger hummed, "sometimes."

"Can you cook?" I pressed.

"Yes." He pushed his shoulders back. "I make great grilled chicken and fish. My rice turns out perfectly, and everyone compliments my roasted vegetables."

"Do you season your rice or veggies?"

"Aunt Reeva—"

"Sorry, I know, I'm keeping you from your jobs. Just keep in mind, both of you, that when you cook for other people, you have to cook that meal with their tastes in mind. What would they like to eat? How would they like it prepared? There's nothing wrong with cooking your favorite meal but keep them in mind as you do so." I took a step back. "Lesson over. You should both come if you can. If you need to skip out early, that's fine. At minimum, you'll get to hang out with other guys and learn some knife skills."

"I have excellent knife skills." A naughty smile turned Jagger's mouth.

"I don't think she means those kinds of skills," Martin corrected. "Or those kinds of knives." He kissed my cheek. "We'll do what we can. Depends on if the tourists behave."

After stopping back at my bike, I'd forgotten about the coffee from Violet, I found Gardenia sitting at a small table on the front porch. Ruby was with her.

"How are you doing, sweetie?" I held out the mug. "I don't know what's in here, but it's from Violet, so you know it'll be wonderful. She says she'll stop by after work."

Before answering, Gardenia removed the lid and took a long swig. She let out an equally long sigh. "Violet always knows. I don't think I had any coffee yet today. This is a butterscotch latte she makes for me by adding brown sugar and butter to the Grinder's brew." She sipped and sighed again. "So comforting and exactly what I needed right now."

I settled into the open chair next to her, gave her a minute to enjoy her first sips of the coffee, then asked, "You said you're concerned that Iris stopped taking her medication. Do you really think she would do that?"

"I pray she didn't, but she seemed to be going downhill so fast." Gardenia took on a pained, distant stare, as though remembering some of the bad days. "She felt awful and couldn't do many of the things she loved to do. I mean, look at Mimi's gardens."

She flung a hand at a nearby bed filled with irises. There were more weeds than flowers, and those that did bloom weren't anywhere near as vibrant as I remembered them being. Almost like her beloved irises had been fading right along with her.

"What happened last night?" Ruby asked with that slightly confrontational tone again.

I gave her a pointed look. She shot it back at me.

"She was so tired," Gardenia began. "After that episode at your cottage, the tea and scone perked her up but only for a little while, then she started getting worse again. That's why we left so suddenly. By the time we got back here, she could barely walk. Stairs became too hard for her a month ago, so I had her bed moved to the main level. We weren't using the dining room, so I converted it."

"How did she feel about that?" I asked.

"She liked it actually." Gardenia smiled and laughed a little. "Said she could see her flowers and all the 'critters' from the bay window there and wondered why she didn't have a bedroom added onto the main level years ago. Anyway, I tucked her in, read from the book I'd been reading to her every night, and told her I loved her."

She stared again. Lost in memories for so long, this time, I gently prodded, "And then what?"

She blew out a breath. "Mimi had always been an early riser. Up between four thirty and five every morning without needing an alarm clock no matter how sick she was. I usually woke to the sound of her shuffling around, making tea and whatnot. When I woke up today and saw it was almost six, I knew something was wrong. I ran down the stairs and found her in the exact same position she was in when I left her."

"So she passed not long after you left her last night," Ruby concluded.

Sipping more coffee, Gardenia nodded. "That's my guess. She always started on her back and flipped onto her right side.

Hands together, tucked up beneath her chin. She was still on her back."

Unsure of what else to do, I asked, "Is there anything you need? Anything we can do for you?"

Gardenia stared, unblinking, the shock of reality hitting her. "I don't think so."

I rested a hand on her arm. "I know you have Violet, but if there's anything Ruby or I can do, please call. Okay?"

"Okay." She gave us a small smile. "Thank you. I appreciate you coming over. I knew this day was coming, but it's been coming for so long I started to think maybe it never would. You know? Guess Dr. Bundy was right about the overwhelming thing." She blinked repeatedly as though fighting tears. "I need my phone. I need to talk to Violet."

I stood. "I'll get it for you. Where is it?"

"In the kitchen on the counter."

Ruby followed me inside the cottage that felt very empty without tiny sassy Iris filling it up. As with Laurel's apartment, it had been more than twenty years since I'd been inside here. Gardenia had been a baby. Eighteen months at most.

"How old is Gardenia?" I wondered aloud.

"Twenty-four? No, twenty-three. I think. Right around there. Why?"

I shook off the question. "Just trying to remember when I was last inside here. Some of it is the same, but there are a lot of new things too."

Iris had always preferred a traditional Asian influence in her home—feng shui arrangements, hand-painted wallpaper, calming colors. Now I saw plenty of modern Asian pieces and Western touches as well. A beautiful blend of both women.

As Ruby paused to admire a curio cabinet filled with pottery and small paintings, I continued to the kitchen and came to the makeshift bedroom in the small dining room first. A shoji screen printed with cherry blossoms must have served as a privacy wall for Iris. It had been pushed to the side making her barely mussed bed visible. I smiled at the view through the five-panel bay window. It was lovely. I could just make out a blur of white hidden in the weeds. Blue emerged, seemed to stare directly at Iris's window for a long moment, and then wandered off.

"Isn't there a saying," I began and then turned to check that Ruby was close enough to hear me. I jumped when I found her directly behind me.

"What saying?"

"Maybe not a saying. More of an old wives' tale, I guess. Something about cats knowing when someone is going to die and will stay with them until they do."

"I've heard that," Ruby confirmed. "That's why some residents at nursing homes are conflicted about having cats around. They're both comforting and foreboding. Why do you ask?"

"Blue is out in the garden. I wonder how long he's been there. And Dot ran straight to Iris last night and climbed onto her lap."

"Dot did? That's unusual."

"I thought so too. Guess it makes a little more sense now." I glanced at a nearby clock on the wall. "Is that accurate? Almost ten? I need to get to the shop."

"You called Bee to come in early. Remember? I, on the other hand, don't have an assistant to open Twisty for me, so we do need to get a move on."

While Ruby grabbed the telephone from the counter, I filled a glass with water. Gardenia should stay hydrated. As the glass filled, I noticed a basket full of Iris's medications near the sink. There were at least a dozen bottles of pills. Most of the witches I knew, myself included, preferred old-world ways of healing. I was always amazed at what Briar, Morgan, and the other green witches could do with the right herbal blends. Being one of them, I wouldn't be at all surprised to find that Iris had stopped taking pharmaceuticals. But had she tried any natural remedies, or had she simply given up and let nature do what it would as Gardenia seemed to fear?

"Here you go." Ruby set the phone on the table next to Gardenia.

I added the glass of water to the table. "We need to leave, but I'm serious about you calling if you need anything. Any reason, any time."

She nodded, thanked us again, and reached for the phone. We helped, but what she really needed was someone familiar. The thought made me even more grateful for Ruby. I was so glad to have her in my sphere.

"Can you come over later tonight?" I asked her once we were back at the shops.

She studied me suspiciously. "What's wrong?"

"I'm not sure," I admitted. "Something's poking at me. Talking it out might help."

"I'll be there. Seven o'clock?"

"See you then."

CHAPTER
TEN

I parked my bike in the stand outside Hearth & Cauldron and inside found Bee in the kitchen area, surrounded by boxes of meat, dairy products, and produce.

"Our order came already?" I asked. It didn't usually come until closer to noon.

"Newt is running early today." Bee gave me a saucy smile. "You missed him."

Newt James was the village's delivery guy. Had been for years. He stood six-foot-two and after so many years of loading and unloading boxes, had developed a physique that made us stare. And he was a nice guy. Which was more important.

"My concern is that I wasn't here to help you," I insisted.

"Right." Bee winked at me and pulled a sack of lemons from a box. "Anyway, Newt says he's got 'a thing' to attend this afternoon so came early. Good that you called me in. I used the spare key to let him into Twisty." She paused then asked, "How's Gardenia?"

Over the next hour, while putting away produce and baking supplies and tending to customers, I filled her in on what I knew, doing my best to remain neutral and accurate. If I let my opinion about anything seep in or got a crucial detail wrong, it would spread through the village like fog off Lucy Lake. Like the time I commented that I don't always worry about whether my butter is salted or not. The firestorm that innocent remark caused among the kitchen witches went on for a week. Busy Bee was a dear woman, but with her love of being in the know and loving even more to share that knowledge, she and Violet could be sisters. Except that Bee was a middle-aged white Jewish woman and Violet was a twenty-something black Wiccan woman. Practically identical otherwise.

After we got the order put away, it was time to prep for my class. I slipped my onion-skin-gold apron over my head and set thirteen baskets on the table. Next, I took out all the ingredients for the hand pies and placed enough potatoes, sweet potatoes, carrots, onions, rutabagas, and parsley for today's meat pie recipe into each one. I'd hand out the refrigerated ingredients when we were ready for them. Once my students arrived, they'd find a filled basket covered with a gingham tea towel at their spot. They obviously knew what we'd be making, but like opening a wrapped present, everyone's eyes lit up when they went to lift that towel.

Tripp walked in, first for class as usual.

"Jayne wants hand pies for dinner," he announced. "And then she wants me to make and keep plenty on hand for our afternoon hikes or kayak rides. Can I help you with anything?"

I was filling large bowls with flour and small ones with sugar. "You can set these on the table. One set for each pair of students. Bee already assembled utensil packs. They're in the crate by the fireplace. We can set those out too."

"Looks like you've got your process down now," Tripp noted. "Even handing out tool packs."

As one of my first and most dedicated students, Tripp had been through my multiple attempts at making class as efficient as possible. Letting students claim their own produce took too long. While learning the proper way to measure was part of my instruction, setting large bins of dry ingredients on the table meant too many hands reaching in and contaminating my stock. Turned out, there were as many definitions of what *clean hands* meant as I had students.

"I'm so grateful I tested everything on the villagers first," I told him. "Word of mouth is huge. If my classes don't run smoothly, eventually I won't have any students. As for the tool packs, part of class is learning how to properly use the gadgets. I could let each student pick for themselves, but if everyone is using the same tool, I don't have to give individual instruction and class runs . . ."

My words faded away, and Tripp asked, "What are you thinking?"

"Individual instruction. I could give private lessons during the off-season."

"Don't tease me." He laughed but turned serious a second later. "Actually, that might be perfect for Jayne. She wants to learn and almost signed up for tomorrow's scone class but balked at the last minute."

"Why? No skills are necessary for my classes. The point is to learn. Plenty of my students have never used more than eating utensils in the kitchen."

He shook his head. "It's not that. It's like we talked about yesterday. Other than seeing our guests and a select few friends, she's becoming a recluse."

It was obvious from the pained look on his face, he wanted everything to be perfect for her. "Give her time. It takes a while to get used to a new lifestyle."

The rest of the students started to arrive just as Tripp set the last of the tool packs near the baskets.

"You made it," I proclaimed when Martin and Jagger walked in.

"Things have been quiet"—Martin patted the walkie-talkie at

his side—"but if we get a call, we'll have to leave right away. And we can only stay for the first run-through. We are on the clock, after all."

As if a small-town sheriff or deputy were ever off the clock.

"Not a problem," I replied. "While you're cooking, I'll bundle up the ingredients for the second batch. You can take them and the recipe with you when you leave or pick them up later and make them at home."

Next, Mr. Powell walked in. He was a dear man but also the klutziest human ever born. He loved to cook and came to many classes. After one lesson on the difference between chopping and dicing onions where he nearly ended up with stitches, I insisted he use a set of child-safe nylon knives. I also had an induction plate for him to cook on because open flames and Mr. Powell would never mix. Fortunately for the other students, he never hurt anyone else. Still, safety first took on a new meaning with him.

"Brought a change of clothes this time." Mr. Powell held up a string bag as proof . . . and somehow got tangled in the string.

Oh, that man.

"Your apron is on the counter." I got an oil cloth one just for him. That way, most of the inevitable spills would slide off him instead of soaking into his shirt and pants. Regardless of the extra cleanup required, it warmed my heart to see him in my classes.

Three tourists entered next—blond, bald, and bearded. They said they were staying a week with a group of friends distributed between four of the rental cottages on the east side of the village.

"It's our turn to make dinner for the group tonight," the blond explained.

"We heard about your class," the bald man added, "so we opted to have the Hearth & Cauldron experience rather than just picking up takeout from Grapes, Grains, and Grub or something from Sundry's deli again."

The bearded one looked especially eager for the class. "I haven't had anything homemade in a long time. And making it myself? My mom will be impressed."

"I hope you enjoy it. Choose your spots at the table and we'll get started shortly."

I greeted Verne, Schmitty, and Rourke next. The trio had taken classes with me before. They could be a challenge to keep in line because they tended to be chatty. I nearly collided with my next student when I turned to welcome him, and my hopes of remaining in control of things wavered.

"Gabe. I don't remember seeing your name on the list."

And I would have noticed it immediately. In fact, it would have pulsed at me like an emergency light.

"I'm switching places with Oren. I hope that's all right."

I gazed up at his dark face and into his gentle black-brown eyes, and my knees went weak. My voice cracked as I replied, "That's fine."

Pull yourself together.

I had been in love with Gabe Grace since we were teenagers. He had been the kindest, funniest, smartest boy I knew. My best friend at the time, Rae Crain, also liked him, and being the pushover people-pleaser that I was, I said nothing when she told me he asked her out. With two broken marriages, three children, and four somewhat disastrous decades between Gabe and me, my heart still wanted him.

I cleared my throat and asked, "Is Oren okay?"

"He's fine," Gabe responded. "Lily Grace is having a bad day, and Jola is working the night shift at Unity."

"Missing her mom." I smiled gently. "I miss her too."

Then I blushed. I had no right to express sorrow with the Grace-Crains. My sister was the reason Rae was dead. If I would have—

"Stop," Gabe ordered, reading my thoughts. "Rae's death is so far from your responsibility it's not even a blip on the radar. Same with Flavia's actions. She was *never* your problem. I mean that, so please believe it. Don't listen to the hateful words of small-minded people."

He put a hand on my shoulder, and electric tingles shot through me. What was I, a fifteen-year-old giddy schoolgirl? No, I was a fifty-eight-year-old businesswoman ... who still had an unshakable crush on the man she still couldn't have. His daughters needed him far more than I did right now. That didn't mean we couldn't talk to each other, however, and if I could quit acting like such a twit, we could have a solid friendship.

"Thank you, Gabe. Your support means a lot to me." I was happy with my now stronger voice.

My last student arrived two minutes after class had officially started. We all turned to look at him, and this time, I wasn't the only one who froze. Standing well over six feet tall with broad shoulders and big arms, this man looked like he could give Jagger a run for his money. He wore his blond hair shaved around his head from his temples down and the rest pulled back in a ponytail. His neatly trimmed beard followed the strong V-shape of his jaw. His eyes were an intense but bright, clear blue. A band of tattoos encircled both upper arms and peeked out from beneath his T-shirt sleeves. He reminded me of a Viking.

"You must be ..." I glanced at the class list. *Jozef Lykke.*

"It's pronounced yo-zef lou-kah." His Scandinavian accent made him sound like a Viking too. "I apologize for being late."

"Not at all. Welcome, Mr. Lykke." I held my hand out to the last open spot at the table. "That's your place. We're just getting started." I stood at the far end of the farmhouse table by the fireplace. "This is the first men's only class I've held, so I'm glad to have you all here. Normally, I never segregate, but my dear friend, Ruby, at the hobby shop a few yards up the Fairy Path, held a very successful men's only class a few weeks ago. How's that afghan coming along Rourke?"

"Slow," he admitted, "but at least all my little granny squares are holding together. I'm hoping to have it done for April's birthday in October."

"That's four months away, man," Verne teased him. "You must do, what, three stitches a day?"

Rourke pushed his shoulders back proudly. "I make one square a night. I could do more, but I have to wait until April goes to bed. It's supposed to be a surprise."

Stay on track. You know better.

"Anyway," I raised my voice, "Ruby polled her group and they said they'd attend more men's classes and would like one here too. I thought it was a great idea. We'll be making both dinner and dessert hand pies today, six of each. If you prefer a vegetarian version, let me know. I've got tofu or a plant-based meat substitute you can use instead of diced beef."

All the men, except Schmitty and the bearded man, looked at me like this was an absurd suggestion.

"What? I'm trying to watch my cholesterol," Schmitty defended.

The bearded man nodded his agreement. "Vegan is the way to go."

I took wrapped sticks of butter from the refrigerator along with a bottle of vodka. "No, this is not for drinking. Gluten makes bread tough. Since gluten needs water to form, using equal amounts of vodka and water helps make a flakier crust. And the alcohol will bake off so no worries there." To Schmitty and the vegan man, I added, "I've got a non-dairy option for you two."

After forming their dough into two discs, wrapping them in waxed paper, and putting them in the refrigerator to chill, we moved on to preparing the meat and vegetable filling.

"Cutting everything approximately the same size," I told them, "will help ensure more even cooking."

Once the meat for the pies had been cooked and the vegetables chopped, mixed, and stuffed into the crust rounds, we put them in the oven and worked on the dessert pies.

"Same crust," I explained, "but with a sweet rather than savory filling this time. At home, your flavor choice is pretty much up to you. I put a list of possible options on the recipe sheet. Today, your choice is chocolate cream or blackberry."

"I like chocolate," Schmitty announced. Tripp, Martin, Verne, and Gabe agreed.

"Which do you prefer, Reeva?" Jozef asked.

I shrugged. "Blackberries are in season now and taste amazing. They're full of vitamin C and high in antioxidants. They can be tart, so if you prefer a sweeter flavor, add a bit more sugar or a drizzle of honey."

"Blackberry it is," Jozef agreed and reached for the bowl at the center of the table.

Once the savory pies were done baking and the sweet ones were in the ovens, the men had the option to assemble the pies again and bring them home to bake. Martin, Jagger, and Schmitty had to get back to work.

"These brave souls," I joked and indicated the customers who had gathered to watch the process, "can sample your first attempts in our dining room if they choose."

I informed the customers that they could purchase the pies from Bee, which were sold at the cost of ingredients plus a slight markup. Morgan's tea and Violet's coffee were also available. If they wanted to purchase beans or tea bags, I had stock available for sale.

"For those of you trying again," I announced, "I'll be hands off and quiet this time, but I'm here to answer questions. And remember, you'll only be assembling this time and bringing them with you to bake later. Jozef, where are you staying?"

"I'm renting one of the cottages," he explained, "so I'll make them for dinner tonight."

I went around the table to talk more with him and Gabe as the two stood next to each other. "You both have impressive knife skills. Gabe, you cook a lot at home, right?"

"Have since the girls were little." A quick shadow crossed his face. "Meals were often left to me. I had to figure it out or be satisfied with bland food. I like to eat so . . ."

"What about you, Jozef?"

He kept his eyes on the cutting board as he explained, "I've held positions in many restaurants at home in Denmark. I'm traveling right now and enjoy learning about foods in different countries." He glanced up at me, his blue eyes filled with what looked like pain. Food tended to stir up a lot of emotion, both when preparing it and eating it. What was his story? "Ironically, I prefer home cooking to restaurant food. Since I'll be in your village for a few more days, I may be back for more of your classes before I leave."

"I'd be happy to have you here." I turned to chat with my other students and this time did collide with Gabe. With my arm pressed against his, I looked up at him. "Sorry. Good thing you didn't have a knife in your hand. You could have cut yourself."

"No harm, no foul," Gabe assured. "You're a natural at teaching, you know. You've known forever that this is what you were meant to do, haven't you?"

"Maybe not forever, but a very long time. I'm blessed. Opening this shop is all I ever dreamed it would be."

I paused by each of the other men. Tripp gave me a sly grin. "What's that look for?"

"If you flirt any harder with Gabe—"

"I'm not flirting." But the heat rising in my cheeks told me I might be.

"That's not what it looks like from this side of the table." He batted his eyelashes at me.

"I don't do that." Did I?

Verne scowled at me when I stopped by his station. He'd been giving me strange looks since the class started. "Something wrong?"

He blinked and shook his head. "No, sorry, everything's fine. I'm a little distracted by a project giving me trouble."

"Working with your hands frees up the mind. Are you coming up with any solutions?"

"Maybe. I have to think this through a little more." He seemed to be taking out his frustrations by aggressively chopping his rutabaga.

"I assume you'll split these with Luna tonight?"

"I hope so." He shrugged. "The girl spends more time with her friends now than her old dad."

"The pains of being a parent." They were gone long before we were ready. Or for some, I suppose, nowhere near soon enough.

Once the second recipes were packaged to bring home, a few of the men stayed to help clean up.

"Just place your dishes near the sink," I instructed. "Bee and I will send them through the dishwasher."

Keiko walked in a little after four with an envelope in her hand that she handed to me. "I'm done at Shoppe Mystique for today. Do you need any help?"

Reeva was handwritten on the envelope in a scrawling script. I tucked it into my apron pocket. "Your timing is great. Class just finished, and dishes need to be washed."

I expected her to object and say that washing dishes had nothing to do with Wicca. But as I had told her last night, when we were cleaning up from the gathering, any task could be performed with intention. A large part of following Wicca was doing things intentionally. Therefore, washing dishes could be either a job that was rushed through or a meditative process. I often found it to be the perfect time to reflect on the day or something that might be weighing on me. Seemed she'd been listening because I could almost see a bubble of concentration form around her as she filled the sink with warm soapy water and the dishwasher with dirty dishes.

I said goodbye to the men, invited them all to come back anytime, and once they were gone, took the envelope Keiko had given me from my pocket. It was nothing fancy. Just a standard white envelope anyone might use. Inside, the message was anything but standard.

The scone was meant for you, High Priestess.

ELEVEN

I wasn't a woman who panicked often. A lifetime with my sister had taught me to be prepared for things to happen unexpectedly and for plans to veer off course without notice. Not sure how anyone could prepare to be threatened, though, and that's what the message in the envelope felt like. A threat of some kind.

Who would threaten me, though?

Flavia. Did she ask someone to deliver it to me?

No. First of all, she would *never* refer to me as high priestess. That was a title she had wanted since Briar led the coven. She took Morgan naming me to the role as a personal attack.

"Are you all right, Reeva?" Bee placed a hand on my shoulder. "You look like someone just told you your cat died." She became concerned. "Dot is okay, isn't she?"

I put the note back in the envelope and the envelope back in my pocket. "Everything's fine, including Dot. Nothing to worry about." At least I didn't think there was. Unless I really had been threatened. "You know, since Keiko is here to clean up and you came in early, why don't you go on home?"

She immediately began untying her apron. "I think I'll do

that. Do you mind if I snag a few of those hand pies? Benji will love them. If there are any left, that is. We sold a lot of them. Venting the ovens toward the Fairy Path was a brilliant idea."

"Nothing draws people in like the aroma of something baking in the oven. Help yourself to some pies."

"Do you know which ones that Norse god made? I heard him say he's a professional cook. Anything Tripp makes would be second on my list."

Laughing at my sassy assistant, I informed, "The Norse god is Jozef Lykke, and his pies have an *R* etched on top. Although it's not really an *R*. The lines are all straight instead of curved on the top, and the line extending to the right only goes halfway. I believe it's a rune, but I don't know what it means."

"I'm impressed that you know that much."

I tapped my head. "All sorts of trivial information stored in here. As for the pies, microwaving is convenient but tends to make things chewy. Warm them gently in a three-hundred-degree oven for fifteen to twenty minutes."

Keiko had finished cleaning up the dishes and kitchen just before six o'clock. There was a steady enough stream of customers that I could have stayed open a little longer, but I'd been distracted since reading that note, and Ruby said she'd meet me at my cottage at seven. I flipped the sign on the door to *Closed*, spent fifteen minutes helping the customers still browsing—I'd never kick anyone out—and turned to Keiko when it was finally just the two of us.

"Who gave you that envelope?"

"No one gave it to me." She pointed toward the main entrance. "It was taped to the door when I got here. What's wrong? You seem upset."

I shook my head, not wanting to bring her into whatever this was. "More puzzled than upset. Whoever left it didn't sign it."

"Weird. Anything else you want me to do?"

Keiko was technically on my payroll as I paid her for any hours she worked, but I hadn't given her a set schedule yet. She'd stop by when she was available, as she had today, to see if I could use her.

"You can lock the back door," I told her with a tired sigh. "This has been a long, emotional day. Time to go home."

"Emotional?" Her look of confusion brightened to one of understanding a moment later. "Oh, Iris. I heard. Everyone's talking about her and Gardenia."

"You know what, there is something you can do. There are a few hand pies left. Since you'll be heading that direction, would you drop some off with Gardenia? The last thing she needs to worry about right now is cooking."

"Sure, I can do that." She watched as I bundled together the pies in parchment packets—savory in one, sweet in the other—and stated, "This is the first thing you do, right?"

"What is?" I asked. "When?"

"Cooking. When something bad happens, you go right to your kitchen, don't you?"

I tied the packets together with a length of twine. "Very astute of you. I've trained myself over the years to not let worries enter my kitchen. Sort of like Scarlett O'Hara."

"Who's she?"

My jaw dropped. "Don't tell me you've never heard of *Gone with the Wind*."

She narrowed her eyes, thinking. "That's a movie, right?"

"It was a book first. Scarlett is the heroine and when things get too upsetting for her, she says she'll think about it tomorrow. I borrow her method and tell myself to deal with whatever's worrying me when I'm done cooking. Then I clear my mind by disappearing into whatever I'm making and am centered when I'm ready to get back to my problem. And I have something good to eat."

"Smart," Keiko praised. "That way your food doesn't get ruined because you're distracted."

"Exactly. It's been years since a recipe has gone wrong." Then I remembered back a couple of months. "I take that back. A few things failed in April after my sister put a hex on me."

"She what?"

"A tale for another time. That's too much drama to add to an already drama-filled day."

Keiko took the packet from me. "That's what you did when you heard about Yasmine, isn't it? Headed straight to your kitchen?"

I froze. Why did kids pick the worst times to open up involved topics?

See you later, honey. I have to scoot, or I'll be late for that auction. The dining set my customer wants is up for bids early.

"Mom, why did my birthmother give me up?"

"I did," I replied to Keiko. "I made blondies with walnuts, white chocolate chips, and toffee chips, I believe. You know what? I have a lot of questions about your time with Yasmine, and we will talk about it, I promise. But now isn't the time for that either."

"That's cool, I get it." She patted the parchment bundle in her arms. "I'll drop this off. Just follow the dirt road on the other side of the highway?"

"Yep. Turn left after you cross the creek and keep going until you see the twin cottages. Gardenia's place will be next. It's surrounded by hundreds of irises." I smiled, picturing the sight.

"Then cross back over the creek and the highway and go west to the campground."

"Are you doing all right there?"

"At the campground? Yeah. As long as people obey the quiet hours, it's great. I like sleeping outside. Outside-ish. Not technically outside if I'm in a tent. I really like sitting by a campfire at night and watching the stars."

"You sound like Jayne and Tripp. No bigger stargazers in the village than those two."

"Do we have to do some sort of closing ceremony here?" She waved a hand at the shop in general.

"Normally, I do a simple candle ceremony to close the day and a full sweep, like the coven did to my cottage, on Sundays. Tonight, I just want to go home, but with all that happened today, I think I'll come in a little earlier in the morning and do another sweeping."

"Can I help?" she asked immediately. "I can meet you here."

She was so eager to learn anything and everything. I considered her offer while locking the day's cash received and credit card receipts into the safe in my office. "Sure. Be here at eight o'clock."

After locking the front door, I jumped on my bike and found that my back tire was flat. I must have run over something sharp earlier. Looked like I was pushing my bike instead of riding. When I finally got home, Dot and Sanny met me at the side door. Dot wound around my ankles while Sanny flew up and perched on my left shoulder. I picked up Dot and offered my finger for Sanny to gently nip.

"After a day like today, you two are just what I need."

I closed my eyes and inhaled deeply. Something was off. My cottage, brimming with positive energy this morning, felt a little tarnished now.

"It's probably just me. Between my pans getting stolen, Iris's passing, that note, and my tire going flat, this was a rough day."

I went to the kitchen, put a kettle of water on the burner to heat, then took the back staircase upstairs to change clothes. That's when I realized I was still wearing my golden apron. Guess I was more flustered than I'd realized. After stripping off my jeans and blouse and tossing them in the hamper, I reached for my favorite pair of soft, flowing pajamas. Never one to mess with anything that was working properly, except to tweak a recipe now and then or try a new kitchen gadget, I had purchased multiple pairs of these pajamas in different colors. Tonight felt like a soothing lavender night. Deciding I needed Ruby's input on that note, I tucked the envelope in the pants pocket. Thank the Goddess I'd asked her to come over.

When I got back to the kitchen, I found her there, taking two mugs from the cupboard.

"When did you get here? And what are you wearing?"

"About ten seconds ago." She grinned when she saw me. "I had a feeling it would be a PJs night."

Her top, too long to be a shirt and too short to be a dress, had a ten-inch-long ruffle along the bottom. The wide-legged pants were cropped to mid-shin. Both were made from fabric that was a patchwork of colors. "You look like you're wearing your grandmother's quilt."

"Thanks. My grandmother had great taste. What flavor tea?"

"Chamomile with honey, please. I need to relax."

"Perfect, I do too."

After eyeing her outfit a little longer, I said, "I hope you drove your car."

"Hey, this is Whispering Pines. If Sister Agnes can ride her bike around the village wearing a habit, I can do so in my jammies."

"I meant that those legs are so wide they'll get caught in the chain." Honestly, each leg had to be a good twelve inches across.

"I worried about that too, so yes, I drove my car."

While our tea steeped, I slid on a pink apron.

"Did you make that one too?" Ruby asked.

"I did. Made the dye out of strawberries that had gone past their prime." I lit the unscented white jar candle sitting on the table and then pulled ingredients from the pantry, giving a grateful thought to each item as I did. One of the many good things about working where I did was that I could partially prepare my dinner there. I'd do a quick demonstration for the customers—"I'll be spatchcocking a chicken for roasting if any of you are interested in watching."—and have the main part of my meal ready for when I got home. Plus, wonderful aromas filling Hearth & Cauldron made for happy customers. Pumping that smell into the woods brought in more.

"What's for dinner?" Ruby took her favorite spot at the table that ran parallel to my work area. Most people liked to watch chefs cook, so I designed my kitchen to allow my guests to do just that. It also provided an extra surface if they wanted to help and meant I wouldn't trip over them if they didn't.

"I made a chicken yesterday and have some leftover. So we're having a green salad with chicken and plenty of fresh veggies," I answered. "I think I have some dinner rolls too."

As I chopped and assembled, Ruby sipped tea, played with Dot by dangling feathers on a string tied to a stick for her to bat at, and told me about her day. My mind kept slipping to the note in my pocket, but I forced myself to listen to my friend and focus on dinner. As I'd just told Keiko, sustenance first, deal with the upsetting topic afterward.

"The hot craft item of the day was resin bookmark kits."

I smiled, letting her chatter distract me from my thoughts. "Resin bookmarks?"

"India ordered some kits from me a few weeks ago and made a bunch to sell in Biblichor. The resin is a liquid that you pour into bookmark-shaped silicone molds. You can color the resin with dye and add things like glitter or small trinkets. India sold out of all that she made but kept a few on hand as samples and is taking orders for more."

"And her more crafty customers came to you to make their own," I guessed.

Who could have left that note?

"Exactly," Ruby agreed. "It's fun, fairly easy, and you can make more than bookmarks. Keychains, coasters, plant tags, jewelry, trinket boxes . . . I could go on and on."

"I'm sure you could." Her enthusiasm made me happy.

One day, I watched a hummingbird eating from one of my feeders. It hovered there, dipping its beak into the flower-shaped opening again and again. Then it moved to the next opening and the next. Then it darted into the trees, only to return a few seconds later and repeat the dipping process. Ruby often reminded me of a hummingbird, never able to stay on target for long. When we met, her obsession had been crocheting. A few months later, it had been watercolors. She was constantly switching to something new and had so many interests she'd filled an entire room in her cottage with her stash. That's how she ended up opening the craft store. Working there and instructing her customers allowed her to get a little taste of many different crafts every day.

I set Ruby's salad on the table in front of her and mine across from her. While we ate, the topic shifted to Gardenia and the online signup sheet April O'Connor had made to help her through this time. Folks could choose a day and either bring over a meal, offer to tidy the cottage, weed the gardens, or whatever Gardenia might need help with.

"I hope that many people hanging around isn't too much for her," Ruby mused. "She's sort of an introvert."

"She's also not shy. She'll let us know when it's time to back off." I loaded my fork with salad and almost mentioned the note. Not yet. Nothing that negative was to be discussed while enjoying a meal together. "Keiko stopped by Hearth & Cauldron to help today. She sure likes to stay busy."

"Willow must have kicked her out of Shoppe Mystique again."

I shot her a *be nice* scowl as I chewed.

"What? The girl isn't meant to be a green witch. Those are Willow's words, not mine."

"Willow didn't kick her out. Keiko is on their schedule from eleven to three every day. Or most days."

What scone is that note referring to?

Sanny flew over and perched on the edge of the table as though she had asked the question and was waiting for an answer.

"Perhaps Keiko needs Morgan's guidance," I suggested. "As talented as Willow is, you know how standoffish she can be. And patience isn't one of her virtues. If Willow's right and green witchery isn't Keiko's path, the girl does have potential. The kitchen gleamed when she was done cleaning it this afternoon."

Ruby considered this and decided, "You're right. Everyone needs a mentor witch when starting out and as we said, that isn't Willow. I hear Morgan is starting back on Friday. She's got dibs."

"She doesn't have dibs," I blurted with a laugh. "Keiko *wants* to follow the green witch path."

"But just wanting something doesn't mean it will happen. Sometimes you have to search awhile."

"True. Morgan is also not shy. She'll send Keiko in a different direction if she feels green witchery isn't the right path for her. In the meantime, Keiko wants more work. I've got plenty she can do, and you need help at Twisty."

"Part-time at Shoppe Mystique and split the remaining hours between us?"

"I'll mention it to her in the morning. She's going to help me bless the shop."

I looked down when Dot stood with her front paws on my lap. She tapped my pocket where the envelope was, gazed at me with those big orange eyes, and tapped it again. Sanny flew to my shoulder.

I scratched Dot's ears and stroked the top of Sanny's feathery head. "Okay, you two, message received."

"What message?" Ruby asked. "What's going on with you tonight? I've been waiting for you to tell me why you're so distracted. Before you say you're not, our salads don't match. And you promised me dinner rolls."

As she jumped up to get the rolls from the breadbasket in my pantry, I noticed she was right about the salads. Presentation was important. When I prepared a dinner salad, everyone got the same ingredients in the same quantities. An allergy to something being the exception. While both salads were perfectly edible, I had given Ruby all of my red pepper strips and gave myself more chicken. A small detail to some, but Ruby knew me well enough to recognize this as a mistake.

I took the envelope from my pocket and set it at the center of the table.

"What's that?" She placed a plate with rolls and the butter dish between us and then reached for the note.

"Keiko found that taped to the front door at Hearth & Cauldron this afternoon."

I buttered two rolls and gave one to each of us as she slid the note out of the envelope and read it.

Her eyes were wide when she looked up at me. "This sounds like a threat, Reeva."

TWELVE

R uby inspected both sides of the note and the envelope. "No signature and no hint of who left it. What's it supposed to mean? And what scone? Are you in danger?"

"I've been thinking about all of that. The obvious answer is the scones Laurel brought to the coven gathering."

"No one else has offered you a scone recently?" Ruby shoved half a roll into her mouth. She really liked bread.

I chewed a forkful of salad and pondered that. "I stopped by Treat Me Sweetly a few days ago to say hi to Sugar and Honey. Honey wanted me to taste her new hot cocoa blend. She steeped the milk with desiccated coconut first. Very tasty. She offered me a scone to go with it."

"Press the pause button." This meant Ruby had something off topic to say and it couldn't wait. "First, what is desiccated coconut?"

"Coconut that's been shredded and dried."

"Why not just say dry, then?"

I wasn't sure, honestly, but guessed, "Desiccated sounds more culinary than dry?"

"I'll accept that. Second, am I the only one shocked that Laurel was brave enough to bring scones last night? She makes excellent muffins. Why didn't she bring those?"

"No, you're right, everyone knows that Sugar makes the scones in this village." They'd been Treat Me Sweetly's signature item for forty years. Mr. Graham perfected them and passed the recipe on to his daughters.

"Had to get that off my chest. And we need to prepare for retaliation from Sugar."

"You think she'll be that upset?"

Ruby looked me in the eye and stated gravely, "Laurel's scones were *good*." She held my gaze then blurted, "Okay, hit play. The note says that the scone 'was meant for you.' That implies you didn't take one that was offered to you. Did Honey want you to take a specific scone or did she say to pick one from the case?"

"She said I could pick one. I chose the last chocolate with almonds on top because almonds and chocolate go so well with coconut. The customer behind me was literally angry because she'd wanted that one. I was going to give it to her, but she was being so rude I took it to make a point."

Ruby slapped an air high five at me. "Has anyone else offered you a scone recently?"

I thought back over the last couple of weeks. "The same day I stopped to talk to Honey and Sugar, I stopped to see Violet too. She also had a beverage she wanted me to try. A new Drink of the Day to add to her lineup. The butterscotch latte she made for Gardenia this morning. It's fantastic. I don't understand why she hasn't already been selling it. And I don't understand why everyone feels they need my approval on new menu items."

Ruby paused while sopping up the last of the balsamic dressing on her plate with a roll. "Because you're Reeva Long. The greatest kitchen witch in the Midwest. I think it's less about getting your approval than wanting your opinion. People do the same thing to Briar and Morgan regarding their gardens. A thumbs up from them ensures it'll be beautiful." She resumed sopping. "So, Violet offered you a scone?"

"She got two varieties from Sugar to determine which would go best with the butterscotch drink, then she planned to sell them as a pair. Maple-pecan or vanilla. Since I'd just had one at Treat Me Sweetly, I didn't take one, but it's not like Violet got upset about it. I told her not to underestimate vanilla. Despite the saying, vanilla is anything but plain. It enhances nicely without overwhelming. Besides, the star of the pair should be her coffee."

"You're making my mouth water. Okay, so not Sugar, Honey, or Violet."

"And not Laurel."

"You're positive?" Ruby took our now empty plates to the sink, started the hot water, and squirted in some dish soap.

"About Laurel? Yes."

"It can't hurt to talk it through a little more."

"Fine, but after we're done with the dishes."

Since there was only chopping and no cooking involved tonight, it didn't take more than five minutes to wash the dishes and wipe down the counter and table. I left the candle burning on the countertop.

Hearth Witch Tip
To prevent a tunnel from forming
in the center of your jar candle,
burn it until the wax melts to the edge.

With the kitchen clean, I added more looseleaf chamomile and hot water to the teapot and secured a crocheted cozy around it.

I set the teapot, a beehive-shaped honey pot, and our mugs onto a tray along with a plate of gingersnaps. Then we moved into the sunroom. Other than my kitchen, this was my favorite room in the cottage. Decorated in shades of sage green, brick red, and ivory, the room was cozy and comfortable year round. Ruby dropped onto her favorite chair covered in floral fabric. I sat across from her in a tone-on-tone striped wingback. We both propped our feet on the matching floral ottoman.

"Regarding Laurel," I began, "I decided yesterday she wasn't involved with anything nefarious. I still believe that." I held up the note. "Besides, this isn't her handwriting."

"But didn't you notice how upset she seemed when you said you hadn't tried one of the scones?"

"Yes, but it's more like the Honey and Violet situation. I think she simply wanted my opinion."

"Why didn't she just ask you then? Why hope you'd taste one and get upset when you didn't? Why didn't she ask Sugar for that matter?"

"For the same reason Honey and Violet didn't directly ask my opinion on their drinks. Laurel's been working for years to improve her baking skills and isn't confident. It started when we were kids. She could never quite get to my or Sugar's level. As for asking Sugar, would you go to the queen of crochet for advice?"

She leaned forward, a look of excitement brightening her face. "There's a queen of crochet?"

"Shush. You know what I'm saying. Regardless of her motive behind those scones, I'm positive she wouldn't tape a threatening note to my door to scold me for not trying one."

"Fine," Ruby relented. "It wasn't Laurel."

I sipped tea and reviewed the facts. The biggest one was that things started going sideways after Monday night's blessing. "It was probably a coven member."

"You think a coven member left the note?"

"That surprises you, but you don't hesitate to accuse Laurel of threatening me?" Before she could reply, I continued, "Your claim that they love me is sweet, but you know full well that half of the coven wasn't happy when Morgan named me high priestess." My fingers went to the Triple Moon Goddess pendant at my throat. Like a crown on a queen's head, the pendant represented my position in the group. "There are times when I feel like choosing me was simply a strategic move."

"Why do you say that?"

"Morgan wanted to step down, and I'm one of the few people my sister can't manipulate. I'm not sure who else she could have chosen, but if that person wasn't strong enough, it wouldn't have been any different than letting Flavia lead."

Ruby stared at me, stone faced. "That's insulting. You think we can't stand up for ourselves? Or stand together for that matter? We're stronger than you give us credit for."

I tilted my head side to side to release the growing tension in my neck. "I'm sorry, I didn't mean it that way. It's just that Flavia can be very sly, and after growing up with her, I can tell when she's up to something."

"You lived with her for the first eighteen years of your life. You haven't lived with her for the past forty. And for twenty of those years, you weren't even in the same village."

"True but as the saying goes, a leopard can't change its spots."

"Yes," Ruby agreed, "but if an antelope hasn't been hunted in a long time, its instincts may not be as keen."

Silence descended between us until I said, "Well, that turned gruesome."

Ruby laughed, pulled her legs into crisscross, and held her mug in both hands. "Why do you keep questioning Morgan's choice? She wouldn't hand over the coven she, her mother, and her grandmother had so carefully cultivated to someone incapable of guiding it. And Briar would never allow it. Along with being a skilled witch, you are devoted to Wicca. You have been all your life. You listen to all sides and weigh them before making a decision. Just like you're doing with this scone situation. I can't think of anyone better to lead us. If you hadn't decided to stay, Morgan wouldn't have stepped down. I'd bet my shop on that."

I let that simmer in my brain for a minute. "You're probably right. Growing up with Flavia, I expected things won't go the way I want them to. Especially here in the village. That's why I was content to walk away from it. The bright side was that I got to raise Yasmine, but Flavia warned me I'd regret it if I dared to step foot in Whispering Pines again."

Ruby frowned and was left speechless. A rare occurrence.

"Ever since I returned last year," I continued, "I've felt like a teenager and not in a young and vibrant way. During the twenty years I was away, I didn't have these kinds of doubts. If I tried something and it didn't work, that was okay because I knew she had nothing to do with it."

Ruby sipped her tea, letting me talk.

"Coming back here, knowing I could run into my sister at any time?" I shook my head. "All my insecurities and doubts returned. Hearth & Cauldron is doing well, better than I dreamed, and I'm terrified that every day will be its last."

"Oh, Reeva. I had no idea. How can I help?"

I inhaled and let out a shaky breath. Then another. "I *know* Flavia is somewhere she can't pull her tricks anymore. As more time passes, I'll start to believe that too. For now, saying it out loud, getting those thoughts out of my head helps a lot. I hear how ridiculous it sounds. Thank you for listening."

"Any time. You know that." She took a cookie from the tray. "Do you need to talk more, or can we try to figure out who's threatening you?"

"I'm good now." Time to deal with real problems rather than the ones in my head. "I think we need to focus on coven members."

"I agree. The question is, which one of them could be this upset with you?"

"I know which members aren't happy with me being high priestess. Lorena, April, Luna, maybe Aster—"

"Aster? Really?"

"I'm on the fence about her. She tends to mold her personality to those she's around. She's sweet as pie to my face, but I was at Sundry one day and heard her, Lorena, and Luna badmouthing Morgan for choosing me."

Ruby shook her head. "Lorena would talk nasty about Goddess Hecate."

I burst out laughing. "That really happened, though. Talking about me, not badmouthing Hecate. They were saying that they didn't think I should have been chosen because I clearly didn't care enough about the village."

"What?"

"Because I left for twenty years."

"Well, thanks to Jayne figuring out how Yasmine died, the truth about why you left came out. Did they happen to mention who they thought should have taken Morgan's place?"

"They didn't get that far. Peyton stepped in, sent Luna and Aster on their way, and gave Lorena a warning about talking about people at work. 'I told you before to keep your blacklisting to personal hours,' he said."

"Good for him."

I grew quiet and clutched my warm mug between my hands. "Something else just occurred to me. Remember how Aster and Alder asked me to help with Clover and Peony yesterday morning?"

She nodded and grabbed another cookie from the plate.

"Did I mention that I gave them an assignment as well?"

"Alder and Aster? No, you left that part out."

"They weren't exactly happy. The thing is, they're going to others more and more to 'help' with discipline. I get it, parenting is hard, but they can't pass off the hard stuff. If they ask, I'm happy to offer advice, but I did my time in the parenting trench." Although, if I had stayed in the trench just a little longer, my daughter might still be here.

Ruby pointed at me. "I heard what you just thought. Stop it. There's no way you could have known what would happen to Yasmine. Regarding the Flowers, do you think they're upset enough to threaten you? Were they at the gathering Monday night?"

I squinted, trying to remember if they were there. "I think Aster was. Are they upset enough to threaten me? Maybe. It's probably worth pursuing."

"Anyone else on your unhappy list? What about Gardenia?"

"What makes you suspect her?"

"Because she was too calm when we were there. I never saw even a single tear."

"That's a little harsh, Ruby. She was in shock. Her mimi just died. Like we said, knowing something bad is coming doesn't necessarily lessen the blow when it finally arrives."

Sanny swooped over from her perch atop her cage by the windows, landed on the ottoman, and pecked at the note I'd tossed there.

"You're right," I told the little owl. "We're losing focus."

"You give that bird too much power."

Sanny swiveled her head backward to look at Ruby and released an ear-piercing screech.

"Hey!" I scolded. "You know better. None of that in the house." To Ruby, I added, "Don't antagonize her. You know better too." I picked up the note. "'The scone was meant for you, High Priestess.' *The* scone. One I was meant to have."

Ruby leaned forward and set down her mug. "It has to be one from the coven gathering. You said you took the one Sugar offered and that Violet wasn't upset that you didn't have one with her latte."

"She didn't think twice about it," I murmured, absently wandering to Sanny's cage to check on her water and food supply. As I added more pellets to her food dish, a sickening thought came to me.

"You're white as the moon," Ruby noted. "What are you thinking?"

"I gave my scone to Iris. I took a chocolate one and then traded for a cinnamon because she liked chocolate better."

"You think someone put something in it. That was the one meant for you."

My legs became weak, so I returned to my chair. "Do you think someone meant to murder me?"

Ruby blanched. "I don't think we can jump to that. Iris has been sick for a long time. If there was something in that scone, it could have been something mild that would have made you sick but was too much for Iris's heart to handle."

True. I suddenly felt nauseated, though. *Did* someone want me dead? If so, why? Because of a leadership role in the coven? Or was there something else going on?

"Blood test!" Ruby blurted. "Gardenia asked Dr. Bundy to check Iris's blood because she thought Iris might have stopped taking her heart medication."

That was a very good point. "Gardenia isn't involved with this. She wouldn't ask him to check her grandmother's blood if there was something harmful in it."

"Yes, but that's not what I'm getting at. I don't know anything about how these blood tests work. Will they check only for the heart medication, or will the test reveal anything foreign in the blood?"

"I don't know, but I'm tempted to call Dr. Bundy and ask him to check for a poison."

Ruby grabbed my tablet computer from the basket on the side table and searched for . . . something.

"What are you looking for?"

"Dr. Bundy's phone number."

"Ruby, you can't—"

"Yes, I can." She picked up my phone next and dialed the number she'd found. "Yes, hi, Joan. I'm calling from the Whispering Pines Sheriff Station. Dr. Bundy picked up a body here earlier today and the woman's granddaughter requested a blood test. We now have reason to believe there may have been foul play involved. Will you instruct the lab to search for poisons as well?"

She hung up.

"Well?" I asked.

"No one's there. I left a message."

"And now Joan will call Martin tomorrow to verify the request. When he says he didn't make a request, they'll track the phone number to my house."

Ruby frowned then shrugged. "Well, that's one way to get their attention."

THIRTEEN

Claiming to be afraid for my safety, Ruby stayed the night in my guest room. I wasn't exactly sure how she would protect me, but I also had Sanny hanging out in the trees surrounding the property. Her screech worked better than any security alarm I could have installed. Of course, neither could do much if someone was intent on harming me. Ruby was tiny, just over a hundred pounds. I guess she could call Martin, while Sanny swooped and pecked. Regardless, it was nice to have someone in the cottage with me. When Sanny let loose with a single screech around three in the morning, I was doubly glad Ruby had stayed.

"Did you hear your bird last night?" Ruby asked while settling in at the kitchen table for an easy breakfast of soft-boiled eggs, yogurt with berries and homemade granola, and tea.

"I did. I couldn't tell if it was an alarm or just her making noise, though."

"Right around the time she cried out, I woke up to use the bathroom. Maybe it's just because she startled me, but something's still not right in this house. I don't think the blessing stuck. I feel like I'm being watched."

"It might not be perfect, but it's significantly better." I stroked the top of the owl's head as she perched on the table next to my placemat. "What bothered you? Did you see Ruby wandering around?" To Ruby, I noted, "Owls have incredible vision, you know. And there are plenty of non-human possibilities, like a rival bird or an animal wandering around the woods. Also, Litha is in two days. The veil is thinning, and three o'clock is the witching hour."

Ruby shook her head. "I hate that excuse. Three o'clock in the morning is no different from any other time of day."

"Plenty of people believe that the hour between three and four in the morning is prime time for paranormal activity." I drizzled some honey into my tea. "Of course, the most reasonable explanation is that you got up to use the bathroom, Sanny noted unusual activity inside the house and alerted me. The feeling of being watched might have been her." I scooped up a bite of egg. "Another reason could be that this house was so full of bad energy, the coven missed some during the blessing. I should probably do another smudging."

"I don't know how you've lived here for a whole year." She stirred her yogurt parfait.

"The first week or so was rough, but it got a little easier each day after that. Asking the coven to come over wasn't because I've been afraid here. With Flavia getting locked up and me deciding to reset my life, it felt like a good time to clear away those dark bits hanging around."

"But there's still something left."

After a bite of berries and yogurt and a sip of tea, I admitted, "I never smudged the reading room. It probably needs extra attention."

"Have you even stepped inside it yet?" Ruby asked gently.

The house was Karl's before we got married. He used the

small room off his bedroom as a study. It was a cozy little space with windows lining every wall and giving the feeling of sitting in the treetops. When I moved in, we converted the main floor bedroom into his office, and I installed built-it bookcases beneath the windows in that little room. Then I brought in two comfy reading chairs and set a table between them that was just big enough to set two beverages and two books on. We called it the reading room and spent many nights in there reading or talking before going to bed. Along with whatever darkness was lingering in there, the small space held many good memories. And, unfortunately, a ghost.

"No, I haven't been inside yet," I replied to Ruby's question.

"You've cleared every other room of him. Is there a reason you're avoiding that one?"

"I haven't been in his garden shed either." Mostly because I returned to the village in the summertime and was focused on clearing out the cottage. By the end of summer, I had decided to stay so planning Hearth & Cauldron took up most of my days. I didn't even think about the yard. Thankfully, some of the green witches came over to tend it for me.

Ruby wouldn't back down. "You sleep eight feet away from that room every night. Don't you think it's a good idea to rid it of him? I mean, if you'd had a good marriage—"

"We did have a good marriage," I insisted like I did anytime people asked if I regretted marrying Karl. "Right up until that day." When my sister seduced him.

"I'll restate. If your marriage had ended well, having him here could be nice. Considering how those last twenty years went, I'd find it infuriating to have him hanging about. And yes, I realized you don't actually see his ghost." She set down her spoon. "It's time. Let's go."

I laughed at her. "Not right this minute. Besides, it isn't a two-person job, and it's something I need to do on my own."

With a softer voice, she repeated, "Is there a reason you're avoiding this?"

"Probably, but now isn't the time to explore my feelings about it."

She scowled at me. "Fine. When are you going to smudge it?"

"Tonight," I blurted, wanting to move past this. "I'll do it tonight. No more talk of Karl. Eat your egg before it's cold."

A few minutes later, Ruby noticed, "You look tired."

Wrapping my hands around my teacup, letting the heat seep in and soothe my joints, I shrugged. "Guess I didn't sleep as well as I did Monday night. Sanny woke me at three a.m. too. I went back to sleep after the one screech but woke again at quarter to five and couldn't fall asleep again. I should have just got up and done something productive instead of lying there for forty-five minutes."

"What were you thinking about?"

"That scone and who could have messed with it."

She frowned at me while chewing her last bite of egg. "You do think it was poisoned then?"

"That's what I lay there thinking about. I can't get myself to believe it."

"What else would you call a substance that caused the person who consumed it to die?"

"A severe allergic reaction?" I offered half-heartedly.

"Possible," she agreed, "but not probable."

I set down my spoon and sat back in my chair. After a few seconds, I forced myself to ask, "Did someone try to kill me?"

"Glad you're taking this seriously. I don't know the answer, but we'll figure it out, and if it's true, we'll make the responsible party pay."

My fear quickly turned into anger. "But why? Why would someone do this to me? Because my sister did all those horrible things?"

She straightened. "What would make you think that? Her actions aren't your fault."

I reiterated the discussion I'd had with Tripp about serial killers' families.

Ruby dismissed it. "I can understand strangers thinking such a thing, but we all know each other here."

"Except in the eyes of plenty of the villagers, I returned and then all hell broke loose. People were murdered, stabbed, and kidnapped." I held up a hand, silencing her objection. "I know, it had been brewing for years before the deaths started. That isn't what some see, though. Only a small handful knew about all the secrets until Jayne exposed them. Those same folks who think I'm somehow responsible blame Jayne too."

"I can't argue with you about that."

We finished our breakfasts in silence. I smiled when Dot jumped onto the chair across from me and watched me, only her eyes and her pointy ears appearing over the table's surface. Yasmine used to do that when she was little. First her fingers would appear on the counter, then the top of her head, her forehead, and finally her eyes. She did it because it made me laugh. I laughed because she did it. Oh, how I missed my girl.

"Okay," Ruby began. "Who's on our suspect list?"

"That's also what I was thinking about at five in the morning. I think we're right. It has to be one of the coven members."

"I agree. And the scone in question has to be the one you were given at the blessing. Who gave you that scone?"

I stared across the table into Dot's eyes and recalled the gathering in my backyard. "Basil rushed over with a chair for Iris, and I knelt on the grass next to her. She was starting to feel a little better when Verne appeared with the tray."

"Verne is our suspect!" Ruby slapped her hand on the table as though she'd cracked the case.

"We can add Verne to our list," I corrected. "He handed them out, but that doesn't mean he was responsible for adding a poison." I cringed at the word.

"True. There were others associated with this. Laurel made them . . ."

I knew what she was thinking. "Laurel did not try to kill me."

"We don't know that for sure. We only know that she didn't steal your pans. That doesn't mean she didn't slip something into your scone. Work the scene. What do you remember?"

"Work the scene," I murmured and slipped back to two nights ago. "I stayed at Iris's side, and Gardenia went inside to make tea for her."

Ruby jumped up and got a notepad and pen from the corner of my counter.

"What are you doing?" I asked.

She looked at me like it should be obvious. "Making a suspect list. Verne, Laurel, and now Gardenia."

"Gardenia? I was only recalling events. We decided last night that she wasn't responsible because she asked for that blood test."

"That's one of the things *I* was thinking about in the middle of the night. She'll inherit everything. Greed makes otherwise wonderful people do horrible things. Dear Iris had been standing on death's doormat for months. Maybe the stress became too much for Gardenia. What if she saw an opportunity that night and poisoned the tea?"

"It wasn't the tea."

"We can't know that for sure."

"We can." I flung a hand at the note Keiko found on my shop door where it lay on my counter. "'The scone was meant for you, High Priestess.' The scone was the weapon."

Ruby softened. "Okay, but I'm keeping Gardenia on the list for now. Continue with whatever you were going to say."

I took a centering breath. Ruby was simply exploring all the options, not purposely being aggravating. That was a good thing. "Verne stopped by with the scones. He asked if we had a preference of flavor. I said no, so he handed a chocolate one to me, and Gardenia took a cinnamon chip for Iris."

"He handed it to you? You're sure?"

"Yes."

"And Gardenia chose one for Iris."

"Yes." A shiver skittered through me.

"What are you thinking? Don't keep anything inside. Say your thoughts out loud."

"Verne couldn't have known which flavor I'd ask for, so there had to be a tainted one of each available." I envisioned him standing next to me. "The tray was half empty. What if someone else had taken one meant for me?"

"Presuming he knew they were tainted he'd stop them. Maybe he kept those ones close to him? Folks don't usually reach across a tray. They'll take whatever's closest."

"Unless they want something specific. The biggest or the smallest or whatever." I blew out a breath. "We're getting stuck on details. We're supposed to be creating a suspect list."

"Right," Ruby agreed. "Laurel brought them, Verne and Luna handed them out."

I remembered looking in the kitchen windows at one point. "Lorena was in here too. Possibly others but, from where I stood in the backyard, I only saw those four."

"They could have been in on it together," Ruby suggested. "Which means Gardenia could have been too. You said she chose one for Iris. She could have known which one to take."

"Except I switched with her. Remember?"

Ruby deflated a bit. "Right."

"Maybe Verne unknowingly got mixed up in this caper."

"And whoever is responsible for messing with the scone told Verne which one to give you? That's possible." She tapped the pad with the pen. "We've got four suspects. We need to investigate."

I shook my head. "If we believe that one of the coven members tried to kill me, we have to tell Martin." I glanced at the clock on my microwave. Ten past seven. "Let's clean up the kitchen and get to work. I told Keiko I'd meet her at the shop at eight."

"I'll drop you at the Fairy Path." She motioned at her pajamas. "I need to go home and get some clothes."

Once the kitchen was clean, I hung the dish towel to dry, and Ruby presented another thought. "Martin will want proof."

"I was just thinking the same thing. He's got enough on his plate with his first season as sheriff. He doesn't have time to chase after hunches. We'll have to wait for the results of the blood test to come in."

"Who knows how long that will take. We could do a little legwork and gather some facts for him in the meantime." When I didn't agree right away, she stated, "This is serious stuff, Reeva. If someone has painted a target on you, they won't stop because someone else got the scone."

She wasn't wrong. Suddenly, my messed up firepit area yesterday morning, my flat bicycle tire last night, and that note taped to my door felt connected. Like they were warnings. Someone was messing with me.

"All right. I'll stop at the station on my way to Hearth & Cauldron and have a chat with my nephew. If things are easy for him right now, I'll broach the subject. If things are crazy . . ."

"Yes?" Ruby practically vibrated with glee.

"If things are crazy, we'll do some legwork."

She pumped a fist. "Yes!"

CHAPTER
FOURTEEN

After making sure the girls had food and water, Ruby and I stepped outside and found broken plant pots on my patio. Not just one, but three of them. And not merely cracked but smashed to pieces with dirt and flower bits everywhere.

"This could have been what Sanny alerted us about," I said, pushing the large shards into a pile. I'd clean it up when I got home tonight. "I'm amazed I didn't hear the breaking."

A few minutes later, Ruby pulled into the Unity parking lot near the entrance to the Fairy Path. "I should go with you to talk to Martin."

"Why?"

"You might forget a detail."

I shook my head. "I'm not going to bother him with this until we have proof. Remember? This could simply be kids causing problems. Maybe Clover and Peony are retaliating against my punishment."

"But the note—"

"Goodbye, Ruby." I shut the car door before she could plead her case any further.

As I strode across the lot, I looked toward Whispering Pines' healing center. Their offerings of not only medical services but yoga, meditation, massage, acupuncture, and other holistic treatments made them the perfect mind, body, and spirit center. Gabe's older daughter Jola was one of two licensed RNs specializing in holistic and preventative healing. Currently, she and Lily Grace were walking through the Zen yard together. When the pair looked my way, I raised my hand in greeting, but they turned away without acknowledgment.

Gabe and others had told me to give them time, and they'd been right. Jola stopped me one day last week as I rode past on my bike.

"We don't hate you," she'd assured. "Well, I don't, and Lily Grace won't forever. I promise."

I wanted to take her in my arms and hug her. Jola was a very mature twenty-three-year-old and while she'd likely never admit it, she still needed a mother in her life. I sure did at that age. With Rae gone now, I'd gladly step up, but I wasn't welcome that way. Besides, Gabe had never given any indication that he wanted my or anyone else's help with them.

"Thank you for saying that," I had replied to her. "I know what it's like to lose someone who you love so much. I'm available if you ever need someone to talk to." I blushed then. "Sorry. That's awfully bold of me, isn't it?"

"It is," she'd agreed, "but I know it was sincere."

Aside from the cold treatment I'd just received from the Grace-Crain girls, it was a beautiful late-spring day, almost summer, and the sky was crystal clear. The woods along the wooden Fairy Path were teeming with life. Along with flowers in full bloom, I spotted dozens of squirrels, chipmunks, bunnies, and birds.

I made it to the sheriff's station in less than five minutes, although I was enjoying my morning walk so much I almost strolled right past it.

Through the windows on the front of the plain rectangular building, I saw both my nephew and his deputy. They were standing side by side, looking down at something I couldn't see. I pulled open the door and walked inside just as they both called out, "No, wait!"

The next thing I knew, I was flat on the floor. I looked up to find a furry face with a long snout and a set of very sharp-looking teeth staring at me. By the time I'd figured out it was a German Shepherd, it was washing my face with its tongue.

"Aunt Reeva," Martin cried. "Jagger, I swear to the Goddess if you don't get this beast under control . . ."

"I am so sorry, ma'am." Jagger swiped the dog aside with a big arm and then helped me to my feet. "He's learning."

"He's been learning for a year," Martin exclaimed. "That's why they said he wasn't going to work for the Madison police force." To me, he said, "Jagger decided we needed a new K-9 since Meeka left with Jayne. I cleared it with River, and he said we should talk to a handler in Madison or Milwaukee. I gave that assignment to my deputy, and they delivered this beast yesterday afternoon."

Jagger and the dog stood to the side, both staring down at the floor. They both looked so ashamed I almost laughed.

"This is what happens," Martin hissed through gritted teeth, "when you choose a dog without actually interacting with it. I knew there was something suspicious about how fast they brought him here. Are you all right, Aunt Reeva?"

I did a quick mental and physical assessment. "Fortunately, I caught myself, or I would have landed on my face." I rotated my wrists. "My palms will be a little sore, but nothing appears broken."

"We were told," Martin continued his tirade, "that he was great at apprehending criminals but was a little too friendly."

"He can track anyone," Jagger explained on the dog's behalf, "and he's fast, so he can catch up to anyone who runs. I figured that would be a positive during tourist season. When there are larger crowds, he can squeeze through places we can't. And a friendly dog in a tourist town is another positive trait."

"What we weren't told," Martin added, "is that his apprehension style is to knock people to the ground by pushing their knees out from under them."

"Like he just did to me. It's effective, I'll give him that."

"They also didn't explain," Martin concluded, "that he'll do that to anyone, whether criminal or civilian, at any time without warning."

I glared at the undeniably beautiful beast, which he took to mean I wanted to play. In a flash, he was standing with his front paws on my shoulders. Before either of the men could respond, I demanded, "Stop! Down."

The dog immediately dropped to his belly, chin on the floor.

Martin's and Jagger's jaws dropped.

"He obeyed you," Martin stated.

"Neither of you has ever raised a child," I noted. "Tone of voice is very important."

I locked stern eyes on the dog again. It was hard to stay angry when he was practically smiling up at me, tongue lolling a bit out of the side of his mouth. He understood I wasn't happy with him because he whined and then rolled over onto his back to present his belly to me.

For some unexplainable reason, I gave in to his doggie superpowers, dropped to my knees, and rubbed his belly. The moment I did, he flipped over, knocked me to my butt, and covered me in kisses again.

"That's it," Martin roared. "He's going back."

"No-no, my fault this time," I insisted as Martin helped me up again. "I've never owned a dog and haven't even spent much time around them, but I know better than to give praise so soon after a scolding. I have to say, though, luring folks into his goofy web that way is also an effective method of capture."

Jagger shot a grateful glance my way and then pleaded, "Give him a chance, boss. Let me work with him."

Martin stood there for a few seconds, hands in his pockets, then let out a sigh. "I know I'm going to regret this. The only way he can stay is if he's trained. He can't go around knocking tourists down and licking them. Take him up to the circus and talk to Igor."

Good idea. If anyone in the village could help, it was the circus veterinarian. What Igor didn't know about an animal he could figure out in minutes.

"Jayne might also be willing to work with him," I suggested. "I happen to know she's got time in her schedule."

"Excellent." Jagger looked relieved. He'd clearly already bonded with this dog. "I'll take him up to the circus right now, talk to Igor, and contact Jayne later."

"What's his name?" I checked his collar tag which read *Tyrann*. "Like tyrannosaurus."

Jagger explained, "It's German and means bully or tyrant."

"Doofus would suit him better," Martin mumbled as Jagger stepped outside with their goofy tyrant. Then he kissed my cheek. "Sorry about that."

"That he knocked me down or that my cheek is covered in slobber?"

He grimaced and wiped his lips. "Yes."

"I'm fine. I promise. You do need a dog that won't hurt innocent people, though."

"Agreed. Come to my office. I've got some wipes."

I smiled as I passed by the *Sheriff Martin Reed* plaque on the door. He was the fourth sheriff in the village's history. First Karl's father, Kent Brighton, then Karl, and Jayne O'Shea. Now my nephew, who had never been given credit for being capable of much as a child. Jayne had no idea how much she'd done for my boy by simply putting a bit of trust in him.

"Did you need something, Aunt Reeva? Or did you just stop by to say hi? Which, by the way, is always fine."

As I cleaned my neck and cheeks with the wipe, removing most of the makeup from the lower half of my face—fortunately I had a backup supply in my desk at Hearth & Cauldron—I reminded myself to be neutral and not give anything away. If Martin thought someone was out to hurt me, he'd drop everything else until the person or persons were caught.

"I'm on my way to the shop and thought I'd see how things are going for you. We haven't had a good visit in more than a week." I arched a brow at him. "You basically live in my backyard. Stop over now and then. Check on your old aunt."

"Old." He chuckled. "Hardly. Sorry I haven't stopped by. Litha is the first big tourist gathering. I've been a little sidetracked with making sure no one dies." He winced. "That was rude, considering poor Iris."

"But valid after last year. A death per month? Is that right?"

"Thirteen in thirteen months, but no one died in November." He paused to think. "Or April, I think."

"And now? The tourists are behaving?"

"So far so good. I heard some of them talking about the bonfire on Friday. They heard that dancing naked around it helps with fertility. I understand there are three or four couples here together who plan to test that theory."

"That's happened in the past," I reminded him. "At least, it did twenty-some years ago."

He shook his head and teased, "Jayne got off easy. She wasn't named sheriff until a few days after Litha. So how are things with you? How's the season starting? Great class yesterday, by the way. Rosalyn came over, and we made that second batch of hand pies."

"It's busy already. I need to hire another employee. Bee can't commit to all the hours I need filled."

Martin leaned back in his chair and propped his foot on his knee. "That's a good problem to have, though, right?"

"It is indeed. I think I know who I'm going to hire. Do you remember a young woman named Keiko Shen?"

His expression cleared as he remembered her and then it clouded again. "I do. She was friends with Yasmine."

My heart clenched every time the topic of Martin's half-sister came up between us. "I'm so sorry you never got to know her better. She was such a bright, vibrant person."

He nodded. "I'm sorry too. I always wanted a sibling."

He'd said that more than once. Despite Flavia's insistence that no one ever tell him what happened between her and Karl, Martin found out. When he told me he'd known for years, I felt even more awful that he couldn't have had some kind of contact with his "cousin" while growing up.

"You have nothing to be sorry for," he scolded the last time I'd said it. "You weren't given much of a choice."

That wasn't the whole truth, though. I found the escape route and took it. I didn't think about the others I was leaving behind, even my nephew. A fact I would regret forever.

"Keiko is back," I told him.

"Is that a good thing?"

"It seems to be. I wasn't here when she was last year, but Morgan told me about how Keiko was sure negative magic was the answer to her woes. She now sees that it's not and wants to figure out her true Wiccan path. She thinks it's green witchcraft, but I hear things aren't going so smoothly for her at Shoppe Mystique."

"Willow isn't much of a teacher."

I chuckled. "That's what I said. Anyway, she's only got halftime hours there and wants more."

"Sheriff Reed?" a low voice called over the walkie-talkie on his belt.

He unclipped the unit and pressed the talk button. "Sheriff Reed here."

"This is Basil. We've got someone trying to lower himself down the Negativity Well. Someone else is threatening to cut the bucket rope if he does."

"Be right there," Martin replied.

"This is how it's going to be all weekend, isn't it?"

"This is how it'll be all summer. With increased popularity comes increased challenges. You and the other shopkeepers need more employees. I have to deal with tourists who are either naked or willing to submerge themselves in negativity."

That's what I thought. I wouldn't bother him with my issues until I had proof that there really was a problem. Ruby was going to be over the moon.

"I'll walk with you," I announced and stood. "I've got to meet Keiko at the shop anyway."

We chatted more about their new K-9 as we walked along the Fairy Path. They had two weeks to return him to Madison if he didn't work out.

"I think he's got one more try after us, because another station already sent him back." Martin frowned. "I'm not sure what will happen to him if he doesn't work as a police dog."

"Surely they wouldn't euthanize him," I gasped. "He's a beautiful animal. Someone could adopt him, right?"

We stopped in front of Hearth & Cauldron. "Who will want a dog that knocks people down?"

Thinking of Keiko and the other outcasts who found this village, I looked him in the eye. "You do. He ended up in this village for a reason. Don't give up on him."

He kissed my cheek. "Yes, ma'am. I hope you have a great day. I better run."

And he literally sprinted toward the commons.

FIFTEEN

Keiko knocked on one of the glass panes of the front door shortly after I got there. The moment I let her in, she blurted, "I'm sorry I'm late. There was a line at the showers this morning."

I glanced at the three-sided train station-style clock hanging between the kitchen and dining room. "It's two minutes after eight."

"You said to be here *by* eight. I'm working on punctuality."

"You can mop the dining room floor as punishment if it'll make you feel better."

She blinked at me, unsure if I was serious or not.

"The floor really does need mopping, and I still need to total the receipts from yesterday, but let's get to the cleansing first."

It was my goal to make every customer who entered my shop feel welcome. And whether they left with a new treasure in hand or only what they entered with, most left a bit happier than they arrived. This meant any negativity attached to them had dropped onto the floor as they wandered about my shop.

I marked a sage water *X* on the sill over the front and back doors like Morgan had done with the external openings in my cottage and declared, "By this mark, no evil shall enter here. So mote it be."

Leaving the back door cracked open, I led Keiko to the retail room and gave her a broom, handmade from a wooden dowel, sorghum grass, and twine at one of Ruby's classes.

"You work the front half of the shop," I instructed, "and I'll do the back. Together, we'll move slowly and make small widdershins circles. You don't need to touch the broom to the floor. We're upsetting negative energy, remember, not sweeping up dirt. That will come later."

"Sweep in counterclockwise circles," she repeated. "Got it."

"Before we start, we need to clear our minds and focus on what we want to achieve."

Keiko closed her eyes, inhaled deeply, and exhaled slowly. "Okay, I'm ready."

"Fill your head with three words. Creativity, curiosity, positivity. Those are the feelings I want my shop to instill in me and my customers. I want them to be creative and curious with their cooking and all aspects of their home. And to always be as positive as possible." I centered myself with a deep breath and then pronounced, "With this cleansing, I ask the spirits to protect my shop and all who enter it from evil and negativity. Fill it, me, and them with creativity, curiosity, and positivity. So mote it be."

Keiko peeked open one eye. "Now?"

"Now," I agreed with a nod. "Creativity, curiosity, positivity. Say it aloud if you choose."

She did and for the next fifteen minutes, we swept in a grid pattern through the retail room and kitchen. Once we got to the dining room, we both moved to the front wall. She went to the far corner, I took the inside one, and we swept everything toward the open back door and out onto the patio.

"With that," I announced with a smile, "Hearth & Cauldron is clean."

"So mote it be," Keiko called out a little louder than necessary. I appreciated her enthusiasm, however.

I breathed deep. "So much better."

"And you only do this once a week?" Keiko asked.

"On Sunday afternoons," I confirmed, "after the tourist traffic lightens, or like today when I feel the energy is off. Otherwise, I light a candle every day and ask the same blessing from the spirits. I should have done a cleansing last night, but I was too upset about Iris's death."

And the note Keiko found taped to the front door. And the theft of the pans. I wouldn't tell her about that, though. A death, a threat, and a theft in two days? I didn't want to scare her off. She was just starting to prove her abilities.

As I hung our brooms on a hook near the fireplace, I asked, "Do you need to leave, or can I talk with you for a few minutes?"

She stiffened. "Uh-oh."

It took me a moment to understand what she meant. "There's no problem. I promise. The opposite actually."

"Okay." She still eyed me suspiciously. "I don't have to be to Shoppe Mystique until eleven."

Her comment made me pause. "You don't have to work until eleven, but you still agreed to meet me here at eight?"

"Well, yeah. I want to learn. If you're doing a cleansing at eight and you'll let me help, I'll be here at eight. If you want to do it at midnight, I'll come then." She patted my shoulder and gave me a smart-alecky grin. "But I understand you don't usually stay up that late."

I pointed a warning finger at her.

She held her hands up in surrender. "Sorry, couldn't help myself. What's up? What did you want to talk about?"

"I wanted to ask about putting you on the schedule."

Her jaw dropped, and she twirled a finger around the shop. "Here?"

"Yes, here," I said through a laugh. "Your schedule at Shoppe Mystique is eleven to three every day?"

"Right. Sundays and Mondays are sometimes less, depending on traffic."

"Perfect. Bee prefers earlier hours. What would you think about starting here at four and working until close?"

"Don't forget me."

We turned to see that Ruby had entered through the dining room door. A hedge enclosed the patio in back, so in order to access that door, she must have followed the hidden path that ran behind our shops and through the woods from The Inn to the schoolhouses. The only way tourists found out about that path or the others, like the one we took to get to Gardenia's cottage, was by accident. They were a little secret the villagers kept for themselves. Taking that route, Ruby could have squeezed between the hedge and my soap shack where I would eventually give instruction on soap making. It was a tight squeeze, though.

"Should've told me to lock that door," Keiko deadpanned.

"Watch it, wannabe witch," Ruby countered, "or I'll rescind my offer before I've made it."

"What offer?" Keiko asked, looking between us.

"Starting at four gives you an hour after leaving Shoppe Mystique to do whatever you need to do."

Ruby nodded. "That works for me."

"What works?" Keiko asked.

"Ruby also needs help over at The Twisty Skein. What do you think of dividing your afternoons between us, working with whichever of us is more in need?"

"Normally," Ruby began, "that will be Reeva. Until you know more about the crafts, you'll really only be able to point out where things are in the shop, stock the shelves—"

"And run the register," Keiko finished. "That's all I do at Shoppe Mystique right now. Yeah, I can handle that." She paused and almost hesitantly added, "For the record, I like crafts. My grandma taught me how to do origami. Not just the cliché crane but 3D swans, cubes . . . all sorts of things. I'll show you. Maybe I can do a kids' class for you sometime."

Ruby's eyes widened, and she paled a bit. I grabbed her shoulder when she jokingly started to lean to the right. At least I was pretty sure she was joking.

"No one else has ever taught a class at Twisty," I explained. "You'll need to be patient with her."

"Like handing your baby over to a new sitter," Keiko stated. "I get it."

I frowned when Ruby's face went from pale to deep pink. "Are you okay?"

"I'm fine. Can we talk a minute?"

"Sure. Keiko, why don't you start familiarizing yourself with the retail room? And the floor really does need mopping."

As she wandered off to look around the shop, I looked closer at my friend. "Seriously, are you okay? Your color isn't good."

She brushed off my concern. "I saw you walk past with Martin earlier. What did he say?"

She was hiding something, but now wasn't the time to press her on it. "I didn't even mention the potential poisoning to him. He's too busy with tourists and the new station K-9, Tyrann. Wait 'til you meet him."

"So we need to investigate?" Her expression was now one of gleeful hope.

"I figure we can stop by and have a chat with . . . who's first on our list?"

"Luna and Verne were handing out the scones at the coven gathering. I think we should start with them. I'm pretty sure Luna is working at the rental cottage office tonight."

"The office stays open until seven thirty for any late check-ins. If we close as close to six as possible, that gives us plenty of time. Let's go have a chat with her after work."

"Yes!" Ruby pumped her fists. "Long & McLaughlin Investigations has its first case."

At least she listed me first.

CHAPTER

SIXTEEN

ednesday morning and early afternoon at Hearth
& Cauldron had been busy but calm, just the way I
preferred. Maybe it was the cleansing Keiko and I
performed. Maybe it was that weekends always tended to
be the rowdier days with folks blowing off steam from the
workweek. Weekdays, in contrast, were generally quieter.
Whatever the answer, the morning hummed along.

"Time to prep for class," Bee told me at two o'clock.

"You're like a human alarm clock."

"The job of any good assistant is to keep her boss organized
and on schedule." She checked the sign-up sheet. "A full baker's
dozen today. I suppose you know where that saying came from
too."

"There are many tales of how this phrase came to be, so I'm
not sure which is accurate. The one I believe comes from bread
bakers. Handmade bread loaves, even made by the same person,
will never be exactly the same size and weight. If a customer
orders a dozen loaves and one baker's is larger and heavier and
another's smaller and lighter, the baker with the bigger loaves
will get more business. To make up for this, some savvy bread

makers began throwing in a thirteenth loaf when a dozen were ordered."

Bee considered this a moment. "That makes sense."

"Personally, the number thirteen appeals to the witch in me, because I like to think that all cooks have a little witch in them."

Bee gave a crooked grin at that.

As for my baker's dozen of students, thirteen was the most I'd allow in a class because that was the most that could comfortably fit around my twenty-four-foot-long by seven-foot-wide farmhouse table. This gave each student just about four square feet of workspace. If the recipe of the day required more room for spreading out, I limited the class size to six with the students zigzagged down the table instead of across from and next to each other. My lectern, so to speak, was the far end of the table in front of the fireplace, complete with cauldron, and directly across from the front door. That way, I could see all my students and any customers who walked in.

I filled large bowls with flour and lined them up down the center of the table. Tool packs and baskets with the other ingredients were set at the individual stations. Baking sheets lined with silicone baking mats sat ready and waiting on the stoves.

"All set?" Bee asked.

I was pulling a khaki-colored apron, colored from water dyed with already used coffee grounds, over my head. "Just need students."

Hearth Witch Tip
Scrub your hands with used coffee grounds
to help remove onion and garlic odors.

Bee pointed to the retail room. "A man in there is asking about the pine tree-shaped cutting boards. They're only for decoration, right?"

Blind Willie Haggerty, one of our elder villagers, was a master woodworker. Along with all the hand-carved direction signs posted around the village, he made furniture and household items that I sold on consignment for him.

"Yes, decoration only," I confirmed. "Or serving, I suppose. Pine is too soft for cutting on."

As she went to relay this information, my students started to arrive. Today, all of them were tourists, but there was one familiar face in the crowd.

"Mr. Lykke—"

"Please, call me Jozef."

I smiled. "Jozef. You're back already."

"I told you I would be. Taking your class yesterday was the first time in a long time that I've baked just for the fun of it. You, Ms. Long—"

"Call me Reeva," I insisted with a wink.

He bowed his head obligingly. "Reeva, you helped me find the joy of baking again, and it's like a drug. I want more."

My hands went to my heart. "You have no idea how happy that makes me."

He pointed at my clipboard. "I am not, however, on your list. Do you have room for one more?"

"This class is full, but sometimes people don't show up. If you want to wait, we'll see what happens."

With a few minutes to go before class started, there were two spots left unclaimed. I motioned Jozef over from where he was browsing through my cookbooks.

"Looks like you might get to bake," I told him, feeling happier about this than I probably should have. "If they don't show up by the time we start measuring, you're in."

I'm not sure which of us was sadder when the couple walked

through the door. They were awfully lovey-dovey with each other, and it was clear they were going to spend more time making googly eyes at each other than making scones. An idea struck me.

"Hi, I'm Reeva, your instructor and the shop owner."

"Hey, Reeva," the guy answered, full of swagger. To impress his date, I'm sure.

"Hiya," the girl chirped and waved at me with both hands.

"You're together?" I asked.

They gazed sappily at each other. She sighed and breathed, "We are."

I pointed at Jozef. "That man was hoping to get a spot in the class. Would you two be willing to share a spot and work together so he can have the other? I'll only charge you for one lesson."

"We've shared spots before." He stared at her, making her blush. "I think we can handle it."

I smiled tightly. "You two are obviously crazy about each other, and I'm happy for you. Let's keep this a family show, though, okay?"

He stood straight and cleared his throat. "No problem."

"Sorry," she whispered. "We haven't been together very long."

The starry-eyed young woman hidden deeply inside me sighed at the young lovers, while the fifty-eight-year-old, well-seasoned woman in me thought, *that'll pass.* "Thank you. Have fun, but not too much fun."

She giggled. He waggled his eyebrows at her.

Oh boy.

After everyone had paid for their spot at the table, I started class with a short history of scones.

"Records tell us that scones originated in Scotland, and it seems every country puts their own twist on them. Some prefer them sweet like we do in America, and others prefer savory with ingredients such as cheese and dill. Some add fruit or nuts.

The English like them with jam and clotted cream. Some make them plump like an American biscuit while others resemble pancakes. And here's a fun fact. Anna Maria Russell, the Duchess of Bedford in England, started the tradition of afternoon tea with scones in the mid-1800s."

Afternoon tea. That would be lovely. While Hearth & Cauldron wasn't a restaurant, there was no saying I couldn't do themed events now and then.

"I like that," Jozef said with a nod. "Do you give the history behind everything you teach?"

"I try to. Personally, I love knowing how recipes came to be. All right, let's start by measuring the flour, sugar, and baking powder into your larger bowl. The best and most consistent method is to weigh your ingredients. I don't have that many scales, however. Instead, fluff up the flour a bit, scoop it into the measuring cup, and level it off with the back of a knife or a wooden spoon handle."

Once they'd measured and mixed their dry ingredients into one bowl and their wet ingredients in another, it was time to add the butter to the dries.

"You need cold butter, straight from the fridge, for things like scones or pie crusts," I explained. "If it's too warm, it tends to soak up the dry ingredients. Using tiny cubes of cold butter and mushing it all together with your fingers or a pastry blender will leave small blobs of butter in the flour mixture. As the butter melts when it bakes, it will leave behind little air pockets. Those air pockets are what make your pastries flaky. Work fast when using the mushing method. You don't want the heat of your hands to melt the butter."

Once everyone had done that much, we added either heavy cream, lavender buds, and lemon zest or heavy cream, lime zest, and ginger.

"If you prefer lemon to lime with the ginger, that will work too. It's easy to make your own crystalized ginger, but it's a long process. That's why we're using premade today. And if you're doing the lemon-lavender"—I paused to get their attention —"don't be tempted to add more lavender than the recipe calls for. Your scones will end up tasting like soap."

Once the butter was properly mushed and they'd added the wet ingredients, they formed the dough into a large disc, cut it into eight wedges with a pastry cutter, and placed the wedges on a sheet.

"Bake at 425° until golden brown. Eighteen to twenty-two minutes."

I surveyed the condition of my table. Covered with flour, splashes of cream, bits of ginger and lavender, and blobs of dough. Dirty dishes were corralled nicely at some stations, spread out all over at others. Our newly dating couple got through the instructions fine, but once their scones were in the oven, he dabbed flour on the tip of her nose.

"No food fights," I warned as I passed by them.

"Yes, ma'am," he said, eyes on his date.

The rest of the group either blushed or sniggered when the couple announced they had something they needed to take care of rather than make the second batch. Two others left as well, taking their scones with them, and those who stayed opted to make whichever version they hadn't made the first time.

"Do you get a lot like them?" Jozef asked, zesting a lemon like the pro he was for the lemon-lavender version.

"Of lovebirds? Not a lot, but there are plenty who look at it as something to do and aren't really interested in learning. As long as they pay the fee, don't break anything, or ruin the experience for the others, I let it go."

"How many stay for the second lesson?"

"About two-thirds. Even if they don't take the ingredients for the second round, everyone takes a copy of the recipe home, and some even email me with questions. Overall, it's been a very good experience."

As with every class, I hovered in the background during the second run-through. Since scones only took twenty minutes on average to bake, and the dough didn't travel well, I let them all bake their second batches here. Half of the students helped clean up the table while they waited. The other half browsed in the retail room. One man, who clearly thought this was meant to be a place to pick up a date, asked me question after question about scones, stepping a little closer with each one. That was fine, but when he laid his hand on mine, he'd gone too far.

Jozef arrived at my side at that point and put an arm around my shoulders. "We're still on for later, aren't we?"

It took me a moment to realize he was rescuing me. "Of course we are. I've been looking forward to it."

The other man glared at Jozef but took the hint.

"I didn't mean to come across as a chauvinist," Jozef promised after the man walked away.

"Not at all. I've been rescuing myself for more than twenty years, but I'll take help when it's offered. Thank you."

By that time, the second batches of scones were done. The students waited a few more minutes for them to cool enough to handle, bagged them up, thanked me for the lesson, and left. When I wandered into the dining room to wipe the tables and straighten the chairs, I noticed Jozef sitting out back on the patio with a scone in hand and cup of coffee on the table in front of him.

"Enjoying your creation?"

His blue eyes twinkled when he looked up and saw it was me. "I am. You're a very good teacher."

I laughed. "You barely listened to my instructions. If that pastry is worth eating, it's because you already knew what you were doing."

He held out a hand to the chair across from him. "Have a seat and take a taste. You tell me if I got it right." He set one of his scones on a napkin for me.

Before I'd fully settled into the chair, the patio door opened, and Bee strode out with my teacup in hand. "Afternoon scones go better with tea."

"I . . . um . . . will you be okay in there alone?"

From behind Jozef where he couldn't see her, she shook her head like I was clueless. "I'll be fine for a few minutes."

"You'll come get me if you need anything."

She held both hands in the air as though she were attending a revival. "May lightning strike me if I don't. Take a little break, Reeva."

Jozef grinned. "Good to have people watching out for your best interest, isn't it?"

"Does that mean you're in my best interest?" The words slipped out before I knew I was going to say them. Was I flirting with the Viking? I mean, I knew exactly four things about him. His name, that he came here from Denmark, that he used to be a restaurant cook, and he was incredibly good looking. I took a bite of the scone before I could embarrass myself further. "Oh my Goddess. It literally melted in my mouth, Jozef. And the flavor is so intense."

Five things. The man could bake.

He inclined his head in a bow of thanks. "I'm glad you like it. And I was serious before. I haven't enjoyed being in a kitchen this much in years." One corner of his mouth turned up. "The baking was fun too."

I met his eyes over my teacup. Nothing wrong with a little flirtation, I guess. Nothing would come from it anyway. He was only visiting here and would be leaving before long.

I looked down to break off another piece of scone and noticed the same mark he'd put on his hand pies. "What does this symbol mean? It's a rune, right?"

"It is. It's a *raidho*. It stands primarily for a journey but also being in control, decision-making, getting to the truth, seeing past illusions . . . Among other things." He paused before quietly adding, "Those concepts feel appropriate for my life right now."

Mine too. Like attracts like, as the saying goes. "Tell me about yourself. Do you have a family?"

"I have a sister, Stine. She has two kids. Keersten is ten, and Christoffer is six. She decided to marry their father, Dierks, two years ago. As for me, I am not married, and there is no person of significance in my life."

Thank the Goddess or this fun little flirtation, or whatever it was, would be over right now. I almost said I was a widow, but he didn't need to know that. Especially since I'd barely considered myself married for the last twenty years. "There's no one of significance in my life either. Where in Denmark do you live?"

"Up until three weeks ago, I lived in Copenhagen."

I sat back. "What happened three weeks ago?"

"I quit my job, sold most of my possessions, and left the country."

Not what I expected to hear. "Why? I've heard such amazing things about Denmark."

"That it's beautiful. Yes, it is. That its people are the happiest in the world. That's what they say."

"You don't agree with that?"

He leaned forward and rested his elbows on the table. "Here's the thing, not every Dane is happy. There's a lot of pressure behind that designation, so some of us fake it. Do I have good friends? Yes, I have a small circle that I hope to remain close with. Something is missing from my life, though. I've felt that way for a couple of years now."

"About the time your sister got married?" I guessed.

He pondered this. "That may be."

"You're saying you feel like you don't fit in with your country of happy people," I mused and gave him an empathetic smile.

"That is true."

"No wonder you ended up in Whispering Pines. How did you find out about the village?"

"I bought a ticket to New York City and stayed there for a week doing all the things tourists do. Then I went to the Amtrak station and bought a ticket heading west. When the train arrived in Milwaukee, I got off. For the next week, I ate dozens of bratwursts, drank much beer, and attended many Brewers baseball games. By that time, I was ready to go again so rented a car and headed to Chicago. I planned to spend a week there as well, but after a few days, I decided I was tired of densely populated areas. I got back in my car, headed north, and I guess you could say the road brought me here."

When people happened to show up here this way, it was almost always because the village had summoned them. Why had it summoned Jozef? "How long will you stay?"

"Only a few more days. Through contacts back in Denmark, I have two job interviews next week. One in Des Moines, Iowa, and the other in Topeka, Kansas."

My breath caught. He was planning to move to the US. Definitely closer than Copenhagen. Except, "If you're looking for smaller populations, you may not like either of those options."

"I know." He shrugged and took on more of a Zen attitude. "One thing leads to another, so I trust that whatever it is that's missing in my life will present itself."

He stared at me as he drank some of his coffee. The corners of his eyes crinkled when he smiled.

"Are these restaurant jobs?"

"Yes, both are looking for a pastry chef."

"If the rest of your recipes are as good as your scones, you're sure to get one if not both of them."

"Especially now that I've rediscovered my joy."

Maybe that was the reason the village brought him here.

Not everyone needed to experience an epiphany to consider a visit here a good one. Maybe Jozef was simply meant to come, cook in my kitchen, and rediscover the joy of being a pastry chef.

Keiko appeared from around the side of the shop and waved at me. How had she gotten past the hedge?

"What are you doing here?" I asked.

She tapped her wrist where a watch would be. "It's three forty-five. I'm done at Shoppe Mystique and am ready to report for duty here."

"Almost four?" I exclaimed. How long had we been sitting here?

"I should let you get back to work," Jozef commented. "Will there be another class tomorrow?"

"Not tomorrow. I do three a week. Wednesday, Friday afternoon, and Saturday morning. Yesterday's class was an unusual one. More of a test, really, to see how a men's only class would work. It was well attended, so I'll do more. Women's only too. Maybe after hours so villagers can attend. We're fairly laid back around here, but leaving work in the middle of the day to attend a cooking class too often won't go over well with the business owners."

A comfortable silence settled between us for a moment. Then Jozef said, "We talked mostly about me. I'd love to get to know more about you. Do you have plans for dinner?"

Over his shoulder, I saw Ruby appear in the dining room doorway with Bee at her side. Both of them shining full-watt grins at me.

I promised Ruby we'd talk to Luna. "There is something I need to do tonight. But I could cancel—"

"No, don't cancel your plans for me."

I stared straight at him and couldn't think of any reason that would be better. "I haven't had much going on in my life lately worth canceling plans for."

He lowered his gaze to his coffee cup and blushed. "Perhaps tomorrow? I have to leave on Friday morning."

"What a shame. You'll miss the class." I pointed at the firepit at the center of the patio that I'd had designed specifically for cooking lessons. "We'll be grilling stuffed burgers out here."

"I'll see what I can do, but I have to check out of my cabin Friday morning and be in Topeka by Sunday night for a Monday morning interview."

You could stay in my guest room almost popped out of my mouth. Honestly, this man could weave a spell.

"Stop by tomorrow," I said instead. "We'll make plans."

I stood to go back inside, but he took my hand in his as I tried to pass by. He placed a kiss on the back. "I'll look forward to seeing you again."

"I, uh . . ." He had me completely tongue-tied. I laughed. "Me too."

When I was a few feet from the dining room door, Ruby shoved it open, grabbed me by the apron, and dragged me inside. "What was that?"

"I'm not sure. He wanted to take me to dinner tonight, but—"

"But what?" she demanded.

My eyes darted to Bee and back. "We've got that thing we need to do tonight."

"We can reschedule."

"No, it's okay," I insisted. "He'll stop by tomorrow, and we'll figure something out. That'll give me time to regain control of my faculties."

"Sweetie," Bee purred, "look at that man. Go ahead and lose control."

Then she growled.

I laughed at her. "I'll go, but it's just dinner with a new friend. He's leaving on Friday anyway."

"And if you play it right," Bee advised, "he'll come back."

CHAPTER
SEVENTEEN

"You're thinking about him, aren't you?" Ruby accused later.

"I am not." I *had* been, it was hard to not think about the intriguing Viking, but it was only for a minute, and my mind was back on work now.

"Who?" Keiko asked as she put the mop and bucket back into the cleaning supplies closet, finished with her tasks for the day. "That guy I saw you sitting with on the patio? Who is he?"

"Jozef Lykke," Ruby teased in a singsong voice. She'd closed up the hobby shop in record time tonight. Whether because she was excited to get over to the rental office and talk to Luna or rib me about Jozef, I wasn't sure. "He asked Reeva out today."

"On a date?" Keiko asked, perplexed. "Really?"

I stared at her. "I heard what you just thought."

"I didn't . . . What do you think I thought?"

"That old people don't date."

"Wow," she replied. "You're good. A mind-reading hearth witch."

"Old people do date," I insisted. "Not that I'm old. And not that it would be a date. Just dinner. And I'm not even positive we'll do that, so I don't want to talk about it."

"She seems a little flustered, don't you think?" Ruby asked Keiko.

"Flustered. Hot and bothered. Or maybe hot and flashy?"

I pointed at Keiko and squinted. "I can take you off my schedule as easily as I put you on it."

She held her hands up in surrender, but her smirk didn't budge.

"If you two must know, I was thinking again about who stole those pans."

"What pans?" Keiko asked. "You two never tell me anything."

As I gave her the shortened version of events, I tried to recall all that had happened here on Monday. I'd told Ruby about my life reset, Tripp picked up the aprons for Jayne, and I performed the blessing ritual on the bowl and the wooden spoons.

"It was late morning right after the blessing," I concluded. "That's when Bee told me they were missing."

Ruby's head bobbed up and down in agreement. "You think someone took them while you were doing the blessing."

"I go into a sort of light trance when I do them. I notice people close to me but don't always see people who are further away, so it's possible."

"Bee was here then, right?" Keiko asked. "Wasn't she keeping an eye on people?"

I shook my head. "During a blessing, she stays by the front door. As people come in, she lets them know they're welcome to wander around or stop and observe the ritual but that they shouldn't interrupt."

"Doesn't Bee remember who she let in?" Ruby had started to pace. A sure sign she wanted to get over to the rental cottages now.

"Unless they came in the back door," Keiko suggested.

I took the white candle from the shelf in the kitchen to do

the closing blessing. "The only way to get to the patio is through the store."

Or that path through the woods and slip between the hedge and shack like Ruby did. Then I recalled Keiko appearing from the side of the shop while I talked with Jozef.

"How did you get back there earlier?" I asked.

She pointed absently. "There's a gap between the hedge and the building."

"You trampled my landscaping? Why wouldn't you just come through the front door?"

She shrugged. "I only stepped on the woodchips. I have time after I'm done at Shoppe Mystique before I start here. I sit on your patio sometimes and read or journal or whatever. It's much more peaceful there than by the Pentacle Garden."

"Why haven't I noticed this gap? How big is it?"

"Not very," Keiko assured. "I'm almost too big so can't imagine many adults would try it. I only know about it because I was sitting back there a few days ago and this little kid squirted right through and went in through the back door. She didn't see me and looked like she was trying to be stealthy or whatever."

"Trying not to get caught," I murmured. "What day was this, Keiko?"

She chewed her lip and then her face brightened. "Guess it would have been Monday. I didn't want to hang out at the campground. Too many people packing up to leave. They tend to get crabby and yell at each other during pack up. I came over here until it was time to go to Shoppe Mystique."

"Right around the time of the theft. Do you remember what this girl looked like?"

"Young," Keiko recalled. "Not little but not a teenager. Long dark hair. She wore blue shorts and a pink T-shirt with butterflies and maybe flowers on it. I noticed the shirt because it looked like something I might wear on a day I'm feeling sweet."

"That describes almost any pre-teen girl."

She held her hands up in a shrug. "Sorry."

"You at least narrowed the list to a girl with dark hair," Ruby praised. "Reeva, if we're going to talk to Luna, we need to get going."

"Right. Keiko, please don't enter that way again. You're welcome to sit on my patio anytime, but you'll damage my hedge and flowers going that way."

She hung her head. "Yes, ma'am."

"Okay, I need to do the closing blessing and then we can leave."

Ruby shot me a frustrated look. "Can't that wait until morning?"

"Not a chance. With all that's been happening around this shop lately, I won't let it sit all night with that kind of energy swirling around."

Ruby blew out a hard breath.

"You're not helping with all that pacing and sighing," I scolded. "Head over to the cottages and track down Luna. I'll be right behind you."

"Fine," Ruby agreed, "but don't dally. You're the high priestess, and this happened at your home. It will be better if the questions come from you."

"I said find her, not question her," I called as she walked away.

She swatted a hand behind her, indicating she heard me.

"Dally?" Keiko asked once Ruby left. "Is that even a word?"

"To dally or dillydally. It means to waste time."

"Look at that, I learned something new today."

"Would you check that the back door is locked, please?"

After she'd done that, Keiko stood by the front door while I stood in the center of each room with my candle and murmured my protection blessing. When I returned to the kitchen, I closed the blessing by asking, "In the name of the five elements and under the light of the sun, moon, and stars, I ask that my shop be protected this eve and kept safe until I return on the morrow." I extinguished the flame by dipping the wick into the melted wax using a poultry pin. This kept my good intentions locked inside the wick until I lit it again. I set the candle on the table where it would wait for tomorrow's opening ritual. "That's it. We can go."

I gathered my bag and Keiko stood on the Fairy Path while I locked the front door.

"I wanted to ask you," she started, "what would happen if I didn't focus on those words or if the circle was broken during a ritual?"

So many questions. So eager to learn. "I need to get over to talk to Luna, so we can discuss this in depth later, but the purpose of the words is to enhance a blessing and help set your intention. A broken circle, however, could cause problems."

"Like what?"

"Breaking a circle will either let good energy out or bad in. It really depends on what caused the break and if there was intention behind the action."

"So if—"

"Tomorrow, Keiko. I don't mean to seem dismissive but—"

"You need to go. I understand. See you later."

She turned and shoved her hands into the pockets of her sweatshirt. Something about her retreating figure tugged at my heart.

"Mom, I had the best time last night."

"That's great, honey. I can't wait to hear about it."

"There was this guy—"

"Oh, sweetie, I need to go look at a new storage facility. My collection of home goods has gotten too big for my current spot. Tell me about it later? I won't be gone long."

"Yeah, sure."

Why didn't I ask her to come with me? It had been a

Saturday morning, she had no plans, and touring the location ended up taking a lot longer than I thought. She'd told me all about the boy later, but her giddiness at sharing it with me had tarnished.

Did Keiko feel rejected now like Yasmine had then? I hoped she knew that wasn't my intent. Between Willow not teaching her much and me putting her off, she probably felt disregarded. Had she at least made friends at the campground, or was it a steady stream of new strangers? She insisted she liked it there, but I felt a little bad about her living situation.

I was about to call out to her when a shiver, like a jolt of ice, passed through me. Must be Ruby thinking *hurry up* thoughts at me.

"Yes, dear." With eyes still on Keiko, I thought, *I promise to answer all your questions.*

I turned to get my bike and remembered its flat tire. Ruby had dropped me off this morning. Hopefully she was already at the rental office because I'd have to walk and there was no way I'd make it over there before it closed.

EIGHTEEN

I found Ruby waiting for me in her car in the Unity parking lot.

"We didn't ride our bikes today," she reminded me unnecessarily.

"Thanks for waiting. We'd better hurry."

It was a couple minutes past seven thirty when we got to the rental office. Luna had just locked the door and turned to leave when we got out of Ruby's car.

"Hey, Luna," Ruby greeted cheerfully. "Can we talk to you for a minute?"

The girl scowled. Maybe she had plans. There was a lot going on in the commons, after all. "What do you want, Reeva?"

Or she was irritated because it was me standing before her.

"If this is a bad time," I began, "it can wait."

Ruby gently added, "This won't take long. Just a few minutes."

Luna was a pretty seventeen-year-old with long wavy hair and a perpetual pout. She was so thin I thought *spaghetti noodle* every time I saw her. Verne started spoiling his daughter the day

HEARTH & CAULDRON • 165

he brought her to Whispering Pines. Or so I'd been told since I wasn't here then. I did know that Luna's parents divorced when she was a baby and that it had been a nasty split. Verne got full custody and moved here to live with his father. The pair doted on the child. Shockwaves shot through the village a few months ago when Luna agreed to share shifts at the rental office with April O'Connor.

"Luna's working?"

"At an actual job?"

"She must be bewitched."

Luna dropped onto a nearby bench, arms and legs crossed, right foot kicking with irritation. "Fine, can we move it along, though? I've got a video to make tonight."

"A video?" I asked.

An amused smile turned her pretty face. "I catch short videos of people here doing stupid things and make montages out of them."

"Videos of our tourists?" I clarified.

"I know what I'm doing," she insisted. "I blur their faces to protect their identities."

I blinked at her.

She sighed. "What? You're going to tell me I should be worried about my karma?"

"If you're thinking it . . ."

"Maybe you should be less concerned about me and more about yourself," she challenged.

My heart rate kicked up a few beats. "What's that supposed to mean?"

"No one wants you to be high priestess."

Ruby's face turned as red as her name. "That is a flat-out lie, Luna Witkowski. I personally know that most of the coven loves Reeva." She crossed her arms, mimicking the girl. "In fact, there's only a handful I know of who are unhappy."

She ticked off on her fingers, "Me, my dad, Lorena, Aster, April, Rourke . . ."

Rourke O'Connor? I believed her about the others, but Rourke had never given any hint that he didn't approve of Morgan's choice. He was even one of the first to congratulate me the night she named me.

"Should I go on?" Luna asked.

"Can you?" Ruby confronted, matching her tone. "I don't think you can."

This was met by silence. Whether that meant Ruby was right or Luna was being her sassy self, I wasn't sure.

"Reeva?" Ruby nudged.

I lifted my chin, composing myself. "Tell me, are you and your father upset enough about me being high priestess that you're willing to do something to remove me from that position?"

Her pout relaxed a smidge. "What do you mean?"

No need to drag this out. "I mean, you and your father handed out Laurel's scones at the gathering the other night. Right?"

"Yeah. So?"

"Your father handed me a chocolate one. Gardenia took a cinnamon chip for Iris. A little while later, I traded with Iris because she said she preferred chocolate. She died later that night. After eating that scone."

As I spoke, I watched her every move. She didn't flinch, didn't even blink when I mentioned swapping scones.

"I don't get it." Luna became less confrontational. "What does that have to do with me or my dad?"

"We think," Ruby cut in, "that the scone Verne gave Reeva was poisoned."

"What? Who would do that?" Luna seemed sincere. Then she understood what I was getting at. "Wait. Are you accusing my dad of trying to poison you with that scone?"

Ruby asked, "Who else was in Reeva's kitchen with you and your dad when you were getting the trays?"

"You don't think *I* had anything to do with this." She uncrossed her legs and slid forward on the bench. "Okay. Me, Daddy, Lorena, and Laurel. Why aren't you talking to Laurel? She made those things."

I stepped closer to her. "We did. She didn't do it."

"And you think Daddy or I did?" She shook her head, long waves falling in front of her eyes. "He and I were in your backyard talking about doing a full moon ritual when Laurel came over and asked if we wanted to help hand out scones. I was starving because I'd been working here all afternoon and didn't have time to eat. I said I'd help and inhaled two or three of them before handing out the rest. Since I volunteered, Daddy said he would help too." She rolled her eyes. "Some weird daddy-daughter bonding thing. He's going totally overboard with this stuff because I'll be a senior in the fall, and this is my last year here."

"You're leaving Whispering Pines?" Ruby asked.

"I'd go today if I could. I'm done with this place."

I smiled. "That's how I felt at eighteen. Where are you going?"

"I have no idea what I want to do with my life, so I'm going to do a gap year or two and wander around Europe. Daddy said he'd buy me two one-way plane tickets, but I have to cover all my other expenses. That's why I'm working here." She glared at the rental cottage office like it was its fault she needed money.

"Who's going with you?" Ruby's concerned mother side had risen to the surface.

Luna pushed back her shoulders, shook out her hair, and proudly announced, "I'm going alone."

"Alone?" Ruby demanded, clearly ready to go tear into Verne.

"I've been taking *kyusho-jitsu* lessons from Emery. Daddy

insisted if I'm going to do this, I have to be able to defend myself. I've gotten really good at it. Made Jagger cry uncle." A wicked smile took over her face. "Want a demonstration?"

"No, I'll take your word for it." My respect level for Verne increased a notch. And as a single parent, I may have spoiled Yasmine a time or two as well. It was hard being everything for your child.

Luna turned serious. "Look, I'm really sorry about what happened to Iris, but I swear, I didn't do it, and neither did Daddy. Like I said, Lorena was in your kitchen too." She paused, remembering something. "Lorena was alone in there when Laurel came and asked us to help. She loaded the trays. Maybe you should talk to her."

I thanked her for her time, and Luna shot out of there before either of us could say another word.

"Do you believe her?" Ruby asked as we returned to her car.

"About some of it, yes."

"But?"

"You know how close she and Verne are. Of course she'll say he didn't do it."

"And she's probably only repeating what he says regarding you being high priestess. She can be a sweet girl when she wants to be, but I swear that girl isn't capable of making decisions for herself."

"I don't know." I thought of Yasmine and how excited she was to get out and live life. "A solo gap year in Europe? Is that her idea or his? I say hers."

"Good point. She did say a gap *year or two*. Verne would insist on a timeline. You know how precise he is."

"That's because he's a drafting engineer." I chuckled. "Have you heard about his new logo?"

Ruby rolled her eyes. "*Everyone* has heard about it. A *V* for Verne with a line across the top."

"Rourke told me it's supposed to be a scale. Verne puts the client's wishes on one side and his plans for making it happen on the other. They add and subtract from both sides, and when the scale stays balanced on its point, the design is perfect. Or something like that."

I grew quiet then and Ruby asked, "You're thinking about what Luna said about Rourke, aren't you?"

"I won't lie, her comment upset me."

Rourke was one of the first new-to-me villagers to welcome me back to Whispering Pines last May. We'd talked dozens of times since Morgan named me high priestess, and I'd never suspected a problem.

"Rourke is fine with Morgan's decision," Ruby promised. "Luna doesn't know what she's talking about. He was probably in the area one time when her father was talking about you, and she assumed he's part of Verne's posse."

She was probably right. "If he was upset, he would have showed it somehow. I'm not naïve. I know there are plenty who aren't happy. I can accept that. There are always two sides no matter the situation. Guess I'm just feeling a little tender right now."

"I know you are." She pulled me in for a hug. "Let's go talk to Lorena and see if we can get closer to the truth."

We got to Sundry just as Lorena Maxwell was heading to her car.

"Are you leaving?" Ruby called out.

"I am." Lorena was pulling her blond bob out of its bun as we pulled up next to her. She ruffled her fingers through her bangs, her gaze lingering on me for a beat too long. "Just got off shift. I need to get home to Cordelia."

Her daughter was four, and her mother, Brigitte, watched her while Lorena worked as the assistant manager at Sundry. Similar to Briar and Morgan, Lorena and her mother never married their babies' fathers. Lorena and Brigitte were also practicing green witches. Brigitte tended their impressive garden while Lorena tended the produce section at Sundry. The Maxwells had lived together here just the two of them, now three, for over twenty years. The comparison to the Barlows was undeniable, although the Maxwells were a very distant second in that race. If anyone was jealous of me rising so quickly in the coven ranks, it was Lorena. It was a title she had wanted as badly as Flavia had. I could easily picture her and Lorena drawing pistols, or maybe athames, at high noon for the chance to take the position from Morgan.

"Can you spare a couple of minutes?" Ruby asked, stepping in as good cop to hopefully keep the tension at bay. "We have a few questions we wanted to ask you."

Lorena looked at me as she answered, "Sure, I guess. What's this about?"

"Monday night," I said as simply and lightly as I could.

"The blessing?"

"After that," Ruby clarified. "We were just talking with Luna about the scones Laurel brought."

"Nice thing for her to do," Lorena stated.

"You helped hand them out, right?" I asked. "Luna mentioned that you put them on the trays."

She let out a frustrated sigh. "Sounds like you're building up to an accusation of some kind. How about you move this along so I can get home to my kid. Some of us have those kinds of responsibilities, you know."

Ruby gasped. "Lorena. What a horrible thing to say."

Externally, I didn't flinch. Internally, I fumed over her using my daughter to try and hurt me. People could come after me all they wanted, but they needed to leave Yasmine out of the discussion.

Lorena inspected her fingernails. "No worse than her accusing me of something I didn't do."

"I haven't accused you of anything." It took all my willpower to keep my temper in check. "Are you feeling guilty about something?"

"One of you better say what's on your minds or I'm leaving." She reached for the handle of her car.

Fine. No dillydallying as Ruby might say. "Iris died after eating a scone meant for me. Luna tells us you were alone in the kitchen and—"

"Whoa." Lorena held her hands out in stop position. "And you think what? That I did something to the scones?"

"Just one of them," Ruby replied. "No one else got sick."

"Two actually," I clarified, my voice even and calm. "One of each flavor because you weren't sure which I would want."

Lorena's deep-brown eyes turned almost black. "Why would I do that? What possible reason could I have for wanting any harm to come to you, Reeva?"

"Because you can't get over the fact that she's high priestess and you're not."

The statement appeared to bounce right off Lorena. "Even the great and powerful Morgan Barlow screws up sometimes."

"All right." I appreciated Ruby trying to be the tough cop again, but things were getting unnecessarily nasty. I stepped between them and refused to lower myself to Lorena's tactics. "Dr. Bundy, the medical examiner, is running tests on Iris's blood. If a poison shows up, knowing that you were alone with the scones will put you at the top of the sheriff's suspect list."

"Is he letting you do his job now?" Lorena asked. "Is the little sheriff in over his head?"

"You've got means, motive, and opportunity," Ruby stated, ignoring the jabs at Martin.

"Means?" Lorena laughed. "How would I get poison?"

I pointed at Sundry. "Last I checked, you've got plenty in the housekeeping department. Take a bit of rat poison home and—"

"Okay, I've heard enough," Lorena fumed. "I was in your

kitchen for about thirty seconds before Laurel and the others walked in. Ask Laurel. And you must have heard your freaking bird."

"Sanny?" I remembered her letting out a squawk right after Morgan left. Which was shortly before Verne and Luna started handing out scones.

"That thing started screeching the moment I stepped foot in your cottage." Lorena winced as though hearing the little owl's call again. "Nearly punctured my eardrums. People were in and out all night, and it didn't make a peep. Laurel came in right behind me, and it was silent. Why me?"

"Animals are very sensitive to things that aren't as they should be," I explained, already planning to give Sanny an extra treat tonight. "There isn't a security system made that would work better than my owl."

"You got anything else you want to accuse me of?" Lorena opened her car door and didn't wait for a response. "Didn't think so. Have a nice night, Ruby."

She tore out of the parking lot, spraying gravel at us.

I stepped to the side, avoiding a pebble heading for my shin. "That was fun."

"Think she'll calm down before the next coven gathering?" Ruby asked.

"No clue. I never raised my voice, never said anything remotely nasty to her." I smiled at my friend. "That was all you, bad cop."

She buffed her nails on her shirt and then dropped her hands to her sides. "You know what this means, don't you?"

"That we're out of suspects?"

"Yep. Should we brainstorm, or are you done for the night?"

"We *should* talk to Verne. Martin wouldn't dismiss a suspect simply because someone else said he was innocent." Except I could pretty much predict how a conversation with Verne would go, and I wasn't up for that tonight. "I have a spare tire in the garage, but let's run inside Sundry and grab a tire repair kit while I'm thinking about it. We can change my tire and then have tea while we brainstorm."

"Okay, but maybe something with a little more kick tonight."

CHAPTER
NINETEEN

By the time we'd gotten home and swapped bike tires, it was too late to make anything for dinner. I wasn't that hungry anyway. After eating the ginger-lime scone Jozef gave me on the patio, I grabbed one of his lemon-lavenders from inside the shop. The way he branded them, the way potters put their mark on the bottom of their creations, made his easy to spot. It was just as flaky, buttery, and perfect. So instead of a meal, I arranged cheese and crackers, grapes, red bell pepper strips, and two small bowls of black olives and almonds on a plate while Ruby opened and poured glasses of Cabernet. I had no sooner lowered myself onto my chair in the sunroom when Dot reminded me that her dishes needed filling.

"You couldn't have said something when we were in the kitchen?" I asked.

She replied by turning her backside to me and raising her tail high in the air. I didn't want to know what that meant in cat speak.

"I love dinners like this." Ruby leaned back with her wine in one hand and a small cluster of grapes in the other. "It's not even close to fancy but makes me feel like . . ."

"Like we're breaking a rule?"

"Yes, that's it."

"How much easier would life be if we didn't worry about all the should-dos or the time on the clock?"

"That's how we get to live in the off-season. Yet another reason Whispering Pines is perfect."

"It's close, but I'm not sure I'd call it perfect. Even here, we have our fair share of troubles." I took a cracker and slice of cheese and, before popping the whole combo in my mouth, asked, "Speaking of troubles, do you suppose one of our suspects is actually the guilty party?"

"Let's analyze what we've learned." She got her notepad from her bag and grabbed a few almonds.

I had to laugh. She jotted down notes every time we discussed *The Case of the Poisoned Pastry* as she'd taken to calling it. She was really taking this private investigator role seriously.

"Who should we review first?" She flipped open her pad. "Luna, Lorena, or Laurel?"

"I still say no to Laurel. Yes, she made the scones and had the opportunity to put something in them, but I will hand over the high priestess position to Lorena if Laurel is guilty. I've known her for too long. We were never *best* friends, but we were good friends, and as far as I know, she's never done anything mean to anyone."

Ruby made a slash with her pen. "Not Laurel."

"As for Lorena," I continued, "her reaction was so over the top, it almost made me wonder if she's covering something up."

"I thought so too, but maybe she had a bad day at work or something. I mean, she came out swinging before we'd even said two words."

"It's because it was me standing there." At nearly sixty years old, I didn't worry much about what other people thought, but it still hurt my feelings when someone didn't like me. "Lorena's not a fan of mine, obviously, but it's only because Morgan named me high priestess. We barely know each other. I returned to Whispering Pines in June and needed a few months to myself, to mourn and figure out what was next for me, so didn't attend a coven gathering until October. That's when I met everyone and told them a bit about my history with the village. Everything was fine, Lorena was even friendly. Then in April, Morgan told the coven her plan for stepping down."

"I remember that. Lorena stormed out, insisting she was going to form her own coven."

"Which she was free to do, but Morgan had a talk with her. She explained that while I left the village, I never stopped my practice. Lorena insisted I wasn't qualified, even though I've been following Wicca for a good twenty years more than her. She backed down—"

"But she hasn't let it go," Ruby completed my thought. "To her, you're an outsider."

"Sometimes I *feel* like an outsider." That was on me, though. I left and returned more than once. It was understandable for some to be skeptical of my loyalty.

"Is Lorena on the list or off?"

"Do we think she's upset enough with me to kill me?"

Ruby made a sandwich with two crackers and a slice of cheese. "Not necessarily kill you, but like we said before, Iris's heart was weak. What ultimately might have killed her may only have made you a little sick."

A good point. "Do I think Lorena is upset enough with me to give me something to make me sick?" I munched a pepper strip while pondering that. "After her reaction tonight, I have to say that it's possible."

Ruby put a star next to Lorena's name. "Did we come to a decision on Luna?"

"I don't think she did anything. Her father has been vocal about me, not disguising his feelings even a little. She may simply be following his lead."

"Verne gets vocal about a lot of things. He didn't like that Jayne was sheriff simply because she's a woman. Although he insists he's not a chauvinist and that he was upset with her because the village was a perfectly peaceful place until she came along and ruined everything."

"*Jayne* ruined everything?" I barked out a laugh and then took a fortifying sip from my wine glass. "She didn't create our problems. They've been brewing beneath this village for decades."

"I put it all on Flavia."

"Karl gets a lot of the blame too. Especially over the last two decades. He wouldn't or couldn't stand up to Flavia, and she ran wild with the power. And then all those years of coverup collapsed when Yasmine came to town."

"Hang on. We need more wine." She scurried to the kitchen, returned ten seconds later, and added a bit to our glasses. As she settled into her chair, she said, "You know, we keep saying the problems started when Yasmine died, but really it was Lucy's death. That's what brought Jayne here."

"You're right. Jayne figured out what happened to Yasmine, but it was when she started digging deeper into her grandmother's death that all the secrets came to light. Then she found Lucy's journal." I shook my head as though trying to warn Jayne in the past of what she was about to do. "Opening the cover on that book was like releasing the valve on a pressure cooker."

"Everything came shooting out. Like a geyser straight up through the Negativity Well." She made explosion hands, then asked, "How did we start talking about that?"

"Verne and his dislike of Jayne. Or more accurately, his dislike of women in power." I took a few olives from the bowl, and one dropped to the floor. Dot immediately batted it to the other side of the sunroom, held it between her paws, and nibbled. The mini panther loved olives.

"Back on topic," Ruby announced. "Do we think Verne could be capable of this? He had the opportunity. You said he handed that scone directly to you."

I threw a hand in the air. "Why though? I moved back to the village, opened a business, and became high priestess. Would one of those things be reason enough for him to poison me?"

"It's less one of those things and more that you fall into the strong woman category. I think that stems from his divorce. I say he's at the top of the list but with a big question mark." She put a star and a question mark by his name on her list. "We need to talk to him."

"Not until the results of that blood test come in," I insisted. "If it's negative, we've been upsetting ourselves and our fellow villagers for nothing. Iris's time may have simply run out."

"But what about that note?"

The scone was meant for you, high priestess.

I shivered. We weren't wrong. Someone did something to that scone.

"We'll need to smudge each other," Ruby declared, "and take salt baths to clean off this bad juju."

"Juju?" I laughed, releasing a little tension. "No more wine for you."

"This is only my first." She held up her half-full glass as though it were evidence.

"It doesn't count as one if you keep topping it off."

"Says you. I'll eat more cheese and crackers."

I gave her a minute to put some food in her belly to soak up a bit of the alcohol, then asked, "Is there anyone we're forgetting?"

She paused, finished the mouthful of cheese, and said, "I think so, but you won't like it."

"Who?"

"Keiko."

"Keiko? You think she tried to kill me? Or make me sick. Why on earth would you suspect her?"

"Because things got weird after she started hanging around. She's bringing a bad vibe to the coven."

"That's like saying Jayne was responsible for the troubles in the village last year. Keiko hasn't even been here a month. Things were weird here well before that." I angrily plucked a grape from the bunch. "I was so sure making Flavia pay for her crimes would make a difference."

"It has for some."

"Yes, but now others are all up in arms for different reasons. And poor Iris got caught up in the crossfire. It's absurd."

"You underestimate people, Reeva. They'll always find something to be mad about." Ruby set down her glass and pulled her legs up beneath her on her chair, a handful of almonds cupped in her palm. "Speaking of which, you're getting worked up."

"I know. We need chocolate."

I went to the kitchen and grabbed my tin of dark chocolate from the pantry. Instead of returning to the sunroom right away, I stopped at the refrigerator. Way in the back in an opaque, amber-colored glass container with a tight-fitting lid was my stash of cookie dough. Everyone in this village seemed to have a secret. One of mine, that even Ruby didn't know about, was that I ate raw chocolate chip cookie dough when I got upset.

Hearth Witch Tip
Pre-portion your cookie dough into balls
for quick and easy stress relief.

But the raw eggs, people would warn. *You'll get salmonella.*

"Been eating cookie dough my entire life," I would reply, "and have never gotten sick from it."

"What?" Ruby called out from the sunroom.

"Talking to myself." I restocked the container with dough balls from the freezer, replaced the lid, and returned the container to the back of the fridge. In the sunroom, I held the chocolate tin out to her.

"Thanks." She took half a dozen pieces. "Can we have a discussion about Keiko without you blowing your top?"

I exhaled as I sat. "Sure."

"You get a little defensive when it comes to her. Is that maybe because she reminds you of Yasmine?"

I stiffened. "I'm not defensive about her. I have, however, spent more time with her than you have." I sat quietly for a minute, sorting through my swirling feelings. "Keiko doesn't remind me of Yasmine, but she does make me think about her a lot because they were together during Yasmine's final days."

"That's understandable. I'm sorry if I made you angry."

I nodded but let it go. "What exactly are you thinking regarding her and this scone situation?"

She leaned forward. "Okay, first, what do we *really* know about her? Be honest now. She wanted Morgan to teach her negative magic last summer. How do we know she didn't find someone else to teach her and now she's back to get revenge for the snub?"

My first reaction was to object, but I promised to have a discussion so kept the thought to myself. Also, I'd agreed to let this young woman work in my shop. I needed to be logical about her.

"I don't understand why she would come back here to take revenge over something like that, but I hear what you're saying."

"Next, during the blessing, Keiko was all over your property, inside and out. She could easily have done something to the scones."

My heart sank a little. "I'm not sure when Laurel brought them into the kitchen, so I guess that is possible."

"And afterward, she hung out here. Why? Why didn't she go back to the campground?"

"I think she gets lonely there," I offered, hearing the justification in my words. "People come to camp with their families and friends, and Keiko's all alone."

"That's fair, but why wouldn't she hang out at the commons then? There are tons of people her age there."

"Because she's here to learn more about Wicca. She's eager to learn—"

"A little too eager if you ask me," Ruby interrupted.

"Perhaps, but a year later, she's still interested. That tells me she's serious about this. She's been studying for a year—"

"Presumably."

"—and now has the opportunity to hang out with a coven of talented witches. If I was her, that's what I would opt for." I popped a piece of chocolate into my mouth. "What else are you thinking?"

"That note. That's a big one for me. She said it was taped to the door, but how do you know? How do you know she didn't bring it for someone or even write it herself? We talked about more than one person working together on this plot. I hate to say it, but that could mean Keiko."

Much as I wanted to, I couldn't make an excuse for that. "Before we left the shop today, she asked what would happen if a cast circle was broken during a ceremony or if someone didn't focus on the words of intent during a ritual. It seemed to be an innocent enough question since I'd just done a blessing. But I guess there could have been an ulterior motive behind it."

"I think we need to take a closer look at this girl," Ruby insisted.

"Why would she do this, though?"

"Because we wouldn't let her in last summer."

I shook my head. "That was a Morgan and Wicca thing. My firepit, flowerpots, and bike tire have nothing to do with Wicca or Morgan."

"True."

"And these things only seem to be happening to me. Have you heard of anyone else having trouble?"

"No, but we could ask Violet. If anyone has heard anything, it's her."

Just when I was really starting to like the girl. "I agree we should ask Keiko some questions, but I'm still not convinced it's her. She and I didn't even know each other until two weeks ago."

"But she knew you through Yasmine."

In other words, Keiko was avenging Yasmine's death? My entire body broke out in gooseflesh, but I refused to follow that path. Not without more evidence behind it. "I had nothing to do with Keiko not getting hired at Shoppe Mystique last summer. Why wouldn't she target Morgan? She's the one who told her to learn more about Wicca first."

Ruby shook her head and lifted her shoulders. "A very good question that I can't answer."

CHAPTER
TWENTY

When it came to the consumption of alcohol, there were lightweights and then there was Ruby McLaughlin. One glass, plus a top off or two, and she was feeling no pain. She likely would be in the morning, however. After debating how to get her home—she insisted on sleeping in her own bed rather than staying in my guest room—I secured my bike to the carrier on the back of her car. I'd ride back.

Ruby's tiny Tudor-style cottage with multiple roof peaks and half-timber trim was adorable. The two-story peaked ceiling above the main floor covered the small living room and kitchen. At the back were her bedroom and bathroom. Her craft room, intended to be the master bedroom, sat behind the smaller bedroom she slept in. It also had a cathedral ceiling, nearly doubled the size of the home, and would make any crafter drool with envy.

Her single-stall garage was nestled among the trees behind the cottage. After putting her car away, I helped her inside and tucked her into bed. "Are you going to be okay? Do you need anything?"

She replied with a rattly snore.

I made a mental note to call her in the morning to make sure she got up in time to open Twisty.

It was a fairly straight shot along the dirt road from Ruby's cottage to mine. The moonbeams through the pines and the headlamp on my handlebars provided just enough light for me to see. It had been ages since I'd wandered through the Whispering Pines woods in the quiet darkness. All I heard was the sound of my tires on the gravel, the water in the creek flowing to Lucy Lake, and the occasional scurrying of a nocturnal creature. I'd forgotten how thrilling a night ride could be so took my time returning home.

"Time for bed, Sanny," I announced when I finally got there and found it was after eleven.

By that I meant me, not her. She flew over from where she had perched on top of a doorframe and landed on my outstretched hand. The first night she left the cottage, I was positive she wouldn't be back. It wasn't a matter of her safety since the forest was her domain. Rather, I'd quickly become attached to the bird. Her near window-shattering screech the next morning, announcing she wanted back in, assured me I had been fully adopted.

Now, I completed our bedtime ritual by stroking the top of her head from front to back. Her big round eyes fluttered shut as though she had achieved Nirvana.

"Goodnight, silly bird." I opened the door, and she darted off into the pines.

Upstairs, I took a quick shower, brushed my teeth, and moisturized my face. Then I stood in the doorway of my bedroom and stared across at the reading room. Ruby had nailed it this morning. Since moving in, I had smudged every room in this cottage, some multiple times, but never that one. It had been Karl's and my favorite spot in the house. The one where we ended every day with conversation or reading and a glass of wine or cup of tea. If reading, we'd get lost in our respective books and then discuss what we'd read until it was time for lights out. That was the thing I had loved most about Karl. We could talk for hours on any topic. Then came the night that he comforted my sister.

He insisted it had only been the one time, but a person can tell when their partner has become involved with someone else. I don't believe they ever slept together again or that there was any sort of romantic feelings, but she had total control over my husband. No matter what she asked, no matter if it was the middle of the night or the crack of dawn and despite my objections, he went to do her bidding. I held second place in his life. Third, really. First was her. His job was second. I slid into third and had zero hope of ever rising in the ranks.

I'd decided during my jaunt through the woods that tonight was the night. I crossed the room, then stopped at the threshold of the reading room and peered inside. Karl's memory was heavy in there. I could practically see him sitting in his chair, book in hand, glass of something on the table next to him.

"It's your fault," I told his memory. "You did this to us. You could have come to Port Washington, too, and raised Yasmine with me. I would have forgiven you eventually, but you rubbed salt in my wounds and chose *her* and here instead of me and that sweet baby."

When I returned to the village a year ago, I'd only planned to clean out the cottage and return to the life I loved five and a half hours away. So I ignored the reading room and the memories inside it. What did I care if he spent eternity haunting this house? The room didn't have a door, so I put a large palm tree in the opening. Despite my diligent care, the plant died within two weeks. It had been a clear message.

"Whispering Pines called me back again," I told Karl and whatever else was lingering in that room, "and this time it isn't letting me go. It's taken five decades, but it's finally time for me to have the life here I was meant to have instead of the one forced on me by you and Flavia. I believe I'm meant to stay, which means you have to go."

I turned to my right, toward the dresser that I once thought of moving to the spot where the palm tree briefly stood. There, waiting for me since Samhain Eve seven months ago was a silver tray with a small bowl of salt, a lighter, a white votive candle, and a smudge stick made of white sage, sweetgrass, lavender, and cedar.

"It seems the coven's blessing didn't quite do the job. I'd hoped they would chase you out, but I guess there are some things a person has to do on their own." I lit the candle, held the stick to the flame, and proclaimed, "I call on the Goddess Hecate. I ask that you bless me."

I bent and passed the smoldering bundle from my toes, up over my head, and to my heels.

Then I spun in a slow circle. "I ask that you bless my home and banish Karl's spirit from it as he no longer serves a purpose in my life. Finally, I ask that you guide me as I start down the path I should have taken long ago."

Holding the tray beneath the stick to catch any falling embers, I traced the doorframe. "Any energy still in this room may not exit through this doorway."

Taking a fortifying breath, I stepped inside the reading room for the first time in more than twenty years, stepped left, and opened the window there. Then continuing widdershins around the space, I let the smoke seep into the corners and the pages of all the books. When the smoke started to die, I held the bundle to the flame again and continued. Once I'd made my way around the room just large enough to comfortably hold a twin bed and tall dresser, I stood by the opened window.

"I demand that you leave my house, Karl Brighton, but not my mind. Ignoring history only ensures that mistakes will be repeated. I never want to forget the lessons I learned from you. I fell out of love with you two decades ago and stopped hating you a few years back. Despite the pain you caused me, I will always be grateful to you for giving me my daughter."

With one final sweep of the still smoldering smudge stick, I directed his energy toward and out the window. Then I closed the window and sprinkled a line of salt across the sill that ran along the perimeter of the three outside walls.

"So mote it be."

When I turned back toward my bedroom, I found Dot sitting on the edge of my bed, watching me.

"Is he gone?"

She purred loud enough for me to hear from inside my reading room.

"Good."

I crawled into bed and took off my Triple Moon Goddess pendant, setting it on the half-moon ceramic plate I bought specifically for it. Using my favorite vanilla lip balm, I smeared my lips with the stick. Then I added vanilla-honey-chamomile lotion to my hands.

With the covers pulled up and folded neatly over my chest, I lay quietly and breathed in all the aromas hanging in the air.

"It feels better now," I told Dot. "Don't you think?"

She nestled in next to me, her purr making her little body vibrate against my side.

"I'll take that as a yes. We need to get to sleep now. Tomorrow, we have to figure out who has such a vendetta against me."

TWENTY-ONE

I slept, but not as soundly as I'd hoped. The inside of the cottage felt fresh and positive now, and the reading room practically glowed despite needing a good physical cleaning. It was the scone issue and the thought that Keiko could be involved that poked at me.

Deciding to not fight things, I rolled out of bed at six o'clock and went down to the kitchen to start some tea water. I felt like I needed a boost today so filled the infuser with caffeinated black tea instead of my usual herbal blend. While the water heated, I opened the side door to let Sanny in. She perched on a high shelf and Dot rubbed against my legs as I toasted two slices of bread and sectioned an orange. Normally, I'd add a protein of some sort, an egg or cottage cheese, but all that snacking Ruby and I did last night left my stomach full. That could also be why I hadn't slept well.

As I took the first bites of toast with jam and sips of tea, I got the distinct and overwhelming feeling that something was wrong at my shop. I could practically hear it calling me. Flashes of the day a couple of months back when an arsonist lit my soap shack on fire flooded my head. What was going on? Someone would have called me if there was a problem like that. Although, Hearth & Cauldron was tucked into the woods in a spot where it couldn't be seen unless someone was at The Twisty Skein or walked past on the Fairy Path. Of course, if they hadn't spotted the problem yet . . .

"Did I extinguish the candle after doing the blessing?"

I kept it up on a shelf during the day but removed it from beneath the hurricane to do the closing blessing. With eyes closed, I envisioned myself going from the retail room to the kitchen to the dining room. Keiko stood by the front door instead of following me, and when I finished I set the candle on the table and dipped the flame in the wax.

"Didn't I?"

Was I remembering my actual actions or simply my regular process?

I ran upstairs to the guestroom window. It looked toward the commons, and a good slice of sky was visible above the treetops from there. No smoke, thank the Goddess, but I needed to get over there. I pulled on jeans and the first blouse my hand touched. Silver. The color of vision and intuition. As I transferred my tea into a travel mug, Sanny and Dot gathered in the kitchen.

"You feel it, too, don't you?"

Sanny clicked. Dot gave a short meow.

Maybe they were just sensing my stress.

I glanced from them to my breakfast dishes still on the table. The last time I left the house with my kitchen still dirty, Yasmine had been seven years old. She'd fallen on the playground and got a nasty gash above her left eyebrow. It took three tiny stitches to close it and left behind a small scar. The scar faded somewhat over the years but never completely. She was thrilled when she figured out how to cover it perfectly with a makeup pencil.

"I have to get over to Hearth & Cauldron." I ignored the

dishes but took thirty more seconds to give Sanny and Dot food and water, then headed for the front door. "Play nice, girls."

Fortunately, the cover of my travel mug was on tight because I tossed it in the basket along with my purse instead of securing it with the strap on the side like usual. I didn't even take time to put on my helmet, letting it bounce around in the basket, too, and didn't slow my pedaling until I was a few yards from the shop. It looked okay from the outside. No damage to the front. Dismounting and then pushing my bike the last few feet, I tried to remember if I'd locked the door last night.

"Keiko had been asking about broken circles as I did so."

I remembered putting the key in the lock . . . but did I turn it? Like extinguishing the candle, locking a door was an act done automatically, so I couldn't say for certain. Just like securing my bike in the rack. That's where it was now, but I didn't remember putting it there seconds ago. I approached the front door cautiously, reached for the latch, and exhaled with relief when the lever didn't press.

The first thing to catch my attention when I stepped inside was that one of the freezer doors was standing open six inches. I rushed across the room to push it shut but stopped.

You need to document this, a voice in my head whispered.

From my bag, I pulled out my cellphone—which only worked when connected to the internet because we had no reception anywhere in the village—and snapped a few pictures. Using a wooden spoon so I wouldn't smudge any fingerprints, I pulled the door open further. Nothing appeared to be missing, but frost had formed on the items closest to the door. The air right in front of the unit was chilly, telling me it had been open for a while, and the thermometer indicated the temperature inside had crept up to 0° from where I set it at -5° but still within the recommended safe range. I tapped one of the items up front with the spoon. Still solid.

I pushed the door shut and heard the sucking sound that

told me it was sealing the door tight and stabilizing the temperature inside. I wouldn't be able to open it for a few minutes no matter how much I tugged.

"The front door was locked," I mused aloud. "The freezer door would not spontaneously pop open. It requires a bit of a tug even when not stabilizing."

What about the door to the patio? I darted to the dining room. The back door stood wide open. I thought back to last night. I asked Keiko to lock it—didn't I?—but clearly she hadn't. Had she been distracted by one of her many questions and forgotten? Or had it been purposeful so she could return or someone else could come in?

I shook my head and ordered myself to, "Focus on your shop now. Deal with Keiko later."

The dining room was otherwise undisturbed with tables still in place and chairs flipped on top from when Keiko mopped the floor last night.

I took more pictures and wondered if an animal had broken in. An animal couldn't turn a doorknob, though, or open the freezer. It must have been a person. But why? Were they looking for food or something else?

I turned toward the kitchen to check the contents of the refrigerators and saw straight into the retail room. I froze in place. The room was trashed. Items were all over the floor. Time to call Martin. This early, he'd probably still be home, so I called his cabin instead of broadcasting to the entire village via walkie-talkie.

"I'll be right there," he promised. "Don't touch anything."

While I waited for him, I used my spoon to open the cabinet beneath the sink in the kitchen and retrieve a pair of plastic gloves. Then I went to my office closet. I surely wouldn't be opening on time today so printed a sign for the front door.

Due to a minor issue, Hearth & Cauldron
will be opening late today.
Please come back this afternoon.

As promised, Martin walked in ten minutes later.

"Jagger's on his way with the camera bag and crime scene kit." He peeked into the retail room. "That's a mess. Kitchen seems okay, though. You said the freezer was open?"

"That one." I pointed to the one on the right side. I had two industrial freezer/refrigerator combos, one on each side of the kitchen. "It didn't appear it had been open for long. No more than an hour if I had to guess. I took pictures."

He noted all of this on his pad. The one Ruby said he always had on him. She was right. "You said the back door was open?"

"Wide open. Still is."

He followed me into the dining room. "There's glass on the floor."

My gaze followed to where he pointed. Shards lay between the door and the potbelly stove in the corner. "I didn't even notice. I was too distracted with trying to figure out what had happened."

Using his pen, Martin pushed aside the café-style curtain hanging on the window to the left of the door and revealed that one of the small panes of glass had been broken. "Here's how they got in. Broke the glass, reached inside, unlocked the deadbolt."

We went to the retail room next. Standing in the doorway, he visually surveyed the damage. "What do you notice?"

"My items all over the floor," I replied glumly.

"Look closer," he urged.

I did and after a few seconds, realized, "Nothing's broken."

"Right. It looks as though whoever did this took things off

the shelves and set them on the floor rather than sweeping them off or tossing them about."

"Why would anyone do that?"

Martin shook his head. "Couldn't begin to guess why criminals do the things they do."

Jagger arrived then. "Morning, Reeva. Sheriff."

I gave a little wave. "Where's Tyrann?"

"Outside on the porch. Igor agreed to work with us. We went up yesterday afternoon for an initial consult. Tyrann follows the standard sit, lay, and stay commands well, so Igor told me to work on control. I'm supposed to set a treat a few feet away from him and have him wait until I give the order to retrieve it." Jagger sighed. "I don't like the idea of food as a reward for either humans or animals so used a ball instead. Now all he wants to do is play." He gestured outside. "He's slobbering up a tennis ball at the moment."

Despite being upset over the state of my shop, I couldn't help but laugh at that.

He started taking pictures while Martin took prints from the freezer door. He said too many people would have touched the back doorknob so wouldn't bother with it.

"The only prints you should find on the freezer are mine, Bee's, and Keiko's." I shoved away the thought that Keiko could have set up a break-in. But nothing had been taken and the only damage was to that window. I watched the dusting process with interest then moved to the doorway of the retail room and took in the chaos there.

"What are you thinking?" Martin asked.

"Everything is piled so neatly. I'm wondering what's inside the heap. Can I look?"

"Jagger? Are you done in there?" The big man let Martin check the pictures. "Those look good."

"I'll start outside, then." Jagger jutted his chin at the patio.

"Good. There will be tons of footprints out there so look for any that don't seem right. Like beneath that window."

"Gotcha."

"Go on in," Martin told me.

"Can I take things off the stack?"

"Sure, but if you come across anything broken, let me get a picture before you move it."

I carefully took one item after another off the pile and set them aside. Not one thing was damaged, thank the Goddess. When I got close to the bottom of the pile, I stopped and stood straight.

"What have you got?" Martin asked.

I pointed. "Fluted muffin pans."

"And why are they important?"

"Because they've been missing since Monday." I explained the whole story.

He snapped a picture of where they lay and picked them up with gloved hands. "And you're sure they're yours?"

I twirled my finger. "Flip them over." On the bottom of both were small square price tag stickers. The ones I used had tiny cauldrons and *H&C* on them. "They're mine."

"This means that whoever stole them from you broke in to return them?"

"Vandalizing my building in the process."

Martin shook his head. "Some criminals are brilliant. Others are dumb as rocks. I'll fingerprint these, too, and keep them as evidence until we figure out who did this."

"Do you think you'll be able to?"

"Not every crime gets solved, but there's always a chance."

"Sheriff?" Jagger appeared in the doorway. "Would you come look at something out here?"

We followed him out the back door and around the side of the building. He pointed out footprints near the hedge. "Looks like someone stepped in your flower bed." Jagger pointed out definite foot-shaped impressions in the wood chips.

"Keiko," I breathed.

"What about her?" Martin asked.

"She told me that she likes sitting on my patio because it's quieter than the Pentacle Garden. For whatever reason, she squeezes in right there instead of going in the front door and through the shop."

Jagger pointed out some broken stems. "Whoever did this, they damaged part of your hedge."

"Keiko says she only steps on the wood chips." I paused before noting, "She isn't the only one that slips through here. She said she saw a girl wearing blue shorts and a pink T-shirt squeeze in this way on Monday."

"The muffin pan thief?" Martin suggested.

"Could be," I agreed. "Or maybe Keiko created a coverup and she's the thief."

"Is that all she said," Jagger asked. "Blue shorts, pink shirt?"

I recalled her words from last night. "She said it was a kid, not little but not a teenager, with dark hair wearing blue shorts and a pink T-shirt with butterflies and maybe flowers."

"Those were her exactly words? Butterflies and maybe flowers?"

"Yes. Why?"

"Because people tend to give more details when they're lying. They think that means they'll come across as observant, when we don't normally notice more than a detail or two in passing. If Keiko said the girl had curly platinum-blond hair and wore a pink T-shirt with green and purple butterflies, multi-colored flowers, and the word *magical* in sparkly letters, I'd say she was lying."

Martin blinked at him. "That's really specific, Jag."

"Got a shirt like that for my niece recently. She loves pink and purple so figured she'd like it. She does." He frowned for a moment. "Someone in the village has that shirt. Don't remember who . . ."

If he was right about this, I could be wrong about Keiko. Please, dear Goddess, let me be wrong. "Maybe you saw it on a tourist."

Jagger shrugged a big shoulder. "Could be. I asked where they got it because I figured my niece would like it better than what I was going to give her for her birthday. The kid said her mom bought it at Sundry. I got her a T-shirt, a stuffed unicorn, and some sparkly pens. My niece loves sparkles."

I couldn't help myself. "What were you planning to give her?"

"Pink camouflage night vision goggles."

Martin looked at me. "Those would be cool too."

I nodded.

"You think?" Jagger asked. "I'll give her that for Christmas."

"Back to your hedge," Martin nudged. "You said Keiko and this mystery girl go through here?"

"I saw the footprints, fluffed up the woodchips, and told Keiko not to cut through there anymore. She said she wouldn't."

"And the footprints are back. I'm thinking your pan thief had an attack of conscience. I'll write up a report for your insurance, but have Mr. Powell send someone over to fix your window."

"Thank you, Martin. I'll need to get that glass cleaned up first thing. Don't want anyone to cut themselves."

He made a few more notes and then said, "There's something else I need to ask you about."

"Sure, what?"

"Do you have any idea why someone would have made a call to the medical examiner's office from your home phone?" He paused just long enough to make sure he had my attention. "Joan said a woman left a message claiming to be from the Whispering Pines Sheriff's Station. Since Joan knows there are no women working at the station now, she asked me about it, and recited the phone number on her caller ID. It was yours."

I didn't reply.

"Aunt Reeva?"

"Ruby did it," I blurted and explained how I switched scones with Iris and about the note Keiko found on my door. "We were standing right there when Gardenia asked Dr. Bundy to run the blood work. Because of that note, we deduced that someone tried to poison me but got Iris instead. Ruby called and ordered the tests. I suppose you canceled them."

He stared, giving me a look that made it clear he wasn't happy with us. "No, I didn't cancel them. I figured if you did this, you had a good reason."

I smiled. "Is my reason good?"

He gave me a warning look. "Ask me again when the results come in. You shouldn't be digging around in this. Why didn't you come to me? That note sounds threatening."

"Because you said Iris's case was closed and that you have enough going on with tourists."

He groaned at the mention of tourists. "Remember those couples I told you about? The ones who heard that Litha is a fertility festival?"

"I remember. What did they do?"

"Every night this week, they've lit fires at the Meditation Circle, on the beach, or in the fire rings outside their cabins. Then they dance naked around it and leap over the fire."

I winced, involuntarily clenched my nether regions, and wondered if these were the blond, bald, and bearded guys from my class. "Don't they realize it's supposed to be the Litha bonfire we'll light tomorrow night at sunset and not just any old fire?"

"Really? That's what bothers you about this?"

"I . . . um . . ." I burst out laughing. "No. But see, you've got enough going on. I promise you, if we find anything important, we'll come to you."

"No more digging around." He wiped a hand over his mouth and exhaled. "Did you happen to find anything?"

"We've narrowed it down to Luna, Lorena, and Verne. And maybe Keiko." I gave him the details of what we'd discovered.

"I'll give you a point for properly narrowing down your suspects, but it sounds like you've got nothing."

"Ask me again when the bloodwork comes back."

In a stern voice, he ordered, "Stay out of this now. If someone is after you, you're putting yourself in danger." Then he softened a bit. "I'd be devastated if anything happened to you."

"I know. I'm sorry. We got a little carried away."

"Let me guess, Ruby instigated this."

"She did. Calls us Long & McLaughlin Investigations."

"At least she put you first."

"That's what I thought."

"I'm joking. Stay out of this. If you think of anything important or if anything else happens, you come to me right away. Got it?"

"I hear you. How long until they get those results?"

"Maybe later today. Dr. Bundy said Gardenia reminds him of his granddaughter and called in a favor."

"He's a good man."

"He is." Martin stared at me. "Are you okay? Because of the break-in, I mean."

"I'm all right. Mostly feeling violated and disappointed."

"Understandable. Bee will be here soon, right? You might feel a little uncomfortable by yourself today."

"Yes, Bee should get here any minute. She'll help me put the retail room back together. Fortunately, I don't have a class until tomorrow."

"Don't forget to call Mr. Powell about that window. And call me if you need anything. Anything, anytime."

I kissed his cheek and he, Jagger, and Tyrann went on their way. Keiko would be here this afternoon. He told me to stay out of Iris's death, but he didn't say anything about asking Keiko about the break-in.

TWENTY-TWO

Minutes after Martin and Jagger left, Ruby popped over, moving slower than normal. She listened as I explained what had happened and was appropriately upset, but she was more upset for herself.

"I stopped to thank you for taking me home. I'm going to go see if Willow has a tea or oil or magic amulet . . . anything that will help my head feel better."

"Go see Violet instead. She makes a hangover brew she calls Buzz Killer, I think. In the past, Martin has been known to imbibe a little too freely."

Of course, this would mean Ruby would be hyped up on caffeine, and she was hyper enough drinking nothing but water.

"At this point, I'll try anything. I'm going to the Grinder."

"Good luck."

By the time Bee arrived, she and most of the village already knew that I'd had a break-in. Somehow Violet had heard and warned Bee as she walked past.

"How does she always know these things?" I asked. "I called Martin at his cabin, on his landline, so the only people who knew were him, me, and Jagger."

"Best not to ask how things work around here," Bee advised. "What exactly happened?"

"I think it was right around the time I was eating breakfast. I suddenly got this feeling that something was wrong over here. When I got here, the first thing I saw was the freezer door standing open a few inches."

Bee nodded and made little humming sounds but said nothing as I told her the rest of the story. I ended by pointing out the pile of products in the retail room, as if she could miss it.

"Nothing's broken. Not one thing. *And* I found the fluted pans in the middle of all that."

"You're kidding."

"I'm not."

"If they came in through the back door," she mused, "they must have known about the path through the woods. The thief is a villager?"

"Possibly, but it looks like they squeezed in next to the hedge." I told her about the footprints in the flower bed. "Keiko admitted to squeezing in that way. She says she barely fits and thinks there's no way an adult would."

"A *child* did this? So we have a young hooligan in the village?"

I bent to pick up some of my beautiful, handcrafted, and thankfully unscathed kitchen grimoires. "A hooligan with a conscience."

"Or concern for their karma."

Karma? Like I'd been struck by lightning, I exhaled a sigh of understanding. "I think I know who did this."

Her face lit up. "Who? Tell me, tell me."

"I will if I'm right. I don't want to plant any seeds by saying something bad about this person if I'm wrong." I chewed my lip, wanting to dart over there right now, but we had work to do. "I'll go speak with them after Keiko gets here. If you wouldn't mind staying a little longer, that is."

"To find out who the pan thief is? I'll stay until close if you need me to."

"Thank you, Bee. Let's get this cleaned up so we can open."

"On the bright side," she noted, "this is a good opportunity to dust the shelves."

Rourke arrived about a half hour later to fix the window, and I led him to the back of the dining room.

"Ah, simple fix," he assured. "I'll have it good as new in a half hour tops."

I was about to go back to helping Bee but stopped. "Before you start, Rourke, can I ask you something?"

"Sure, you can. What's on your mind?"

Now that I'd opened the topic, I was almost embarrassed to say anything. "Someone, it's not important who, told me they thought you might be upset that Morgan chose me to be high priestess."

His eyebrows shot to his hairline, and his cheeks reddened. "Me? Upset about you as the HP? Never."

"Now you're offended. I'm sorry."

"Not by you. Whoever told you this needs to check their facts. We haven't known each other long, but I've liked you just fine from the start."

"Me too. That's why I was so shocked when they said that."

"I heard tales about Reeva Long well before you moved back to the village. Seemed to me that you'd been through more than your fair share of trouble with Flavia and Karl. I was glad to learn you kept following your religion."

I smiled gratefully. "The rituals help keep me centered. On days when nothing was going right or Yasmine wasn't cooperating and I had no one to turn to, a few minutes at my altar would settle me."

"And that's why I knew you were the perfect choice. When a person sticks with something for as long as you've stuck with Wicca, they know a thing or two. And while it may not feel like it right now, trust me when I say there are more of us on your side than against you."

A warm flush of gratitude spread through me. "Thank you, Rourke. That helps me more than you know."

Whether out of curiosity to see what had happened here or for some other reason, customers flocked to Hearth & Cauldron in the afternoon. Because there was no class scheduled today, and because I really wanted something chocolatey, I did a quick demonstration on how to make fudgy brownies with pecans and dark chocolate chunks. The shop smelled wonderful, which made happy customers. I started doing demonstrations one day when the weather was cold and dreary but found that the smell of something baking worked no matter what was going on outside. And if it was something they could buy and eat along with a cup of coffee or tea, the customers were content to stay longer. They'd sit in the dining room with a fire burning in the pot belly stove on cold or rainy days. They loved the solitude of the patio on warm, sunny ones.

"Heard we had some trouble this morning." Keiko found me the second she entered the shop.

I explained, again, what had happened.

With clenched hands, she asked, "Any idea who might have done it?"

Her reaction, as though prepared to defend my shop, touched me. "I have an idea and was waiting for you to get here. Bee will stay with you while I go talk with these folks. I'll be back quick as I can."

"But who—"

"I'll tell you when I get back. If I'm right. Go help Bee, please."

Wishing I had taken my SUV this morning, I rode my bike along the hidden paths through the woods and went north on the dirt road that led to the Meditation Circle. It also led to Sister Agnes's unchurch, where my sister was imprisoned.

Thankfully I didn't have to go quite that far to get to the Flowers' cottage.

"Reeva, what are you doing here?" Aster greeted, surprised to find me at her front door.

"I need to talk with the four of you. It shouldn't take long. Are Alder and the girls home?"

"Yeah, they're here. Come on in."

Their cottage, like most of the homes in the village, was compact. The closest thing to a mansion in Whispering Pines was Pine Time Bed-and-Breakfast or The Inn. The rest of us had quaint, well-built homes that taught us to value quality over quantity. The Flowers seemed to favor wood furniture with simple lines that created an airy feel, in the living room at least. That's all I saw of the place.

Alder met me while Aster rounded up the girls. "Is this some sort of follow-up? For the punishment you issued on Monday, I mean."

"Oh, no, that's not it."

"What is it, then?" he asked, somewhere between concerned and annoyed.

Sure hoped I wasn't wrong about this, because the last thing I wanted was to incorrectly accuse children of breaking into my shop. Before I could answer him, the girls walked in wearing matching T-shirts. Pink with green and purple butterflies. And the word *magical* in sparkly letters surrounded by multi-colored flowers.

"I like your shirts," I began.

Peony beamed. She had to perch on the front edge of the sofa cushion; otherwise, her short legs would stick straight out. "Momma got them for us to celebrate the end of the school year."

Rough, tough Clover blushed. Embarrassed to be wearing the same shirt as her little sister?

I noted that Clover had a similar build to Keiko, except she was taller and a little heavier. She would likely struggle to fit between the hedge and the side of the shop. Peony, however, would squirt right through.

"What have you two been up to today?" I asked them.

Clover's eyes narrowed. "Working on research for the papers we have to write."

Peony's feet kicked, bouncing off the couch as she said, "You'll be proud of us, Miss Reeva. We got books from the library, and Miss Morgan says we can use the books at Shoppe Mystique too, but we can't take them home if we don't buy them."

"No," I agreed, "because that would be *stealing*. And I'm sure you both know that stealing is wrong."

Peony didn't seem to understand what I was getting at, but Clover turned bright pink.

"They're working hard on this," Aster assured. "They decided they want to write their papers ASAP. Then they can enjoy the rest of their summer."

"Went to the library bright and early this morning," Alder informed. "I think they got there before it opened."

"That early?" Right around the time I was eating breakfast. My heart fluttered a bit at that revelation.

Clover added, "Indira has a horticulture section at Biblichor that might help too."

"But only bring them home if you buy them." I tweaked Peony's nose. "Right?"

She nodded, her stockinged feet kicking. "Right."

Alder flung a hand toward the back of their cottage. "Not to be rude, Reeva, but I work from home and need to get back to it."

"Of course," I apologized. "I had a break-in at Hearth & Cauldron early this morning."

Peony's feet stopped kicking, and she looked up at her big

206 • SHAWN MCGUIRE

sister. Clover's expression remained neutral, but her cheeks deepened from pink to dark rose.

"I assume you took the Fairy Path to get to the library?"

"Yeah," Clover said with a shrug.

"We went right past your shop, Miss Reeva," Peony volunteered.

"I think this break-in may have happened right around the time you would have been in that area. Did either of you notice anyone sneaking around Hearth & Cauldron?"

I directed the question at both of them but kept my eyes on Peony. She was the weaker link in this sister chain.

"I didn't see anyone," Clover stated flatly. "Neither did Peony."

"Maybe Peony should answer for herself." I smiled at the younger girl. "You don't need people doing things or answering questions for you, do you? You're a big girl."

"Sometimes I can't reach stuff," she admitted, a naughty smile brightening her face, "so I climb up on the cupboard."

"I've asked you not to do that," Aster scolded. "You fell that one time and sprained your wrist. Don't you remember?"

The smile intensified. "I remember. Clover had to do all my chores for a week."

"That's one of the good things about being little," I told Peony to Aster's dismay. "I bet you can squeeze into little places too."

Clover's jaw went slack as Peony said, "I can fit almost anywhere."

"Like between the hedge and the side of Hearth & Cauldron to get to the patio in back?"

Peony froze, chewed on her lips, and then slowly nodded.

"I see you've got a bandage on your right elbow. What happened?"

"She's always hurting herself," Clover supplied.

"Reeva," Aster's voice took on a concerned tone, "what are

you getting at? I mean, it sounds like you're accusing my seven-year-old of something."

"Let me be clear, then. Did you cut your elbow by breaking a windowpane at my shop?"

"Now hang on one minute," Alder protested.

Peony looked down and played with her fingers. "Yes."

"What?" her parents demanded in unison.

As though about to burst, Peony blurted, "We had to bring them back."

"Peony, hush," Clover hissed.

I held out a hand at the older girl. "Please, Clover, let her talk."

"Don't you remember about Carmen?" Peony asked her sister.

It took me a second and then my heart softened. "You mean karma?"

"Yeah. That's when if you do something bad," Peony recited, "bad stuff will happen to you."

I waited, but that's all she had for me. "You know what?"

"What?"

"Karma also means that when you do something good, good stuff will happen to you. Tell me what happened at my shop this morning. I promise, doing so will be a good thing."

She tilted her head to look at Clover, then peeked up at her parents.

"Go ahead, Peanut," Alder encouraged. "Tell Miss Reeva what happened."

Peony blew out a breath, preparing herself, then said, "On Monday, after you gave us our punishment, Momma was really sad and kind of mad. I wanted to make her feel better, so I went to your shop to get her a present."

Aster's mouth fell open in surprise, but she remained silent.

"When I got there," Peony continued, "there were all these

people on the porch. I saw Miss Bee talking to them, and it looked like she wasn't letting anyone in."

That would have been while I was blessing the bowl and the wooden spoons. "So you went around to the back by squeezing past the hedge?"

"Yeah, I saw a girl with long black pigtails do that one time. I like her pigtails. Momma, can you make me pigtails?"

"Sure," Aster smiled stiffly. "Keep telling us what happened, though."

"Okay. I went through the dining room. You were in the kitchen doing something to a bowl, Miss Reeva. Then I went to that other room with all the cooking stuff in it. Momma likes to make cupcakes, and I saw those pans and thought they would make super-cute cupcakes."

"They would," I agreed. "Did you take the pans?"

"I forgot I was supposed to give you money. So I took them home and was gonna bring you some money, but there's not very many coins in my piggy bank. We learned about money in school, so I know it's not enough." She smiled big. "My piggy bank looks like a real piggy. Wanna see it?"

There's no way she did any of this with malice. "Not right now, sweetheart. What did you do when you realized you didn't have enough money?"

"I asked Clover for some. She said I'd be in big karma trouble for stealing and you'd be super mad at me, so we figured we better just put them back."

"But you broke my window and messed up my shop."

"They what?" Aster demanded.

"That was Clover's idea," Peony told us.

We all looked at the older girl. She rolled her eyes and sighed.

"Clover." With the single word, Alder's disappointment was clear.

"Why," I began, "did you think breaking in was the right way to handle this? You could have left the pans on a table on the patio or even on the front steps."

"Yeah, I know." Clover threw her hands in the air. "I hoped the back door would be open so sent Peony back there. I didn't tell her to break the window."

"She didn't," Peony agreed. "That was all me."

"She let me in the front door and when I saw what she did to the window, I figured we'd make it look like someone broke in."

"We didn't break anything but that window, though," Peony insisted. "We were super careful about that."

"You're right. Nothing else was broken." I looked between the girls. "Do you see now what a foolish decision this was?"

"I'm sorry. Really." Clover appeared sincere.

I looked between them long enough to make them squirm. "I appreciate that you tried to do the right thing, even getting a gift for your mom because she was sad. But neither of you handled either situation the right way."

"What's their punishment?" Alder asked.

"This time," I turned to the parents, "you have to decide."

Aster's mouth dropped open again, and Alder mumbled, "We . . . um . . . us?"

"You can do it," I encouraged. "Part of your job as parents is to teach your children that there are consequences for their actions. Another part of that job is issuing a punishment when they do something wrong. I promise you're not being mean."

They stared at me wide-eyed.

"Why don't you two step out of the room and discuss it?" I suggested.

When they returned a few minutes later, Aster told them, "You did the wrong thing, but your intentions were good."

Alder continued, "We decided your punishment will be to go to Hearth & Cauldron every day for two weeks and do chores."

"What?" Clover cried. "Two weeks?"

"You have to do enough to pay for the broken window,"

Alder added, "plus more to clear your karma." He looked at me, "If that's not enough, we'll change it."

"That will be fine." I would've said one week.

Clover slumped against the sofa cushion. "What do we have to do?"

Aster turned to me. "We figured you could decide that part."

"Fair enough," I agreed. "Come over every day at four o'clock. You can clean up the patio and front porch. You'll wipe down the tables and chairs, sweep, and pull any weeds in the flower beds. But ask me first so I can show you what's a weed and what's a plant."

"Okay," they said in unison.

"And I'd like you to keep something in mind for the future."

They both looked expectantly at me.

"I like that you wanted to get your mom a gift. If there's ever a time when you want to get something for someone and you don't have enough money, tell me. I'll either let you pay it off over time or you can do chores around the shop and pay for it that way. There are always floors to sweep or shelves to dust."

"Or weeds to pull." Peony jumped to her feet and threw herself into my arms. "I'm so sorry, Miss Reeva. I'll never steal anything ever again. I promise."

And with that, one mystery was solved. Somehow, I was pretty sure the motive behind Iris's death wouldn't be as innocent.

B y the time I got back to the shop, I was a sweaty mess from pedaling hard. Bee probably wanted to get home . . . and find out who the pan thief was. After quickly securing my bike into the rack, I turned and almost collided with Jozef.

Goddess, please don't let me be stinky as well as sweaty.

"I was just inside looking for you." He nodded at Hearth & Cauldron. "Bee told me you'd be back soon."

"Here I am." I made jazz hands next to my face. Really? Jazz hands? What was wrong with me? "What did you need?"

"Dinner. You promised to have dinner with me tonight."

I scanned my memory. "I don't recall promising but do remember us talking about it."

"I understand you've had a rough day." His voice was full of empathy. "Even more reason for me to take you to dinner. Then you can relax and don't have to worry about cooking tonight."

I smiled. "Cooking is never a worry. I wouldn't mind the company, though."

"When do you close?"

"Six o'clock unless there are customers still shopping." That was only an hour from now. Good Goddess this day flew.

"I'll pick you up here at six thirty, and we'll go to Grapes, Grains, and Grub. How does that sound?"

That wouldn't give me enough time to run home and change. Did I have any clean shirts here? I usually kept one on hand in case of spills and splashes. No, I used my backup last week and forgot to bring a fresh one. I could run up the Fairy Path to Ivy's Boutique and buy something new. She carried the prettiest blouses. A quick bird bath, as my grandmother used to call it, in the shop's bathroom sink and I'd be all freshened up.

"Triple G sounds perfect, but let's make it six forty-five."

His eyes sparkled as he smiled. "See you then."

I entered the shop to find Bee and Keiko grinning like fools at me.

"What did he want?" Bee asked.

"Reeva has a boyfriend," Keiko sang out.

"Reeva does not have a boyfriend," I corrected.

"Reeva's going on a date," Keiko proclaimed in the same singsong.

"I'm going out to dinner with a friend."

"Ooh," they hooted together.

"Stop it." I had to turn away from them or they'd see me blushing. *Was* this a date?

"Were you right about the pan thief?" Bee asked.

"One minute." I pulled out my cell phone, connected to the shop's Wi-Fi, and video called Ivy.

Seconds later, her round face and huge afro filled the screen. "Hey there. Heard you had a break-in this morning."

"I did. Everything's fine. I'll tell you about it later. I need a blouse for tonight, and if I come over, I'll spend an hour and far too much money."

"I'm okay with that," she teased. "Kidding. You want a walkthrough?"

"Please."

She turned the camera to show me a dozen different blouses, all of which I loved. I'd purchased so many items from Ivy over the past year, she knew my size and often knew better than I did what would look good on me.

"I'll take the hot pink V-neck with the gathering across the back," I said, then decided to splurge. "And the black tunic with the white cutwork embroidery." The tunic was gorgeous.

"Charge your card?" she confirmed.

"Yes, please. I'll pick them up a little after six."

My helpers were grinning at me again when I signed off. "What? I don't have time to run home and change. Jozef is picking me up here."

Before they could start razzing me about Jozef again, I told them about Clover and Peony, stopping every few minutes to answer customer questions. When the shop emptied for a short time, I concluded, "It's all because you mentioned a girl in a pink T-shirt squeezing through the hedge, Keiko."

She did a curtsy. "Glad I could help crack the case."

"Mystery solved." Bee brushed her hands together. "I'm going to go unless you need anything else."

"No, you're free. Thank you for staying late and for all your help today."

Fortunately, by quarter to six, the shop was empty. I wanted to ask Keiko about her comment from yesterday, so made the unprecedented decision to close early.

"I don't have long," I qualified, "so we have to clean and straighten while we talk."

"About what?"

"Your question about broken circles."

Since Bee and I had dusted the shelves in the retail room this morning, we headed into the dining room. As I wiped down the tables and flipped the chairs on top of them, Keiko started sweeping.

"Maybe it was my imagination," she began, "but I could have sworn I saw some folks not chanting at the blessing the other night. The one at your house."

"Chanting? When did we . . . oh, outside to bless the whole property?"

"Right. I was saying what Morgan told us to. Peace, comfort, safety. Peace, comfort, safety. I said it over and over, but I looked around the circle at the same time."

"That doesn't break the circle, and you don't have to close your eyes. Doing so simply helps with focus and intent."

The elementary explanation seemed to insult her. "I figured that, but when I opened my eyes, I saw a few people not chanting. And now that I've said it out loud, I guess they could have just been thinking the words." She shrugged. "It just hit me at the moment, I guess. All that energy swirling around and stuff."

This explained why she was so fidgety that night. "Why did it concern you so much?"

She blinked as though surprised. "It could leave you unprotected. I mean, if they weren't taking part, that would make a gap in the circle. Right? You said positivity could leak out or negativity could get in through a gap. I mean, that's why we were there. To clear negativity from your home and keep it away."

My heart swelled. She truly was worried about this. Suspecting her as being the one who poisoned the scones suddenly felt like a textbook case of circumstantial evidence. Keiko Shen was a good kid trying to find her way. I think we were safe to cross her off the suspect list. Did that mean we were closer to solving the scone crime or farther away?

I placed my palms together. "Thank you for worrying about me, Keiko. I can't say that the circle was broken, but something was definitely off that night."

"Does the coven need to come again?" She looked hopeful about this. Keiko liked coven gatherings.

"I think it's to the point where doing my own regular smudging will solve my problems."

She gave me an awkward smile.

"You want to help?" I guessed.

"Can I?"

So enthusiastic. "I took care of a big problem last night, but I'll let you know when I want to do it again." I glanced at the clock. "Time to get ready for dinner."

"When is he coming?"

"In half an hour. I need to clean myself up a bit."

She waved one hand in front of her face while holding her nose with the other. "Yes, you do." At my warning glance, she replied, "Just sayin'. You want me to run over and get your shirts?"

"That would be great. You pick which one I should wear."

CHAPTER
TWENTY-FOUR

Grapes, Grains, and Grub, despite the casual name and appearance, made a little bit of everything from the best greasy burgers, to a prime rib that cut with a butter knife, to a perfectly prepared salmon filet.

When Maeve, the owner-operator, saw us walk in, she opted to seat us herself instead of letting the hostess do so. "Nice blouse. Is it new? Did you get it from Ivy?" she asked while we followed her out onto the huge deck at the back of the building and over to the far righthand corner.

"Thank you, yes, and yes," I replied with a pointed look. Was she trying to embarrass me, or did she simply like the tunic? Or had Keiko told Ivy why I bought the blouses, and that news flash was now making its way around the village?

Maeve led us up a flight of five stairs to a small platform that was covered by a canopy of fairy lights and held a table for two. She winked and said, "The Love Nest is more private, so you two can talk without being disturbed. The tourists are getting more and more excitable the closer we get to Litha. Enjoy your dinners."

"Thank you for saying yes to dinner." Jozef held my chair out for me. "I hated the idea of leaving in the morning without seeing you again."

I kept a smile on my face despite the clench of sadness in my chest. "Thank you for asking."

Our server, Sloan, appeared with menus and glasses of water. "May I bring you cocktails?"

"What do you recommend?" Jozef asked me.

"You want me to decide?"

"If we were in Denmark, I'd suggest we get an Akvavit," he noted. "It's popular for Midsummer celebrations."

"Something specific to Whispering Pines . . ." I pondered this a moment. "Maeve brews her own mead. It's very good, but I say we try the Witches Brew. It's not on the menu. You have to know to ask for it. You can get the same drink at The Inn if you ask."

"That sounds far too intriguing to decline." Jozef looked to Sloan. "We'll take two."

Sloan bowed his head, the big bun of dreadlock strands wobbling as he did. "I'll be right back with your drinks and to take your orders."

"And what do you recommend for dinner?" Jozef asked.

"My-my, you're putting all your faith in me tonight."

He gazed up from his menu. "I'm not worried."

My heart fluttered. Why did this man have such an effect on me? Because I was out of practice and not used to being flirted with. I took a sip of water and cleared my throat. "While not fine dining, the Friday night fish fry is a Wisconsin tradition."

"This isn't Friday."

"I know, but I'm sure they can whip up a couple of plates for us."

"Very well. I like traditions and I like fish."

We heard Sloan returning with our drinks before we saw him. The Witches Brew always caused gasps and whispers of "What's that?" as it was carried past the diners. They came in margarita-style glasses with lime-green sugar around the rim. Shimmery deep-purple and midnight-blue liquids remained separated and were beautiful to look at, but what made people gasp was the smoke rising from the glasses.

"Enjoy only with your eyes until the smoke is gone," Sloan cautioned. At Jozef's questioning look, he explained, "Consuming dry ice would be very bad for your digestion."

Once Sloan left to fill our orders, Jozef gazed at the liquids. "What are the ingredients?"

"I'm not sure exactly but know there's vodka and blue curacao in the blue half, vodka and elderberry in the purple. Luster dust creates the shimmer. They do come in non-alcoholic versions as well. They're called Familiars."

"Clever. And why don't the two combine?"

I smiled and held my hands up in a *beats me* gesture. "Magic." Once the smoke had cleared, I raised my glass. "To new friends."

As our glasses touched, Jozef added, "And to where that path leads."

I drank and then asked, "Have you changed your mind about leaving?"

His head tilted to the side. "I haven't. Why do you ask?"

I fanned myself playfully with my napkin. "Because there's a lot of innuendo swirling around, Mr. Lykke."

He took my hand in his across the table. "When is the last time you've been out to dinner?"

"As in on a date?"

"Is that what this is?"

Now I felt like he was picking on me. I tried to pull my hand away, but he tightened his grip just a little.

"I'm not expecting anything except dinner and conversation," he assured. "I enjoyed talking with you the other day and simply wanted to spend more time with the charming, intelligent woman with whom I share some interests."

Don't be an idiot. Play along. You're sitting across from an insanely handsome man and you're freaking out because he's flirting?

"It's been a very long time since I've been 'out to dinner,'" I admitted. "I enjoyed talking with you the other day as well."

He lifted his glass to me. "To friends?"

I picked up mine and grinned. "And wherever the path leads them."

Sloan brought a breadbasket with a small cup of Maeve's signature cherry butter and another of whipped honey with a hint of cinnamon. She sourced the honey from our local beekeeper, Beckett. A few minutes later, our side salads arrived.

"Tell me about this place," Jozef requested, waving his hand at the restaurant. "It's very unique."

"It does have an interesting history," I agreed. "From the outside, as you can tell, it looks more like a house than a pub. The original owner, Sally Sullivan, had always dreamed of running a restaurant where her customers felt like they were eating in someone's home. She and her husband of twenty years came here for a long weekend sometime in the early 1970s. He had been sick for many months, and they knew it would be their last trip together. He died peacefully in his sleep the night before they were to leave. The owner of Whispering Pines, Lucy O'Shea, heard about the man's death and came to comfort Sally. She told her that if there was anything she could do for her, to let her know."

"And Sally asked if she could open a restaurant here?"

"Yes, but not only that, she asked if she could move her house here."

Surprised, Jozef pointed at the building. "This was her home?"

"It was. She didn't want to leave the place where she'd spent so many years with her husband, but they had already agreed that she should follow her dream once he was gone. They both fell in love with the village, and moving here felt right to her.

Lucy agreed and Sally paid to have her house moved to this spot."

Jozef grinned and shook his head slowly. "I knew there would be a story. That's a good one."

Sloan appeared at our table with "complimentary" second glasses of Witches Brew. "The kitchen is really backed up tonight, so there will be a bit of a delay on your dinners. Is there anything else I can bring you in the meantime?"

"I think we're good right now," I replied.

"What's that smile for?" Jozef asked when Sloan walked away.

"A fish fry doesn't normally come with a salad, just a cup of really good coleslaw, and the breadbasket is usually dinner rolls with foil-wrapped butter pats, not artisan bread, specialty butter, and whipped honey. We're getting *Maeved*."

"Maeved?"

I dabbed some of the sugar from the rim of my glass and placed it on my tongue. "It means she doesn't want our dinner to end any sooner than we do."

Later, when Sloan came to take away our plates, he assured, "No rush. Maeve says this table is yours for as long as you want it."

"In that case," Jozef said, eyes on me, "tell us about dessert."

In all, we sat in the Love Nest for three hours and could have stayed for three more without running out of things to talk about.

"I really hate to say this . . ."

"But you need to get home," he guessed. "I don't like it either, but I understand. You have to work tomorrow."

"And the next day and the next until Samhain. The tourist season is intense here."

"May I walk you?"

Anything for a few more minutes.

"How was dinner?" Maeve asked when we got to the front door.

"Everything was perfect," Jozef praised.

"You're awfully proud of yourself, aren't you?" I whispered in her ear as I gave her a hug.

"I have no idea what you're talking about," she insisted and pulled away.

"Turn down that smile. You look like the Cheshire Cat." She glanced at Jozef and back at me. "Glad your night was so delicious."

Outside on the red brick path that encircled the Pentacle Garden, Jozef took my hand. I stiffened at first and then reminded myself to play along. He was leaving in a few hours, and I'd likely never see him again. There was nothing wrong with enjoying every moment.

We went north around the garden past Biblichor, Ye Olde Bean Grinder, Shoppe Mystique, and when we came to Treat Me Sweetly, I nearly froze in place. Gabe, Jola, and Lily Grace were coming out with paper cups in hand. Probably Honey's hot chocolate. They were all laughing until they saw me.

"Hey, Reeva," Gabe greeted, his gaze lowering to my hand entwined with Jozef's.

"Good evening," I replied, my mouth suddenly dry. *Say something. Anything so this doesn't get weird.* "Is Treat Me Sweetly still open? I thought they closed at nine." *Good enough.*

Gabe glanced behind them at the sweet shop but had no response.

"We stopped in for an ice cream," Jola supplied while Lily Grace stared at me, "and the next thing we knew, Sugar was flipping the sign to closed. They let us stay until they were done cleaning up."

An awkward pause descended and then Gabe turned to my date. "Jozef, right? We took Reeva's class together."

"We did." Jozef released my hand and shook Gabe's. "I am,

unfortunately, leaving in the morning, so tonight I'm enjoying some of the best that Whispering Pines has to offer."

Thank the Goddess the village had a rule about outdoor lighting. We preferred to see the moon and stars instead of fluorescents. Between the few dim lights that were permitted and the thick pine boughs blocking much of the moonlight in this spot, it was dark enough that none of them could see me blushing. I hoped.

"Good to see you all," I stammered and tugged on Jozef's arm. "Have a great night."

"I knew there was something between you two," Jozef teased.

"What are you—"

"Reeva?" Lily Grace called out to me. "Can I talk to you for a minute?"

Not only had the girl not spoken a word to me since her mother died, I'm pretty sure she'd been getting evil eye lessons from her grandmother Cybil.

"Sure." We stepped a few feet away from Jozef. "What's on your mind?"

She sighed and wouldn't look me in the face. "There's something I should tell you about."

Should? "Okay."

"I had a vision."

Uh-oh. Or perhaps yay? One never knew what the young fortune teller's visions would hold.

"I don't know what it means"—she rolled her eyes—"I never know what they mean, but I saw a pastry."

"A pastry," I repeated, purposely keeping any judgment or doubt from my voice. "You're sure this was meant for me?"

"Yeah, because I also saw a flash of your face first. And then I saw a biscuit or muffin maybe, I don't know. I don't think that was the important part. Whatever the thing was, it was marked."

"Marked? How? With what?"

"Some symbol. It was like tattooed onto the top of the thing."

I thought of how Jozef marked his scones. Did her vision have to do with Jozef and me?

"Do you remember what the symbol looked like?"

She shook her head and drew random marks in the air with her finger. "All I remember was a bunch of lines."

That sounded like Jozef's rune.

TWENTY-FIVE

ily Grace saw Jozef's raidho mark on a scone or biscuit and my face. What did that mean? It could signify a connection between us. We did connect, but was this just a passing thing, as we'd been alluding to all night, or was there more? No, there couldn't be more, he was leaving.

Or could there be?

Lily Grace stared at me, waiting for a response. "That must make sense to you because you look like you're going to pass out or throw up or something."

Did I want there to be more?

"It does make sense, but I'm not going to pass out or throw up." At least not right now.

"Thank you, Lily Grace."

She nodded and turned to walk away but stopped and turned back. "Reeva? I know you weren't responsible for my mother's death. I'm just really mad."

"I understand, honey. You're grieving."

Her eyes filled with tears. "She just got here. I was finally going to have a life with my mother and . . ."

"And now you'll never have that." I wanted to hug her, but

that would be the worst thing I could do at that moment. I could empathize, though. "And since you can't take it out on my sister, I'm the closest thing. Believe it or not, I understand."

Other than the tears, her expression remained neutral as she nodded and then returned to her dad and sister.

"Is everything okay?" Jozef asked, taking my hand and tucking it into the crook of his elbow. "You both look upset."

"My sister was responsible for Lily Grace and Jola's mother's death. Long story that I don't want to talk about."

"Then we won't." We continued to the Fairy Path entrance. "Want to talk about you and Gabe?"

I couldn't detect any hint of jealousy in his voice. Only curiosity. Did I want him to be jealous? Lily Grace now had me wondering if there was meant to be more between us. Or maybe her vision meant something entirely different. They rarely predicted the future. In fact, they usually only made sense after the fact.

I hugged Jozef's arm. "There's nothing between me and Gabe except friendship."

"But you have a crush on him. I saw you blush at my comment."

"Crush is a good word for it. Gabe and I grew up here together. As a teenager, I thought he was the funniest, cutest, greatest guy ever. For many very complicated reasons, we never dated, not once, and then he left the village. For forty years, we never saw or heard from each other."

"And now he's back," Jozef supplied. "Do you want there to be something between you?"

I looked up at him. Perhaps I was being foolish and a little giddy from the attention he was giving me, but I felt safe with Jozef. And not just because he had big Viking muscles.

"Even if I did, this is time for him and his daughters to heal and bond."

He chuckled softly, his focus straight ahead on the path. "I don't think that answers my question."

We chatted about less emotionally loaded topics the rest of the way to my cottage. He explained that while he was applying for pastry chef positions, he was also a fully trained sous chef, having studied in both Paris and Milan. My heart clenched with envy. How I would have loved to learn at one of the premier culinary institutes.

At my doorstep, Dot and Sanny made so much noise, I finally had to open the door a crack and assure them that I was okay. "This is Jozef. He's fine."

I turned back, finding myself staring at his broad, muscular chest.

Finer than fine. Should I invite him inside? What are the rules of dating these days?

"I won't ask to come in," he said, reading my mind. "I don't want to risk ruining an otherwise perfect night by potentially making things uncomfortable."

Resting my hand against his chest, I relaxed. "You're a good man, Jozef Lykke. I've really enjoyed meeting and getting to know you. As I said earlier, it's been a long time since I've gone on a date, but tonight may have cracked open the shell I've encased myself in."

He traced a finger along my jaw, sending shivers through my body. "I would like to kiss you goodbye."

He didn't need to ask twice. I leaned against him, draped my arms around his neck, and pressed my lips to his. When he tickled my lip with the tip of his tongue, I almost dragged him inside. He was right, though. Reality had a way of ruining things. This was the perfect ending for us. He left me breathless, with memories and fantasies firmly in place.

"Goodbye, Jozef. Keep in touch. Let me know which job you take."

He smiled, his intense blue eyes sparkling in the moonlight. "You think I'll be offered both?"

"If not one of those, they weren't meant to be, and a better opportunity will appear for you."

"A blessing from a witch. I'm golden."

He opened the door for me, laughed when both Sanny and Dot backed away from him, and then pulled the door shut with a gentle click after I'd stepped inside.

I leaned against the closest wall, my chest heaving for breath as my heart raced. Was this how I felt after my first date with Karl? No, not even close. I wasn't head-over-heels for Karl when we married, I was still in love with Gabe at that time, but Karl was a good man who I came to love over the years. Then I hated him. Then settled in at neutral.

Mrow, Dot complained.

Sanny clicked her dissatisfaction.

"I know, your dinner is late. If you two could spend a few minutes with that man, you'd understand why *my* desires were more important tonight."

There was a message on my phone from Ruby. "Keiko told me you went to dinner with Jozef. I couldn't help myself. I spied on you from the woods near the Love Nest. Call me the second you get home."

Smiling so big my cheeks hurt, I dialed her number and put her on speaker phone so I could feed the girls.

"Good Goddess, Reeva. I haven't seen you that happy since you got accepted to culinary school."

Really? That was forty years ago. "I remember days with Yasmine when I was that happy. In a different way, of course."

"Yes, good that you had her to complete your life," Ruby agreed, but her voice had taken on a slightly dismissive tone. Why did her mood shift whenever children were mentioned? "Tell me about dinner. What did you talk about? Or is there a Viking in your bed at the moment?"

I let Sanny outside and then climbed the stairs to my bedroom. "If he was in my bed, I certainly wouldn't be talking to you right now."

While changing into my pajamas, I told her about the evening and our many discussions. And the kiss.

"He kissed you? Oh, Reeva, I'm so happy for you."

"Technically, he said he wanted to kiss me. I granted his wish."

"Ooh-la-la. And now he's leaving you with nothing but memories."

I could picture her, hands clutched over her heart in unrequited bliss.

"Really good memories."

Before I could tell her about Lily Grace's vision, she stated, "We're getting back to work tomorrow, right? We need to talk to Verne and Keiko."

I told her about my discussion with Keiko earlier.

"She could be playing you. Worse, she could be trying to kill my best friend."

I smiled at the best friend comment. "I trust her. You know why? Because I trusted my daughter and they were friends. Yasmine was murdered and that had nothing to do with me. There is no reason Keiko would be trying to kill me."

Ruby hesitated before replying, "You'll keep your guard up?"

"I promise."

"We'll talk to Verne tomorrow then."

"We need to wait."

"For what?" she blurted, obviously losing patience.

"Martin knows we were snooping around. He confronted me this morning because Joan from Dr. Bundy's office asked who requested further tests. She got my phone number from caller ID, and Martin recognized it."

"Sorry. Is he mad?"

"He's upset that we're snooping around but let the test for

poison go through anyway. Dr. Bundy called in a favor, so the results should be in quickly. I'll stop by the station on the way to the shop in the morning and see if he's got any new information."

"He shouldn't be mad at you for something I did. I'll go with you and apologize for making the call. We'll ride together—"

"Oh crud."

"What?"

"Jozef walked me home. My bike is at Hearth & Cauldron."

"He really distracted you. Shame that he's leaving."

"Tell me about it."

"Can I ask you something?"

"Can I stop you?"

"What about Gabe? You've been in love with him since you were seventeen. He's back now and unattached."

It had only been three weeks since Rae died. If she and Gabe hadn't divorced years ago, Ruby's comment would be highly insensitive.

"First, Jozef and I don't have a relationship, so I'm unattached as well. Second, Gabe moved here to connect with his daughters. I can't interfere with that."

"So you're just going to wait for him again?"

"Wait for him?" I laughed at that. "It's not like I've been sitting at home pining for him, Ruby. I raised a daughter, ran a catering business, and acquired items for people's homes. Remember?"

"But you never dated."

Should I point out she was describing her life as well? Less the child part. "Honestly, I never had the desire. Maybe Gabe was part of the reason for that and maybe not. Either way, he and Rae were married until a few years ago."

She paused again. "I'm sorry. I didn't mean to make you angry. It's just, you deserve to be happy, you know."

Besides giving me a night of fun with a handsome, sexy,

wonderfully flirty man, that's exactly what my date with Jozef taught me. I was ready to be happy again and to get back into life. As much as I loved it, I wanted and needed more than Hearth & Cauldron. I needed a life as a woman too. Maybe that *could* be with Gabe. It would be nice if we could at least give it a try. If I was bold enough to kiss a stranger, I should surely be able to invite a friend over for dinner.

"Are you still there?" Ruby asked.

"Yes, sorry. Got lost in thought. I'm wiped out and need to go to bed. I'll see you in the morning, okay? Come early. We'll have breakfast."

"I'll be there. I'd like two poached eggs, please. And I didn't mean to rain on your date night with comments about killers and Gabe. I really am happy for you."

I thanked her, hit the off button on my phone, and realized I was sitting in my reading room. When had I come in here? Another sign that Karl was gone from my life. It was long past time.

TWENTY-SIX

After a restless night's sleep—dreaming about a band of Vikings that all looked like Jozef, roads that led to nowhere, and mountains of rune-branded pastries—I gave up and rolled out of bed at five o'clock. Dot ignored me except to crawl a few inches and snuggle into the warm place my body had left on the sheets. I pulled the covers over her to make the bed and laughed when I lifted the edge to peek in at her. She didn't even open an eye. It was still dark, so Sanny wasn't ready for our morning routine either.

Ruby arrived at seven to a spotless, wonderfully smelling house.

"Two poached eggs on the way," I announced when she entered the kitchen. "I've also got almond-raspberry-chocolate chip muffins, and a fruit salad of strawberries, bananas, blueberries, peaches, a sprinkle of coconut flakes, and a drizzle of honey."

"I like this restaurant." She made herself some tea and settled into her place at the table. "The muffins are still warm. Did you just make these?"

"Been up since five." I told her about my dreams.

232 · SHAWN MCGUIRE

"You've had a lot on your mind, and I'm not helping," she said after we'd taken our first bites. "Sorry about pushing you regarding Gabe last night. And Verne. I'm just worried about you."

"It's all right." I kicked her shin gently under the table. "Good to have a friend that loves you enough to make you mad for the right reasons."

We chatted about how her week was going—she needed Keiko's help restocking shelves soon—and how I was almost ready to give my first lesson on soapmaking. Ruby had been upset with me when I first built the soap shack on Hearth & Cauldron's back patio. Much like the aprons, she felt I was treading on her territory. I explained that I didn't consider soapmaking to be a craft, though. It fell under the category of household necessity.

"Housewives have been making soap for centuries," I had explained. "They looked at it as another item on their to-do list, not a creative outlet."

She had backed down but still stiffened whenever I brought it up. Like now.

"You can't do every craft in the world, Ruby," I replied to her scowl and cut a muffin in two to share with her.

"I don't teach cookie baking," she mumbled and accepted my peace offering.

"That's not a craft."

"Some people would consider it to be." She shot me a pointed look. "It kind of falls into that odd category where soapmaking is a household chore." She smiled pointedly at me.

"If you want to teach people how to decorate cookies, I won't object." I waited a beat. "Do you know how to decorate cookies?"

She narrowed her eyes at me, but I saw the playful sparkle in them. "Witch."

After breakfast, we washed the dishes and wiped down the

table and countertops. I fed the girls, and as I gave them their goodbye pats, I saw something in the backyard that made me dart out the sunroom door.

"What's wrong?" Ruby called and chased after me.

More damage to my property. Someone had sprayed white paint on my red garden shed and tore up some of the flowers planted around it. From the flowers' wilted appearance, it had happened last night.

"Is that a sigil?" Ruby looked as shocked as I felt.

I stood back and looked at the graffiti. "A sigil is when the consonants of a word or phrase—"

"Are formed into a symbol that represents that word or phrase. I know what a sigil is."

She was unusually defensive lately. What was going on with her?

"Do *you* think it's a sigil?" I asked.

She studied it for a minute. "Could be. Or someone just wanted to mess up your shed." She stepped forward and retrieved something white peeking out from beneath a clump of pulled-up pansies. "Another envelope."

I took it from her and opened it. "Same handwriting. It says, 'Tired of this yet? Your troubles will only escalate if you don't step down. Time for the coven to decide who should be the HP.' The word coven is underlined."

"That's it," Ruby declared. "Bring this envelope, the one Keiko found taped to the shop door, and all the pictures you've taken. And get pictures of this mess. We're going to Martin."

This time, I didn't object.

"Definitely a threat." Martin flipped through the pictures. "You found the damage to your shed this morning?"

"Right after breakfast," Ruby confirmed.

"Any idea of when this might have happened?" he asked.

"Based on the condition of those flowers," I told my nephew, "sometime last night."

"Wouldn't Sanny have alerted you?"

Ruby answered for me. "She would have, so it probably happened earlier in the evening."

My whole body grew warm with frustration. No wonder the girls were so worked up.

"Both Sanny and Dot were agitated when I got home, but I figured it was because it was so late. Someone vandalizing the backyard would explain it."

"Working late?" Martin noted and then cocked his head to the side. "Are you blushing?"

Ruby leaned forward and stage whispered, "She had a date."

He broke out in a grin. "A date? With who?"

He probably expected me to say Gabe. "Do you remember Jozef Lykke from the hand pie class?"

Martin held his hand a few inches above his head. "The big guy? Looks like he should be wearing a helmet with horns and an animal skin cape?" He winked at me. "Good for you."

I don't know why I expected people wouldn't approve of me going to dinner. Maybe because there was a stigma attached to it. Dating was for young people. When someone reached fifty-eight, they should be content with the lot they drew. I now realized mine was the only voice claiming that.

"You feel a coven member is responsible," Martin verified. "I concur. A case of sour grapes. And it looks like you were right about the scone being poisoned." He picked up the first note and confessed, "I'm worried about you being alone."

Ruby placed a hand on my shoulder. "I'll stay with her."

Martin swept the papers and pictures into a stack. "That's great, Ruby, but you can't be with her twenty-four hours a day. You have a walkie-talkie at the shop, right, Aunt Reeva?"

I nodded. "It's sitting on my desk."

"Until we figure out what's going on, I want you to clip it to your waistband and carry it with you everywhere. Keep it in the charger next to your bed at night. If you feel at all uneasy, call me. Or just put out a general call for help. Someone will come to your aid."

Their concern both touched me and made me even more nervous. Did I really need protection?

"Have you used it before?" He pulled his from his belt. Jayne had distributed identical units to the businesses.

"I've looked it over but never had a reason to use it."

"Super easy. If you want to get my attention first, press the call button." He did and Jagger's unit in the other room made an alarm sound.

"Sheriff?" Jagger called.

"Giving a lesson," Martin replied. To me, he continued, "On second thought, don't worry about alerting me first. Just push this button on the side and start talking. I'll hear you."

I smiled at him. "You take such good care of me."

"Just doing my job." He held my gaze and then looked between Ruby and me. "Thought you'd want to know that the results of the bloodwork are in. There was a message in my inbox when I got here this morning. I was about to call Dr. Bundy for an explanation when you got here."

Ruby pushed his phone closer to him. "Don't let us stop you."

A corner of his mouth curved up in amusement. "Under normal circumstances, I wouldn't do this. This directly affects Aunt Reeva, though, and you two seem to have more evidence than I do. Everything you hear stays in this room. Got it?"

"Of course," I assured.

Ruby wiggled her fingers in front of her mouth, copying Violet's version of locking her lips and throwing away the key.

Martin turned on the speakerphone and then hit a button. The medical examiner was on speed dial. Not surprising considering Whispering Pines' track record.

"Good morning, Sheriff Reed," a woman with a strong, nasally Wisconsin accent greeted.

"Morning, Joan. Is Dr. Bundy available? He sent me some bloodwork results that I need some clarification on."

"Oh, sure, he's here somewhere. Let me hunt him down for ya. Hang on a sec."

A minute later, Dr. Bundy answered. "Good morning, Martin. You got the report?"

"I did. Can you decipher it for me, or do I need to call the lab?"

"I should be able to help. Let me pull it up." We heard jazz playing softly in the background. "Ah, yes. Paralytic poisoning."

"What's that?" Martin asked and turned up the volume when Ruby tapped her ear and jabbed her thumb upward.

"Pretty much what it sounds like. A state of paralysis brought on by a poisonous substance. In this case . . . oh, that's unusual. Tetrodotoxin. That's a substance found in some frogs, snails, shellfish, octopi, and some varieties of fish. People most commonly associate it with pufferfish, though."

"Pufferfish?" I blurted and nearly leapt off my chair. Instead, I slapped my hand over my mouth to listen to the doctor.

"You got others there with you, Sheriff?" Dr. Bundy asked.

"I do. Aunt Reeva and Ruby McLaughlin. You met them the other day." He gave us a half smile. "They've set up a sort of private investigation service and have been looking into Ms. Nakamura's death. You can speak freely. How would tetrodotoxin have killed Iris?"

"Want a little background?"

"Of course." Martin leaned back as though settling in to listen to a story.

"Tetrodotoxin is found in the liver and sex organs. It's said that sailors initially discovered this after serving pufferfish flesh to the crew and the innards to livestock they had on board. The crew members got sick, and the livestock died. They steered clear of the pokey little fishies after that. Today, it's a delicacy in some restaurants."

"Wait. Ruby here, Dr. Bundy. People purposely eat poisonous fish?"

"Crazy, isn't it? It takes years of training for the chefs to learn how to properly prepare the dish. From what I understand, patrons are served a paper-thin slice with the goal of getting a tingling sensation in their mouths. The danger is—"

"Too much will kill you," Martin concluded.

"Exactly."

"And how much is too much?" I asked, feeling a little woozy thinking about that scone I passed on to Iris.

"An average drop of water weighs approximately fifty milligrams. It takes as little as twenty-five milligrams of tetrodotoxin to kill a one-hundred-sixty-five-pound person."

Martin whistled in surprise. "The size of a half of a drop of water."

Iris didn't even weigh a hundred pounds. Half a drop would have been more than enough to kill her.

"Now, I could be off on some of these quantities," Dr. Bundy admitted. "I only did a quick bit of research on this stuff. What we know for sure is that tetrodotoxin was found in Ms. Nakamura's blood."

"Do we know if that's what killed her?" Martin asked.

"No, because her granddaughter refused an autopsy. My gut says it's a safe assumption, though."

Ruby spun to face me and mouthed, "Gardenia?"

I swatted my hand at her. Dr. Bundy first, suspects later.

"Paralysis," Dr. Bundy continued, "can begin in as little as ten minutes or as many as three hours."

Gardenia had said that by the time they got back to their cottage, Iris was so tired she could barely walk. The question is, was she tired or was the paralytic already taking effect?

"Most victims die from asphyxiation," Dr. Bundy said.

"When their lungs paralyze, they obviously can't breathe. I know that Ms. Nakamura's heart was failing."

"Right." Martin stared at his computer screen. "We didn't expect her to be with us much longer. Speaking of which, you did test for heart medication as well, didn't you?"

"We did," the doctor confirmed. "There was very little in her system."

"Gardenia's fear was right," I noted sadly. "Iris had stopped taking her prescription."

"This is a death," Dr. Bundy began, "for which we'll never have a solid cause. Not taking her medication didn't help, but tetrodotoxin will kill even the healthiest person."

My body broke out in a cold sweat at those last words.

"With this, my job is complete," Dr. Bundy concluded. "Now the sheriff gets to step in and figure out whodunnit. Can I help with anything else?"

"Not right now," Martin answered. "And hopefully not for a long time to come."

"Hear, hear. Hope you have a quiet day, Sheriff. Ladies."

Martin hung up and then looked directly at me. "What is it? You nearly hit the roof when he said pufferfish."

"Verne Witkowski recently added two of them to his aquarium."

CHAPTER

TWENTY-SEVEN

M artin paced behind his desk, hands in his pockets, trying to come up with a solid reason to bring Verne Witkowski in for questioning. "I've got poison from a fish he has in his collection. I need more. Tell me what you learned. Start at the beginning and give me all the details."

Ruby and I explained how after seeing that first note we figured there could be a poison involved and focused our attention on those who had direct contact with the scones.

"We started with Laurel," I told him. "I wanted to ask her about muffin pans."

"The ones returned at the break-in?" he clarified.

"Right." I took a minute to explain the Clover and Peony Flowers issue. "That's all under control now. Back to Laurel, I don't believe for a minute that she was involved with the poisoning. After leaving her that day, we stopped by the Grinder to pick up my bean order, and that's when we found out that Iris had died."

Ruby nodded along with my words. "We narrowed our list to those who had direct contact with the scones Monday night.

We talked to Luna Witkowski and Lorena Maxwell first. You may want to keep an eye on Lorena."

"You think she was involved with the poisoning?" Martin asked.

"Possibly. Either way, she's very snarly and could be a potential problem for Reeva."

"Can't charge her with snarliness, but I'll start a file." He returned to his chair, opened a document on his laptop, and wondered aloud, "Should I call it *Coven Problems* or *Reeva Problems?*" He typed something, not letting us know what he decided. "Okay, Lorena's snarly. What about Luna? She and her dad are hot and cold with everyone, including each other, depending on the day." He paused to reconsider that statement. "Sometimes, depending on the hour. Did you bring up her dad when you spoke with her?"

"We did," I confirmed. "With both Luna and Lorena, we started by asking them about being involved with handing out the scones. Other than Laurel, Lorena was the only one to be alone with the baskets, and she insisted that was only for a few seconds before Verne, Luna, and Laurel—" I bit off my words as a thought slammed into my head.

"What's wrong?" Martin asked.

"Last night, Lily Grace told me about a vision she'd had. A flash of my face and pastries that had been branded. She said she didn't remember the exact mark, only that it was all straight lines. I assumed it meant the rune mark Jozef put on his scones, but it could have been Verne's logo."

Ruby slid to the edge of her seat. "A *V* with a line across the top. All straight lines."

A shiver raced up my spine. "The mark in Lily Grace's vision wasn't necessarily literal. Marking a scone could be as simple as poking your finger into it or breaking off a bit. Or the mark she saw could just indicate that Verne is the responsible party."

Martin scribbled on his notepad. "You claim the scone in

question came from Verne's tray. He could have easily injected tetrodotoxin into two scones as he carried them over to you."

"Verne is our guy," I stated.

"Yeah," Ruby agreed, "but can we talk about Gardenia for a minute?"

Martin looked up from his scribbling. "What about her?"

"There's just a lot pointing to her being a suspect. First, she's Iris's only relative. Gardenia will now inherit everything, which will make life far easier on a young woman who can't seem to find a path to follow. Second, she fixed a cup of tea for Iris. It would take a nanosecond to put a drop of that tetro-stuff into the cup. And third, she didn't want an autopsy done."

"She did want a blood test, though," I pointed out.

"For heart medication. If Martin hadn't let my request go through, we wouldn't even know about the poison. Would we?"

Jagger appeared in the doorway. "Sheriff? Gardenia is here."

"You two stay right here," Martin instructed. "I asked Gardenia to come in so I could discuss the results. I'll be back in a few minutes."

He closed the door when he left, which meant we couldn't hear him talking with Gardenia in the interview room next door. So Ruby pressed her ear to the adjoining wall.

"Can you hear anything?" I asked after a minute.

"Nothing." She returned to her seat.

"You made some really good points, Ruby. What you said about Gardenia being Iris's heir and having plenty of time to put the tetrodotoxin in her tea. Spot on. Any one of those things could raise flags, but adding them all together? Now I'm wondering if she did it."

"Now I'm about to poke a hole in my own balloon. The big question is, how would Gardenia get ahold of that toxin?"

I thought on that and decided, "She and Verne could be working together. If Gardenia did do this, they'd almost have to be. The possibility of this being a coincidence, that she happened to use a toxin that comes from a fish that Verne just acquired? No way." I slumped in my seat as something else came to mind. "But why would Gardenia do this? Everyone knew Iris was going to die. Why poison her? Why not just wait out the time?"

"A very good question," Ruby conceded. "And we're forgetting about those notes again. Whoever wrote them wants you to step down. Has Gardenia ever expressed interest in becoming high priestess?"

I shook my head. "I've never heard Gardenia express an interest in anything but caring for her grandmother. Honestly, she's a lost soul. Which makes it believable that she might want to speed up getting her inheritance. Poor Iris had been standing on death's doormat, as you call it, for so long."

"You think Gardenia gave her a little shove?"

We sat pondering that possibility for long enough that Martin came back into the room.

"I don't think she's our killer," he announced.

"No? Why?" I asked.

"She was heartbroken to hear the bloodwork confirmed her fear and showed that Iris had stopped taking her heart medicine. She thinks Iris put them in her bathrobe pocket and flushed them when she used the bathroom. Gardenia could be playing me, but her reaction sure felt genuine. So did her reaction to me telling her about the tetrodotoxin. She said she'd been to Japan a few times with Iris so is aware of the fugu fascination."

"Fugu?" Ruby asked.

"The Japanese word for pufferfish. Again, she could be putting on an act, but she told me she knew someone who died from improperly prepared fugu. She said after that incident, she won't touch any kind of fish. Cooked or raw."

I grimaced. "Raw fish. Not a fan. Are you excluding her as a suspect?"

"For now. I didn't ask any questions, only reviewed the test results with her." He held up a piece of paper. "She wanted a copy of them, so I had her put the request in writing." His grin said he was proud of himself. "I've got a sample of her handwriting."

He set Gardenia's request on his desk alongside the notes left for me. Not even close. The notes were scrawly and scratchy. Gardenia wrote in beautiful looping cursive that resembled calligraphy.

"I bet Iris taught her that," Ruby guessed, admiring the text. "I hear they don't teach cursive in school anymore. A lost art." Her face brightened suddenly.

I tapped her leg with the toe of my clog. "You're thinking about teaching handwriting, aren't you?"

She spun on me. "Don't try to tell me it falls under the housekeeping umbrella because for millennia housewives have been handwriting their to-do and grocery lists."

I laughed, holding my hands in the air. "All yours, craft witch. I'll be busy enough with cooking, soapmaking, and fabric dying lessons."

She narrowed her eyes at me.

Martin looked confused.

"Long story," I told him. "This means Verne is our suspect, then."

"Verne is *my* suspect." His tone left no room for interpretation. "I appreciate the information you've given me. Turning in those notes and the pictures is very helpful, but you're done now. No more interviews."

"But," Ruby began.

"No. If you keep pushing this, whoever is trying to intimidate Aunt Reeva could retaliate with more than broken flowerpots and graffiti. Thank you for your assistance, but no more."

We stood to leave, and I asked Martin, "Will you let us know what happens?"

"This is Whispering Pines. Every villager and half the tourists will probably know whodunnit before I do." He laughed. I didn't, so he vowed, "I'll tell you. Since this affects you directly, I will let you know the moment after I put your tormentor behind bars. Hopefully that will be fast enough that Violet won't have heard the news first."

Then I did laugh. "I promise, I wasn't trying to do your job for you or anything like that. I know how capable you are. You had already closed Iris's case as being a natural death, though, and you had tourist issues."

"Tourists," He grumbled. "I'll be shocked if I don't get slapped with a suit of some kind. This naked thing is out of control. A woman was drunk and heading right for the fire last night. I reached out to stop her and, well . . ."

"You caught her in the boob?" Ruby guessed.

"Exactly. Don't tell Rosalyn."

I patted his shoulder. "Just doing your job, my boy."

CHAPTER

TWENTY-EIGHT

With tomorrow being Litha, the village had filled to capacity with tourists eager to celebrate the summer solstice in a Wiccan village. Every room at The Inn and Pine Time was booked. Every cottage was rented. Every campsite full. Even the hotels just over the village border had sold every room.

"The village is going to need another inn," Keiko stated, flipping the sign on Hearth & Cauldron's door from *Open* to *Closed*.

"River is considering that," I told her. "He's worried about it becoming an *if you build it, they'll come* situation, though, and we'll still be turning people away."

"At least another restaurant, then. The lines at Triple G and The Inn are ridiculous on the weekends. Why are you smiling at me?"

"Because you're starting to sound like a villager. We love the tourists, couldn't survive without them, but we all gripe about them at the same time." A yawn sneaked up on me. "Goodness. I'll need a nap, or I won't be able to stay awake from sunset to sunrise."

"And then be back here in the morning. A nap would do you good."

"Being an oldster, you mean."

She put her hands in the air. "You said it this time, not me."

"I'm going to straighten the retail shelves. Will you take care of the dining room?"

"On it."

We both turned to do our tasks and I said, "Keiko? You're welcome to come over tonight and celebrate Litha. I have plenty of traditional solstice food. Fresh fruit and vegetables, barbecue, honey cakes . . ."

She looked surprised by the offer. "Okay. Yeah, I'll think about it. I might check out the bonfire by the marina and the stuff going on in the commons."

"Sure. That would be more your crowd," I agreed. "Well, the offer's open if you decide you want to come."

I had a sinking feeling that for the second year in a row, I'd be celebrating Midsummer alone. I'd mentioned it to Ruby yesterday but didn't get a confirmation from her. That was fine. This wouldn't be the first time I'd celebrated a sabbat by myself. I could handle it.

We finished cleaning and Keiko opted to perform the closing blessing with me tonight.

"I'm so excited for tomorrow," she admitted while I locked the door. "Morgan will be back. I might actually learn something rather than just stocking shelves and running the register."

Or washing dishes and mopping the floor. She was so desperate to prove herself, and I was treating her like little more than a servant. Not that I didn't appreciate what she did for me, someone had to do those chores after all, but there had to be more I could teach her. It might help if I thought of her as an apprentice instead of an employee.

"Reeva?" She waved her hand in front of my face. "You checked out on me. You okay?"

"I'm fine. Just thinking about the future. See you tomorrow. Or maybe tonight."

It only took a couple of minutes for me to get to the spot on the Fairy Path where it split—right to the library and schools, left to Unity and home, straight ahead to the sheriff's station. What had my attention wasn't the diverging paths but the person standing there. Seemingly waiting for me. When I got close, I saw that it was Verne.

"I understand you and Ruby were talking to my daughter."

I stopped and straddled my bike. "We talked with her Wednesday evening, yes. We had a few questions about the gathering at my cottage Monday night."

"What did you want to know?" He stood with his feet in a wide stance, his hands dangling at his side. Ready to strike?

"It was nothing, Verne. She answered and we moved along."

He took a step closer, and his hands clenched into fists. "I asked you what you talked to my daughter about. She was all upset when she got home."

I shifted positions to stand next to my bike, keeping it between us. As I did, I reached my right hand around to the small of my back like I had an itch, pulled the walkie-talkie Martin insisted I carry from my waistband, and pushed the button on the side.

"I don't know why Luna would be upset, Verne." How sensitive was the microphone on this thing? I was probably speaking louder than necessary. "I know a few questions came off as a bit confrontational, but we smoothed things over. She was okay when she left. Maybe something else upset her."

He took another step forward. "She told me you accused us of killing Iris."

I shook my head. "That's not what we said. We told her there might have been a problem with the scones. I knew the two of you handed them out. You brought a tray full over to where I was sitting with Iris. Remember?"

"You told Luna the scones were poisoned, and you thought she or I did it."

I squeezed the button on the talkie harder. If Martin was hearing this, it might be proof enough to bring Verne in. "You handed one to me, and Gardenia took one for Iris. It was shortly after Iris ate the scone that she got so sick, so it seems a normal conclusion that the two were connected."

"Don't play dumb with me, Reeva." His voice turned to a growl so low I wasn't sure the talkie would pick it up. I stretched my right hand closer to my left side, hoping those extra couple of inches would help. "I know you switched scones with Iris. Luna told me you gave her the one you were supposed to get."

My heart raced, and my hands shook. I needed to keep it together. And above all, not lose my grip on the walkie-talkie.

"The one I was *supposed* to get. The one laced with tetrodotoxin, you mean?"

His face went slack for an instant, and then his jaw clenched.

"Why, Verne? Why would you try to kill me? What did I ever do to you?"

He shook his head. "No one was supposed to die. Not you and especially not Iris. She was a sweet old lady who had suffered enough. It was meant to be a threat. Like those notes and the paint on your shed." He nodded at my bike. "See you got your tire fixed."

"And the flowerpots?"

His eyes narrowed. "I didn't do anything to flowerpots." He ran his hands through his hair and blurted, "Why couldn't you just stay away?"

I stiffened. "From the village?"

"Yes, from the village. And don't give me some cock-and-bull story about cleaning out Karl's cottage. That didn't take you more than a couple weeks. You shoulda left after that. Gone back to your other life. But you had to go and get involved with things that weren't any of your business. You ruined everything."

My body went cold. I turned slightly, willing Martin to hear every word. "What things? What did I ruin?"

Verne's eyes lowered to my waist then. "What are you doing? What have you got there, Reeva?"

He stepped forward, hand reaching for the walkie-talkie, but before he could grab it, a flash of something dark brown and furry raced out from behind a nearby pine tree. Verne's knees buckled, and he dropped to the ground face first. The next second, Tyrann climbed onto his back and sat.

Verne reached around, like he was about to grab the Shephard by the foot when Jagger appeared from behind the same tree.

"I wouldn't do that, Verne," he warned. "You do not want him to clamp down on your hand. Those teeth are sharp, and his jaw is like a vice."

"Aunt Reeva?" Martin emerged while Jagger was dealing with Verne. "Are you okay?"

"Completely fine. You heard everything?"

Martin grinned. "The whole village heard. You can release the button now."

"What?" Verne demanded. Tyrann growled.

"That was brilliant," Martin praised. "Absolutely brilliant. The station phone started ringing like crazy with people letting us know you seemed to be in trouble."

"It did?"

"Oh, yeah. Many of them asked if we needed help looking for you. For the record, I could see you through my office window. We were giving you time to get Verne to incriminate himself. Great job."

While Jagger and Tyrann escorted Verne inside to the

interview room, Martin pushed my bike to the station's porch and then brought me to his office.

"Will you be okay in here for a bit?" my nephew asked. "I need to talk with our suspect."

"I'm fine," I insisted but suddenly felt drained. "I wouldn't say no to some coffee, though."

He made me a cup and left his office door open this time so I could hear Verne's words. In fact, he placed a chair at the threshold so I wouldn't miss a thing.

"I'll be recording this conversation," Martin announced as he entered the interview room.

"This whole thing with the walkie-talkie," Verne complained, "it's entrapment."

"Reeva isn't a deputy. She's a resident of this village like you and all the others. She was fearful for her safety and opted to carry a walkie-talkie with her in case she needed help."

"She's nothing like us," Verne hissed. "She might've lived here first, but . . ." His words faded away.

"But what? I heard you tell Reeva that she ruined everything. Sounds like something's going on that I need to know about."

"Why? Because you're the sheriff? Or because you're an *Original?*" Ice coated that last word. "Considering what happened to your mother, you should understand better than anyone."

"Understand what?" Martin asked.

"Everyone's angry about how new blood is taking over the village. First Jayne and Tripp, then Reeva, then River Carr. Morgan Barlow struts around like she's royalty or the first lady of Whispering Pines or something."

"The Barlows have always been like royalty here. Second in line after the O'Sheas."

"They changed, though," Verne insisted. "Got all high and mighty. Morgan didn't even consider one of us when she stepped down. There are members of our coven who have been here longer than Morgan. We understood when Briar named her high priestess, but none of us get why Morgan would hand over the title to an outsider."

I knew that's what they thought of me. There was the proof.

"Reeva isn't an outsider," Martin insisted, his tone dropping.

"Just because she was one of the first to live here doesn't mean anything. Loyalty is proven by longevity. She left and came back twice now. That's not loyalty. Why should we believe she'll stay?"

"Was that the point of those notes? To scare her into leaving? To make her step down from the high priestess designation?"

There was a pause before Verne replied, "Either would've been fine."

"I assume that's what the vandalism was for as well. The graffiti on her shed, the messed up firepit, punctured bike tire, and the broken flowerpots."

"What is it with you two and those pots? I didn't touch any flowerpots."

That was the second time he'd denied it. If he didn't break them, who did?

"But you were responsible for the other things," Martin clarified.

Another pause. I could practically hear him shrug. "Had to let her know we were serious."

He kept saying *we*, making it very clear that he wasn't the only one unhappy with me.

"Let's talk about the other more serious warning you tried to deliver," Martin continued. "The poison in the scone."

"It's exactly what you said. It was just supposed to be a warning. It was supposed to make Reeva a little sick. Make her feel tingly and a little weird."

"But it ended up killing Iris. Blood tests revealed tetrodotoxin in her system, and I know you recently bought a pair of pufferfish."

Seconds later, the sound of crying . . . no, sobbing came from the interview room.

"It wasn't meant for Iris," Verne insisted. "I just wanted to scare Reeva off. Figured maybe if she knew we don't want her here, she'd leave again. Everything was fine until she came back and caused all those problems with Flavia."

Just like he did with Jayne. Accuse me of causing problems that were already here. Verne reminded me of a mosquito. I'd suffered far worse blows in my life than his pesky buzzing about, and I was still standing.

"Are you admitting," Martin stated, "to putting the poison tetrodotoxin into a scone that ultimately killed Iris Nakamura?"

"Iris wasn't supposed to get it," Verne moaned. "I gave that one to Reeva. She shouldn't have switched with Iris."

From the doorway, I watched as Martin escorted Verne to a cell and locked him inside.

When he saw me sitting there, Verne called out, "See? Special treatment. Which other villager would get to sit in your office like that? Go back where you belong, Reeva."

"Tyrann, come," Martin called. The dog went right to his side. "Sit. Stay."

The station's new K-9 kept an eye on their prisoner while Martin went to Jagger's desk. A moment later, Jagger reached for his phone. When Martin returned to his office, I moved the chair back by his desk.

"Deputy Atkins from the county sheriff's office will be here shortly to take Verne away." He sat in the chair next to me. "You heard all that?"

"I heard. Sounds like this war isn't just about me. Jayne, Tripp, River, and maybe even the Barlows should be warned."

"I'll talk to them," Martin promised, "but I think of this as less of a war and more a . . . skirmish. Verne is trying to make it sound like half the village is upset, but I know these folks. I've lived with them my whole life and am out and about with them every day. If real trouble was brewing, someone would have said something by now."

He was probably right. "How many people should I be worried about, then?"

"I truly don't think there are as many as Verne is alluding to. What the villagers ultimately want is to live a peaceful life."

"Don't dismiss this, Martin. We ignored Flavia and look what happened."

He winced at that. "I'm not dismissing anything."

"Then tell me. I need to know. How many are we talking about?"

He shrugged. "If I have to guess, maybe six or eight."

I held his gaze. "That's a pretty large percentage of the coven."

"But a small percent of the villager population. I promise I'm taking this seriously. I'll be out talking to people and so will Jagger. And while I know it's not much of a comfort, nor is it intended to be, remember that Verne wasn't referring to only you. He talked about outsiders and Originals. *This* attack was aimed at you, but I don't believe he meant to kill you. He wanted to irritate you and make a point. If he meant for you to die, he would have come at you with more than a tainted scone."

"I guess that's true. And you're right, it doesn't comfort me."

"Consider that we may have cut off the snake's head. Verne's mistake with the tetrodotoxin might be enough to show the others how stupid this was. I don't want you to be scared, just cautious. That's what I'll tell the others who might be targeted as well."

"Okay," I agreed after some thought. "I trust you. If this is what you believe, I'll believe it too."

He patted my hand. "Good."

I forced myself to move on to a happier topic. "Do you have plans for tonight? Getting together with Rosalyn?"

"She's going to come to the gathering in the commons. She

254 • SHAWN MCGUIRE

and Tripp are trying to get Jayne to rejoin society. Since most villagers will be celebrating at home tonight, Rosalyn thinks this is a good chance for her to make a public appearance. As for me, Jagger and I will be patrolling the commons. It's going to be a long night."

I stood and pulled my nephew in for a hug. He held on a little tighter than I expected.

"Excellent job on wrapping up your first solo case," I told him and gave a final squeeze before releasing him.

"Thank you. What about you? Do you have plans tonight?"

I smiled. "Just a quiet night at home."

He frowned but didn't respond.

I headed for the door and stopped. "By the way, your new K-9 should stay."

"Yeah," he replied. "Tyrann isn't going anywhere."

CHAPTER
TWENTY-NINE

Once I got home, I greeted the girls, changed into yard clothes, and headed out to the shed. I tossed the wilted and dried-up flowers that had been yanked from the ground into the compost bin. If I'd been able to replant and water them soon enough, they might have made it. They were past hope now, however. And try as I might to scrub off the white paint, that was also hopeless. My shed would need to be repainted. Good opportunity to go through it and give away anything I didn't need or want. Karl had owned as many garden tools as I did kitchen gadgets.

My cottage was far too quiet tonight. Dot and Sanny hovered nearby, but I felt especially lonely and would have preferred a friend or two to help me welcome the Holly King's ascension. After changing clothes again, into something comfortable and clean, I went out to my triad, stepped inside, and felt the world slip away. The firefly-fairies were very active tonight. The veil was thin, after all, which meant there was lots of activity to stir them up.

I sat in the middle of my oak, ash, and hawthorn, then closed my eyes. After a few deep breaths, I thought of how easy it would be to slip through the veil to where I would no longer have to worry about the problems that came with life. My parents were on the other side. More importantly, my daughter was too.

"If only I could see you again, Yazzy. Of course, if I see you, I'll want to hold you. And if I hold you, I'll never want to let go." Tears trickled down the sides of my nose. "I miss you every single day, sweetheart. They say that pain is the price we pay for loving someone. I have loved you with every cell in my body since the day you were born, and some days the pain is almost too much to bear."

Images of my date last night flashed through my mind like a slideshow.

"Something good happened this week, though. Maybe you already know. I suspect you do." I smiled, recalling the feel of Jozef's lips on mine. "I went on a date. He's a very nice man, and I think you'd like him. He had to leave this morning, so it seems we were only meant to pass through each other's lives, but it gave me hope. If the Universe brought us together, there could well be someone else out there for me too." More tears fell. "I'm just so lonely sometimes. I have good, dear friends but—"

I felt Sanny land on my shoulder, and Dot crawled into my lap. And then a hand on my other shoulder startled me. Verne and his posse came to mind, but when I opened my eyes, I found Ruby, Laurel, and Maeve standing behind me.

"We didn't mean to eavesdrop," Ruby promised gently, "but we heard what you said."

"Friends aren't the same as a Viking," Laurel teased, "but we're not going anywhere."

"And we're proof that you can have a full life without a man," Maeve added. "Although, if your Viking has friends, we wouldn't say no to some blind dates."

I laughed, dried my eyes, and looked to Maeve. "Shouldn't you be at the pub?"

She shrugged. "I never take a night off. They can handle a few hours without me."

My tears flowed again but for a different reason. I missed my daughter, but I was so grateful to have these strong, smart women in my life.

"Quite a quartet," I managed through my thick throat. "Give me one more minute and I'll come out."

When they stepped away, I looked toward the spot where the air sometimes shimmered.

"It's not time yet. Turns out, I've got more friends than I realized to prop me up. No one will ever replace my daughter, but these women will do until it's time for us to be together again." I blew a kiss at the shimmer and imagined her on the other side catching it and pressing it to her heart. Our way of saying goodbye since she was little. "I do love you, beautiful girl. Hold my spot there, okay?"

My tears turned my vision into a watery blur, and I swear I saw her standing there, hand to her heart. I blinked and she was gone.

"Are you three still out there?" I called, wiping my face.

"We're here," Ruby replied.

"I have no idea how long I've been sitting here, but I could use a little help up." I held my arms out wide.

"Knees locked up on you, did they?" Laurel asked, stepping back inside.

"Happens to the best of us," Maeve muttered.

"I've got some food in the kitchen. It won't take me long—"

"We took care of everything." Ruby pointed toward my firepit where a tower of logs was ready for lighting. Four chairs with blankets surrounded the pit, and a small table filled with food sat nearby.

"I brought plenty of my Midsummer Mead," Maeve bragged, knowing how much we loved the honey, orange, and spice drink.

"I brought salmon and veggies to grill," Laurel announced.

"And I," Ruby said, "brought candied ginger, fresh fruit, and lemon balm tea."

My tears threatened again. "You ladies are the best."

We lit the fire and settled into our chairs and talked as the sun got closer to setting.

We'd been sitting there for at least an hour when Keiko appeared from in front of the cottage. "Y'all are a noisy lot. I could hear you halfway to the Barlow place." She stood there awkwardly. "Got room for one more single lady?"

"Of course," Laurel stated while Maeve told her to, "Go find a chair and join the circle."

After she'd settled in with me on her right and Ruby on her left, Ruby asked, "Hanging out with the oldsters, hey?"

Keiko shrugged. "I can think of worse company."

We laughed and told stories and laughed some more and ate all night long.

"I've got something in my freezer," I told them as the sun started to brighten the horizon. I returned with five bowls and a container from the freezer. "Briar shared her Sunrise Gelato recipe with me."

"Briar!" Maeve threw her hands in the air. "Another single lady. We should have invited her."

"Next time," I vowed, thinking of how gatherings like this could be a good way to heal any lasting wounds she and I had. "She's still so obsessed with those grandbabies you can barely pull her away from them."

"True," Laurel agreed. "By this time next year, they'll be walking and getting into everything. She'll be happy to let their parents deal with them."

We enjoyed the lemon, lime, orange, and strawberry dessert and watched the sky turn from indigo to purple gray to red orange and finally a bright clear blue. After helping me clean up the remains of our celebration, Ruby, Laurel, and Maeve headed home to catch a few hours' sleep before opening their respective businesses. This was the one day of the year when everyone stayed closed until noon. Except for Violet, but she didn't open the Grinder until nine.

"Guess I should get back to the campground," Keiko said with a yawn.

I shook my head. "It's only a few hours. Use my guest room."

"Really? Thanks, Reeva."

As we went inside, I said, "After work tonight, we should go get your stuff from the campground."

"And put it where?"

"Here."

"You want me to camp in your backyard?"

I laughed. "No. I've been thinking about it and decided that the problem with my cottage wasn't that it held too much negativity. It's that there hasn't been enough positivity in it or my life in more than a year."

Keiko blinked and her voice quavered the tiniest bit as she asked, "What are you saying?"

"I'm saying that I'd like for you to move into my guest room. Your parents are far away, and my daughter is even farther. Not that I'll act like a parent, although there will be rules you'll need to follow."

She threw her arms around my neck. "Yes. Yes, yes, yes. Thank you."

She kicked off her shoes, leaving them in the middle of the floor, ran up the stairs to the guest room, and closed the door a little too hard, making it slam.

Mrow?

"Think of it as a new adventure," I told Dot. I wanted excitement in my life and was willing to bet every penny I had that Keiko Shen would provide it.

ALSO BY SHAWN MCGUIRE

HEARTH & CAULDRON Mystery Series

WHISPERING PINES Mystery Series

GEMI KITTREDGE Mystery Series

THE WISH MAKERS Fantasy Series

ABOUT THE AUTHOR

Suspense and fantasy author Shawn McGuire loves creating characters and places her fans want to return to again and again. She started writing after seeing the first Star Wars movie (that's episode IV) as a kid. She couldn't wait for the next installment to come out so wrote her own. Sadly, those notebooks are long lost, but her desire to tell a tale is as strong now as it was then. She lives in Wisconsin near the beautiful Mississippi River and when not writing or reading, she might be baking, gardening, crafting, going for a long walk, or nibbling really dark chocolate.

Made in the USA
Monee, IL
30 October 2024